# WENDY'S WINTER GIFT

Debbie Viggiano

ISBN: 9798362011864

www.debbieviggiano.com

*For my Joe*

*Always and forever*

# Chapter One

I stumbled over a tree root, arms briefly windmilling, before recovering my balance.

'Careful, Wends.' The caution came from my canine-walking partner-in-grime, Kelly. Her breath made clouds in the early morning November air. 'You're lucky you didn't slip on that pile of doggy-do over there. It's bang out of order that some owners can't be bothered to pick up after their pooches.'

'Perhaps the person had run out of poo bags,' I said, automatically fishing for one from the pocket of my Barbour.

'You're never going to pick up after someone else's dog, are you?' Kelly asked incredulously. Her huge brown eyes widened. She looked like a middle-aged Audrey Hepburn, but with swishy long hair.

'Absolutely,' I replied, bending to the task.

'*Ewww.* Rather you than me.' Kelly wrinkled her nose.

'Surely it's no different to picking up after Alfie,' I countered.

Alfie is Kelly's ancient German Shepherd – not an incontinent husband, in case you're wondering.

I stooped and scooped, then knotted up the chemically

perfumed little sack. A moment later and it had been deposited in one of the handy red waste bins, dotted throughout Trosley Country Park.

'It's different picking up after your own dog,' said Kelly, as we resumed our pace. 'It's like when your kids are babies. I never thought twice about changing my sons' nappies, but could never do the same for my niece. My sister used to get really annoyed with me. She'd say, "For heaven's sake, Kelly. Poo is poo!" But it isn't really, is it? I mean, it's like wiping one's bum. You just do it. But you wouldn't do it for anyone else, would you?'

'Erm…'

I tucked a strand of blonde hair behind one ear. How on earth had we got on to this subject?

'I mean' – Kelly persisted – 'you wouldn't stroll over to a stranger – like that guy coming towards us – and waggle a pack of wet wipes at him while saying, "I'm offering a bottom wiping service. One wipe for a quid or a polish for a fiver."'

'No,' I agreed.

So far, our Friday morning conversation had been a far cry from the usual topic; namely, our husbands. And whether to stay with them or leave.

Like me, Kelly had been married for twenty-seven years. And also, like me, she insisted there was little companionship and a lack of marital bliss. But – *unlike* me – she was having a terrific flirtation with a married man. She'd met Steve in Costco, of all places. At the time, he was being publicly rebuked in the bread aisle by a sergeant major wife. This had been seconds after Kelly had had a public row with Henry. She'd left him sulking in *Beers and Wines* because she wasn't prepared to blow the housekeeping on twenty crates of the store's Whisky of the Week.

Henry's drink consumption was a topic that frequently caused huge arguments. As Kelly had swung past shelves stacked with seeded loaves, she'd locked eyes with the henpecked man, and something unspoken had passed between them.

He'd made his move just after his wife had declared him useless. She'd ordered him to stay put while she, and she alone, went off to source the next item on the shopping list. A hasty conversation had taken place between Kelly and Steve and numbers had been furtively exchanged.

Flushed with excitement and derring-do, they'd been secretly meeting in various supermarkets ever since, enjoying peaceful shopping excursions and sparky conversation.

However, at their last meeting, things had taken a different turn. While the pair of them had lingered in *Breakfast Cereals*, Steve had dared to lean in and drop an impromptu kiss on Kelly's lips. Flustered, she'd put out a hand to steady herself and sent several boxes of porridge cascading everywhere. She was now in a continual state of overexcitement, wondering if this was the universe's way of saying that Steve should have his oats.

'Anyway' – I hauled my mind back from its meandering thoughts – 'I don't have any truck with poop scooping. After all, as a professional dog walker' – I affectionately glanced down at Sylvie, a sweet Golden Retriever, at my heel – 'it's something that sometimes has to be done.'

Sylvie belonged to Jack and Sadie Farrell who were occasionally overtaken by their respective work commitments and needed a hand exercising their two dogs. Sadie was a talented potter who mostly worked from home, but this week she'd been involved in an arts and crafts pre-Christmas exhibition at nearby Paddock Wood's Hop Farm.

'Sylvie isn't mine' – I reminded Kelly – 'but nonetheless I love her to bits and am happy to do the right thing by her.'

'She is a lovely dog,' Kelly agreed.

Sylvie was one of the calmest dogs I'd ever had the joy to take out. Unlike William Beagle who – along with Kelly's dog – had long disappeared amongst the woodland in search of hares and squirrels.

'ALFIE!' Kelly fog-horned, making Sylvie and me jump. 'ALFIE, WHERE ARE YOU?' She stopped and did a three-hundred-and-sixty-degree turn, scanning the undergrowth. 'Where has he gone?' she tutted. 'He's far too old and arthritic to keep up with William.'

'He'll be back,' I assured.

'Yeah, hopefully not with a dead squirrel hanging out of his mouth. I'm not good with bodies. Every time the cat dumps a mouse on the doorstep, I end up asking my neighbour to dispose of the body.'

'Doesn't Henry do it for you?' I asked in astonishment.

Kelly rolled her eyes.

'Henry doesn't "do" anything other than make me gnash my teeth. He's drinking way too much, blaming his excessive alcohol consumption on work and stress.'

'I know,' I soothed.

'I should leave him.'

'And I should leave Derek.'

'Do you think we'll ever be brave enough to take the plunge?' she asked gloomily.

But before I could reply, William Beagle shot out of a side path. He powered towards us with Alfie in stiff pursuit.

'Oh no,' I moaned.

'Bugger,' Kelly hissed.

William had a dead hare swinging from his jaws, while Alfie had found Mr Fox's calling card and had a marvellous time rolling in it.

'Never mind our husbands,' Kelly muttered. 'Right now, we have a far more pressing problem. How am I going to clip the lead on Alfie's slime-green collar, and how are you going to persuade William to drop that furry corpse?'

# Chapter Two

'*Ewww*,' wailed Kelly.

She attempted wiping her hands on a small tissue I'd found in the depths of my coat pocket.

'DON'T RUB YOUR FACE ON MY LEGS!' she shrieked at Alfie, as he proceeded to wipe himself against her denim-clad thighs. 'Oh God,' she gasped. 'Why did I ever get a dog?'

'Because they're great company,' I said, snapping the lead on William's collar.

Feeling like a murderer's dodgy accomplice, I swiftly hurled the little beagle's "gift" into the undergrowth.

*Don't think about your actions, Wendy. It's not a cute bunny. It's a dead body.*

'I can't believe you just did that!' Kelly blinked in horror.

'What else could I do?' I asked helplessly.

'Well, I don't know. Shouldn't we have buried it, or something?'

'Unfortunately, when I left home, I didn't think to pop a shovel in my handbag.'

'No need for sarcasm,' my bestie tutted. She dropped the soiled tissue on the woodland floor, then kicked some dead leaves over it. 'Let's turn around and head to the public toilets. I need to properly wash my hands. I'm not looking forward to going home. There's nothing I loathe more than wrestling an enormous dog into the bathtub and trying to remove the stench of fox crap.'

'I've heard that tomato ketchup is a must when it comes to getting rid of the pong.'

'Really?' said Kelly hopefully as we headed back to the visitors' area. 'I'll give it a try. And then I'll have to wash my clothes and deep clean the bathroom before I can even *think* about bathing myself. That's ninety minutes of my life gone on a joyless task.'

'Text Steve,' I said slyly. 'See if he's able to skive off work and wash your back.'

Kelly's eyes lit up.

'I'd like nothing more than that.' She flashed me a furtive look. 'Lately, I've been fantasising about what he looks like without his clothes on. He seems to be in good shape for someone not far off fifty. Probably because of his job.'

Steve had his own construction company but wasn't averse to mucking in with the labourers. Consequently, he had broad shoulders and big biceps – from what Kelly had glimpsed when Steve had been wearing t-shirts.

The guy sounded very different to Kelly's husband. Henry had a blue whisky-nose, the paunch of a drinker, and spaghetti-skinny legs.

'Do you think it's wrong to daydream about another man?' Kelly whispered as we passed a pair of joggers.

My answer was immediate.

'No.'

Heavens, I'd fantasised enough about men myself. Mostly actors in their heyday. Brad Pitt. Bruce Willis. George Clooney. More recently my thoughts had turned to my hunky neighbour. Ben was a whole decade younger than me with a wife who was rapidly going to seed. Lately, I'd been running a mental scenario on repeat. Ben saying, "You're locked out, Wendy? Why of *course* I'll shimmy up a ladder and climb through your bedroom window. Thank goodness you left it open." And then, when Ben reappeared downstairs, flushed and triumphant, me flashing him a smile and asking if he'd like a cuppa and a slice of cake by way of thanks. Except this was the point he'd waggle his eyebrows and say, "I have a far better idea about how you can repay me." And naturally I'd oblige. Energetically. Joyfully. Enthusiastically. Him sweeping me into his arms. Me swooning prettily. Him lowering his mouth to mine. Me closing my eyes as the tip of his tongue–

'Why are you panting?' asked Kelly.

My thoughts scattered like confetti.

'Er, because we're walking faster than usual. It's making me a bit, you know, out of breath.'

Kelly narrowed her eyes.

'Hm.'

'Anyway,' I chirped, keen to avoid her scrutiny. 'I expect sooner or later you and Steve will take things to the next level. I mean, you can't keep lurking in Lidl or skulking in Sainsbury's.'

My friend was instantly distracted, as I had known she

would be.

'You're right,' she sighed. 'But it's one thing to keep flirty company and have a stolen kiss. It's quite another to do the deed. And anyway, where would we go? I daren't risk inviting him back to my place. I have two savvy teenagers who have a habit of turning up when least expected.' Kelly momentarily stared up at the sky as she visualised a scenario. 'Imagine. Ten o'clock in the morning. Henry safely ensconced behind his desk at the office. The boys at their respective universities and conveniently out of the way. And then, just when I'm stripped down to my undies and my lover is admiring the way my boobs haven't quite yet reached my navel, my sons bursting into the bedroom and reminding me they're home for study days and' – she adopted a shocked accent – '"Good GOD, Mother! Why are you breastfeeding a strange man?"' She tore her eyes away from a flurry of cumulus clouds. 'No, it would never work. Anyway, I have nosy neighbours.'

'Everybody in Little Waterlow has nosy neighbours,' I pointed out.

'True,' she agreed.

'What about going to Steve's place?' I suggested.

'Definitely not.' Kelly gave a mock shudder. 'Caroline is a full-time stay-at-home wife who is kept *extremely* busy supervising the cleaning lady, overseeing the gardener, and standing over the ironing lady who apparently even presses the family's pants.' She looked at me incredulously. 'I mean, *who* irons pants?'

'I have no idea,' I said, flushing slightly as I recalled

another fantasy. Me standing over the ironing board. Blasting steam everywhere as I ironed black cotton briefs belonging to Yours Truly. The radio playing. Tom Jones belting out *Baby You Can Keep Your Hat On.* Me changing the lyrics and singing, "Wendy you can take your pants off," just as Ben magically appeared in front of the ironing board and hooked his fingers through the belt-hoops of my jeans… zipper going down… top coming off… until I was standing before him in nothing but my one good lacy bra and a pair of pristine briefs – not a crease to be seen – which miraculously also reflected my face on this occasion. Yes, I thought fervently, recalling my ironed pants. Best to be on the safe side. These days one needed all the help one could get to look good at forty-eight. If that meant ironing one's pants, then so be it.

'Wends? Are you listening to me?'

'Of course I'm listening to you,' I said, snapping to. 'Caroline sounds like a complete nightmare.'

'She is.' Kelly nodded fervently. 'I reckon if she caught me and Steve at it, instead of bawling him out for adultery, she'd more than likely march over and yell, "Not like THAT, you stupid man!" Apparently, she is a complete control freak in all areas, so I can't imagine her being any different in the bedroom.'

'Are they still sleeping together?' I asked carelessly. Kelly's face crumpled, and I realised I'd fluffed up by asking such a stupid question. 'Sorry, that was insensitive of me.'

'It's fine.' Kelly did a few rapid blinks and composed herself. 'Steve says not. He says they haven't done anything for yonks.'

'And do you believe him?'

She shrugged.

'I want to. He's asked me too. You know... whether Henry and I are still active under the duvet.'

'And are you?'

She looked anguished for a moment.

'Well, generally, no.'

'What do you mean *generally* no?'

'I mean, definitely no. Not for ages. Until two nights ago.'

'What happened two nights ago?'

'Something crazy. We're talking totally whacko. I'd eaten a load of blue cheese before bedtime and... did you know that cheese consumed in the evening can make you vividly dream?'

'I didn't.'

'Well, it does. And it did. And...' Kelly trailed off awkwardly.

'Ah.' Realisation dawned. 'You'd eaten blue cheese and found yourself having *blue* dreams.'

'Exactly!' she said, grateful for me cottoning on. 'So, there I was. In bed. Fast asleep and having the most *incredibly* heightened dream starring the delectable Steve and moi. Unsurprisingly, cheese featured. Steve wanted to play silly games. He'd dressed up as a pony with a mask on and I had to guess which cheese he was.'

'Mascarpone?'

'Very good, Wends! Well, the dream progressed, and we were having this bizarre conversation about what sort of music a cheese would listen to–'

'R & Brie?'

She nodded.

'And then Steve was whispering in my ear – which seemed incredibly erotic at the time – and he was saying that the Big Cheese had turned up and needed handling–'

'Caerphilly?'

Kelly gave me a sharp look.

'Were you having the same dream as me last night?'

'Absolutely not,' I said hastily.

'Anyway. Steve began nuzzling my neck and I let out a blissful sigh as he cooed, "I'm right brie-hind yoooo!" But… but…'

'But what?' I prompted.

'But it wasn't Steve behind me. It was Henry. In real life. My eyes snapped open in the dark just as Henry – boozy breath billowing – took advantage of his conjugal rights with a compliant wife who'd apparently woken him up moaning, "Do it! Do it! I Camembert it any longer." Henry has since stocked up the fridge with three vast blue cheeses and spent yesterday evening encouraging me to have a bedtime snack.'

'Oh dear,' I said, trying not to giggle.

'Do you think that counts as cheating?' she asked fretfully.

'Hardly. After all, Henry is your husband.'

'Not with Henry,' Kelly tutted, rolling her eyes. 'I meant with Steve.'

'No,' I said, telling her what she wanted to hear. 'You're not in a proper relationship with Steve, so how can you have cheated on him?'

'Yes,' she said, sighing with relief. 'You're right. Phew.'

'We're here.' I pointed to the Bluebell Café and the public loos alongside. 'Let's clean up and then have a quick cuppa before heading home.'

'I don't think I have the nerve to go inside the café reeking of *Eau de Monsieur Renard*.'

'I'll do it,' I said, stooping to the task of looping three sets of dogs leads around a nearby post-and-rail fence. 'Let me quickly wash my hands first. Do you want a Cheddar toastie too?'

'No thanks,' said Kelly. She flashed me a grin. 'Right now, I'm all cheesed out.'

## Chapter Three

Ten minutes later, we were sitting outside the café, bums on a bench seat, drinks resting on one of the country park's trestle tables and doing our best to ignore the stiff November breeze.

We huddled into our coats whilst admiring the surrounding woodland which was a stunning backdrop of red, orange and gold. The grassy area around our table was heavily coated in leaf fall, indicating winter was just around the corner.

The three dogs sat together, looking on. Alfie and Sylvie were behaving impeccably, but William was having none of it. He kept up a steady stream of barking, baying his displeasure at being excluded from sampling a slice of carrot cake.

'*Arrroooooooo*!' he wailed repeatedly.

We'd already received some pained looks from other walkers who'd paused to enjoy an al fresco coffee and snack.

'Ignore,' I said to a rattled Kelly.

'Who? William or that cross looking elderly couple sitting over there?'

'Both,' I said firmly.

'I know those two,' she hissed, leaning in.

'Me too,' I whispered back.

'Fred and Mabel Plaistow. Little Waterlow's oldest residents who think they're entitled just because they're days away from receiving the Queen's telegram.'

'You mean the King's telegram,' I pointed out. 'Anyway, I don't think they're *that* ancient.'

'Mabel is giving us absolute daggers,' Kelly muttered. She turned and gave them her own ferocious scowl. 'There,' she said, smirking with satisfaction. 'That'll teach them to glare. Now then' – she took a sip of her drink, a regrouping gesture – 'this morning all I did was moan about Henry. Now it's your turn to moan about Derek. Tell me what's going on.'

I took a slurp of my own drink before replying.

'Nothing,' I sighed. 'It's the same old same old.'

'He's still picking his nose?'

'Yes.'

'And hogging the remote control?'

'Yes. But it's not his habits that rattle the chains of our marriage, Kelly.'

'Ah. In other words, he's still a self-opinionated, arrogant prat who treats you like the dog poo you pick up.'

'Yes,' I sighed again.

'Why don't you leave him?'

'Why don't you leave Henry?' I countered.

'I will when the boys have graduated from uni. I can't risk jeopardising their exam results. Do you *really* think you'll ever leave Derek?'

'One day,' I said, but my words lacked conviction.

‘When exactly is *one day*?’

‘Not sure. Anyway, an escape needs proper planning. After all, I have responsibilities.’

My friend rolled her eyes.

‘You mean being a doormat.’

‘That’s a bit harsh,’ I winced, trying to not look hurt. ‘Ruby might not be at uni like your boys, but she’s still living under our roof. Having unexpectedly made us grandparents, I can hardly turf her out along with my granddaughter, can I?’ I felt upset at the very thought. ‘I know your lads gave you the run-around for a while, but at least they got through their early teenage years without falling in with the wrong crowd and ending up pregnant at fifteen.’

‘Well, being male, they could hardly get pregnant,’ Kelly pointed out.

‘No, but they could easily have got someone else’s daughter up the duff, and how would you have felt then?’

‘Awful,’ Kelly admitted. ‘I’m sorry. Now it’s my turn to have dropped a clanger.’

The subject of Ruby was hardly a fresh one between me and my bestie. A little after her fifteenth birthday, my daughter had announced that her pal Simon was more of a mate than Derek and I had realised. Discovering that a missing ten-pound note from my purse had paid for a pregnancy test – one that showed two blue lines – had given me an instant out-of-body experience.

At the time my mind had splintered in two. I’d watched, from somewhere around ceiling level, the scenario that had gone on to unfold in the kitchen.

There was Ruby in her school uniform. And Simon, tall and gangly. Derek, mercifully, had not yet arrived home from work, so was not around to punch Simon's lights out.

On that lifechanging morning, Ruby had left for school with her hemline too short, eyes defiantly outlined in kohl, and her newly dyed hair an interesting shade of purple. Her attitude for the last twelve months had seesawed between truculent and sneering.

Back then, she'd looked down her nose at me. Her expression could shift from pity to disgust faster than a Tesla's acceleration. I was aware that raging hormones were behind the transformation in my previously sweet girl. Almost overnight she'd morphed into a spotty, bad-tempered adolescent with unexpected tantrums fuelled by pre-menstrual tension. Suddenly everyone was an idiot. I was an idiot. Derek was an idiot. Even the cat next door was an idiot.

On this particular day, she'd returned home from school with Simon. Ruby had revealed an emotion never witnessed before. Fear. She'd tried to disguise it by carelessly tossing the plastic tester across the kitchen table but had then slumped down on a chair. I'd not needed any further explanation.

'I'm not having an abortion,' she'd shrieked into the shocked silence. 'Simon and I have already discussed it. We want to be together. If we have a boy, he'll be called Sunshine Lord, and if it's a girl, she will be named Moonbeam Fairy.'

I'd been unable to reply on account of my essence bobbing somewhere around the kitchen's lightshade. I'd looked on – like a member of the audience at a play – as the drama played out.

Ruby's boyfriend had decided not to sit down at the table – possibly in case Derek came home early and Simon needed to make a quick getaway. The kitchen was too small to pace around, so instead he'd had a complete outbreak of the fidgets, shifting his weight repeatedly from one foot to the other.

'SAY SOMETHING!' Ruby had roared, making Simon visibly jump.

Her outburst had catapulted my mind back into my body which had been leaning against the worktop. The edge had dug painfully into the small of my back.

'Erm,' I'd croaked, before hastily clearing my throat. 'Nice names.'

I hadn't dared say otherwise. Who knew what wrath my disagreement might have caused? Yes, I admit it. I'd been a little scared of my teenager. Keeping the peace had been paramount. Avoiding rows, essential. Deflecting temper outbursts had been all. And trying to keep Derek and Ruby at arm's length from each other had been crucial because, if father and daughter went head-to-head, I'd inadvertently end up as whipping boy for the pair of them. Pathetic? Yes, maybe. But unless you've shared your home with a human box of fireworks, you won't know what it's like being permanently on edge. Waiting for one of them to light the emotional fuse – BOOM! – leaving you trembling at the vileness. The hateful words. The breathtaking ugliness of it all.

# Chapter Four

'I really am sorry,' Kelly repeated.

She put down her cup and enfolded one of my cold hands within hers.

'It's fine,' I said wearily. 'Apology accepted. But you must understand that it's not just about Derek. There are two other people to think about if I pack my bags and run away.'

'I know.' Kelly squeezed my hand. 'But remember that Ruby made the decision to have a baby whilst still a child-woman. You said yourself, not that long ago, that in some respects it was one of the best things to ever happen to her. She ditched the bad attitude and did some rapid growing up.'

'Yes, Ruby did. She was in such a state when Simon's parents moved to Scotland, insisting he go with them. By the time she was six months' pregnant, the enormity of the situation had hit her. She had a complete meltdown. Her boyfriend was off the radar and her unrealistic back-up plans – marrying a footballer or getting on *Love Island* and gaining overnight fame before settling down with a reality star – were in ashes. When she went into labour, the only thing Ruby had in common with her celebrity idols was the whacky name waiting for her newborn.'

'Thank goodness she eventually had the sense to shorten

*Moonbeam Fairy* to *Mo*.'

'Well, I don't know about the Moonbeam bit, but Mo is definitely a little fairy. I've never seen such a dainty child. Her hands and feet are so delicate, and she moves with such grace – almost as if there are wings on her back. When music comes on the radio, she dances round the kitchen like a tiny ballerina.'

'Is Derek a little more involved now as a granddad?'

I gave Kelly an incredulous look.

'Do pigs fly?'

'I'll take that as a no.'

'He was never a hands-on father, never mind a capable grandfather.'

'Yeah, I seem to remember him being shellshocked when Mo treated him to some projectile vomiting. But listen, Wends. You're not exactly left holding the baby now, are you? I mean, I know in the beginning it was you who looked after Mo while Ruby studied or whooped it up at the weekend. But Ruby's head is no longer in the clouds. She's studying hairdressing and Mo is at crèche during the day.'

'I know, but despite Ruby having ambitious plans to one day have her own hair salon, the fact remains that she's still some way from qualifying, never mind getting a job.'

William Beagle chose this point to accelerate his attempts to win our attention for the last mouthful of carrot cake.

'ARRRROOOOOOO!'

'I don't know how Sadie puts up with that dog,' Kelly muttered while deflecting another look of annoyance from Fred and Mabel.

'Beagles can be tricky,' I pointed out. 'But they usually have big hearts.'

'And bigger howls,' Kelly grunted. 'Gordon Bennett. Don't you have anything to keep him quiet?'

'Like a dummy? He's a dog, not a baby.'

'Sadie's three months' pregnant. How on earth is she going to deal with a little one *and* William?'

'I'll probably be walking William a whole lot more once Baby Farrell is born,' I acknowledged. 'I don't mind. Anyway, whether it's walking Sadie and Jack's dogs, or helping Ruby with little Mo, I like to be kept busy. It stops me thinking about how empty my marriage is.'

'At least Derek isn't a borderline alkie like Henry,' Kelly countered.

'I'm not too sure about that,' I muttered. It was nip and tuck these days. 'It's not even the booze, particularly. We simply have nothing in common. Thinking about it, we haven't done for years. And, well, it sounds daft, Kelly, but unless I'm busy, I feel so lonely.'

'It's not daft, Wends. I understand.'

'Anyway, I'm glad you've found Steve to lighten things up. Even if nothing comes of it, right now you're happy, and that's good. I haven't seen you looking so animated in a long time.'

'And you have your darling granddaughter,' Kelly gently pointed out. 'Two years old and the light of your life.'

'She is. Ruby too,' I added. My daughter was the apple of my eye, despite emotionally bruising them both along the adolescent pathway.

'I'm glad everything is okay between the two of you now. I know, for a long time, it was challenging. I just wish you could find your own Steve. Not necessarily to have an affair with. Just to, you know, put a spring in your step.'

I rolled my eyes. Another man? That was the last thing I needed.

'I've 'ad ENOUGH!' boomed a crackly woman's voice.

I turned, wondering if, like me, someone was reaching the end of their marital tether. Instead, I was met by a puce-faced, pop-eyed Mabel Plaistow who was already hauling herself to her feet. For a moment her arthritic hips hampered movement, but her intention was set. She was heading our way.

'Uh-oh,' I muttered.

'I dunno 'ow you two can carry on yakkin'' – she remonstrated – 'because I can't 'ear meself THINK. I love Sadie ter bits but was so glad when she moved into Jack's 'ouse an' took William Beagle with 'er. Livin' next door to that dog tested me patience many a time, an' I can't put up with 'is noise a second longer.'

'Sorry,' I apologised, getting to my feet. 'He is a raucous little fellow, but please don't rush off on account of us. We were about to leave anyway.'

'Good,' said Mabel, not beating about the bush. 'I just 'ope, when Sadie's 'ouse is sold, that I don't end up with another dog owner livin' next door.'

My ears pricked up.

'I thought her place was empty while she considered renting it out?'

'It *is* empty,' Mabel affirmed. 'But she must've finally stopped 'er ditherin' an' decided ter put it on the market, 'cause I saw that lad from the local estate agent this mornin'. He was parked up outside, just before Sadie went off ter work. Anyways' – Mabel stuck her nose in the air and pulled her coat together – 'I'm not one ter gossip, so I'll say no more other than that I'm lookin' forward to a peaceful second cup of coffee once you an' yer menagerie 'ave cleared orf.'

'Er, right. Yes, we'll be off now. Thanks for the heads up about Clover Cottage.'

But I was talking to Mabel's back.

'Cranky old bat,' Kelly hissed under her breath. 'And why has hearing about Clover Cottage potentially going on the market lit your eyes up like a pinball machine?'

'Because… because…' I faltered. 'Just for one mad moment, I was thinking about divorcing Derek, taking my rightful half of the marital home, and blowing it on Sadie's little house. It has two bedrooms. Ruby and Mo could easily share the larger one.'

Kelly's eyes widened in astonishment.

'Do it!' she urged. Suddenly she had a messianic light in her eyes. 'Go on, Wends. Be brave. Take back your power.'

'My girl power?' I gave a mirthless laugh. 'I'm forty-eight. Hardly one of the Spice Girls. Mind you, they're all knocking on a bit now. Hardly girls themselves. Brooklyn Beckham recently married. Maybe he'll soon make Victoria a granny, like me.'

'The Spice Grannies,' Kelly chuckled. 'Nothing wrong

with granny power.' Her eyes twinkled mischievously. 'You're just as glamorous as Victoria. Well, when you want to be,' she added hastily, taking in the well-worn Barbour overlaying ancient and rather bobbly tracksuit bottoms. 'On a good day you look just like Jennifer Aniston.'

'And on a bad day?' I asked cautiously.

'Maggie Smith,' she said, without hesitation.

'Maggie Smith is nearly eighty-eight,' I spluttered.

'I know. So, think on. Preferably before you find yourself in the queue alongside Mabel Plaistow for that congratulatory telegram. Claim your life back, Wends. You still have a lot of living left to do. Give it some consideration in a quiet moment.'

'Maybe.' I stooped to untie William and Sylvie's leads from the post-and-rail. 'Although I can't see Derek ever agreeing to a divorce. What? Lose his unpaid housekeeper? I've more chance of winning the lottery.'

'Even so, when you were chatting to Mabel, I saw a momentary sparkle about you. Like I said, give it some serious thought. About leaving Derek. Not buying Clover Cottage.'

'Don't you like Clover Cottage?'

'Oh, I *lurve* it,' she gushed. 'It's chocolate-box cute. I just couldn't be doing living next door to Little Waterlow's biggest curtain twitchers.'

# Chapter Five

William Beagle and Sylvie, the Golden Retriever, lived in nearby West Malling.

I could have easily opted to walk both dogs at a nearby park, just around the corner from Jack and Sadie's house. And sometimes I did, unless I was meeting up with Kelly, like I had done today. Fortunately, most of my canine customers were not averse to clambering into the back of Betty, my ancient Citroen Picasso, for a jaunt elsewhere.

I had keys to all of my clients' houses, and codes to several burglar alarms. Sometimes it was a little daunting dealing with different security systems. Recently, I'd had a memory blip and failed to recall Sadie's security code. Within minutes, a modified van with blacked-out windows had roared into the peaceful gated development. A uniformed guy had leapt out, looking for all the world like he was a member of the SAS. After he'd reset the alarm, he'd subjected me to an awful lot of questions. I'd eventually left the premises with a red face and damp armpits.

Today, happily, the iffy menopausal brain cells didn't let me down, and I went inside the house without any issues. Sylvie obediently sat on the doormat, waiting to have her paws wiped. Sadie always left an old towel by the back door.

However, William Beagle showed no such finesse or consideration. He barged past, leaving dirty paddy-paw prints on Sadie's immaculate kitchen floor.

'Hey,' I called after him. 'Look what you've done.'

Muttering oaths, I grabbed a handy roll of kitchen towel. Ripping off several sheets, I dampened them under the tap, and then swiftly cleaned up the marks. My knees clicked as I creaked upright. Balling up the wet paper, I lobbed it into the bin, then did a time check. It was a little after noon. Kelly and I had spent far too much time nattering at Trosley. I needed to crack on, get to the supermarket, and buy the weekend groceries.

I turned to Sylvie.

'Right, lovely lady. Your mum told me she'd be back from her exhibition no later than four o'clock. Now be a good girl and have a nap until she's home.'

Sylvie seemed to understand. She padded out to the hallway and went to her basket. I followed behind her and immediately spotted Rosemary and Thyme, Sadie's cats. They'd invaded Sylvie's space and were currently curled up within the basket's fleecy interior. Sylvie gently nudged Thyme's bottom to one side, then collapsed down next to the pair of them, sighing with contentment.

'You are such a sweetheart,' I said, stooping to rub one silky ear. 'You never give anyone a moment's trouble, but your brother is something else.' I straightened up. 'Where has he gone?'

As if hearing me, William emerged from the lounge and shot straight up the staircase.

'Oy!' I hollered after him. 'You're banned from going upstairs. Your mum doesn't like you lolling over the beds so I think you'll find all the bedroom doors are shut.'

William looked down at me from the landing. "Is that so?" his expression seemed to say. A second later and he'd vertically bounced against the nearest doorhandle. It immediately gave way and the door swung open. He gave me a cocky look – ha! – before disappearing within.

'Terrific,' I muttered.

Now what? Go up and try and wrestle with a beagle that promptly played dead and refused to move? For a small dog he was surprisingly heavy. Or pretend I'd not noticed and quietly tiptoe away? There was a dog crate in the kitchen used for emergency measures, but I knew that Sadie wasn't keen on containing her beloved beagle within its confines. Consequently, William got away with doggy murder.

Before I could make up my mind about what to do for the best, there was the sound of a key in the front door. I turned just in time to see Sadie walking in.

'Hi, Wendy,' she said, giving me a dazzling smile.

Everything about Sadie was warm, from her long vibrant red hair to her radiant complexion, the latter of which was possibly heightened by the early stages of pregnancy.

'Have you just got back with the dogs?' she asked, closing the door behind her.

'Yes, and I'm ever so sorry, but William evaded me and let himself into your bedroom before I had a chance to wipe his paws. That said, I think most of the mud came off on the kitchen floor beforehand. I did wipe it up.'

'I'm not going to worry about a bit of dirt,' she laughed, moving over to the bottom step of the staircase. She sat down and pulled off her Uggs. 'The duvet can be washed. Jack and I gave up a long time ago trying to change William's ways. He may be a handful, but he's good-natured, and that's the most important thing.' She stood up, shrugged off her coat, then tucked it away in the cupboard by the stairs. 'Fancy having a coffee before you head off?'

'Well,' I dithered. Nothing would be nicer than spending a pleasant half hour gossiping with Sadie. 'I met up with a friend earlier and we had a drink at Trosley.'

'Can't I twist your arm to have another? I do believe a certain amount of caffeine is beneficial for one's health,' she dimpled.

'Go on then,' I grinned, following her into the kitchen. 'But let me make it for you. You've been on your feet all morning and must be tired in your condition.'

'Nonsense,' she protested. 'I drove to the exhibition. And to be honest, although the place was manic, I spent most of the time sitting down. I shared the stand with my pal, Charlotte. She said she'd finish the afternoon session off for me. She could see I was getting ants in my pants because I have a pile of accounts waiting for some attention. I'm good at my pottery business, but not so great with paperwork,' she laughed.

'Oh, but if you have your accounts to do, I'm holding you up,' I protested.

'Absolutely not.' She shook her head. 'There's still time for a natter before I don my Admin Hat.' She gave me a rueful look. 'I have to say, since getting pregnant, I've been terribly scatty. Do you think that's normal?'

'Um' – I wrinkled my brow – 'not sure. It's been so long since I was pregnant, I've forgotten.'

'Give over. You don't look a day over thirty-five.'

'You're very kind,' I said, sitting down at the table.

Sadie reached for a kettle that looked as if it had been designed by NASA.

'Not kind at all,' she said, shaking her head. 'I'm being honest.'

She reached for a couple of mugs from an overhead cupboard. Both were captioned. One said *APPROACH WITH CAUTION UNTIL I'VE DRUNK MY COFFEE.* The other declared *MY BRAIN HAS TOO MANY TABS OPEN.* She poured boiling water over granules, then set the mugs on the table.

'That reminds me,' she said, staring at the two captions. 'I must ring the estate agent.'

My ears pricked up like William Beagle's.

'I heard you're selling Clover Cottage.'

She peered at me over the rim of her cup.

'How on earth did you find that out?'

'Mabel Plaistow. She was at The Bluebell Café earlier and happened to mention it.'

'Flaming heck.' Sadie blew out her cheeks. 'That's the trouble with that village. People tell you what's going on in your life before you even know what's happening yourself. I have to say, much as I loved Little Waterlow's community atmosphere, I don't miss living there.'

'I can understand that.' I gave her a sympathetic smile.

A while ago, the spotlight had fallen upon Sadie during an unhappy period of her life. As a result, she'd become the talk of the village. Residents hadn't been able to walk into The Angel for a drink without hearing someone mentioning Sadie's name. She'd unwittingly become the subject of gossip again when Jack's ex-girlfriend had turned out to be a few biscuits short of the full pack.

'So, are you definitely selling?' I asked.

'Yes,' she said firmly. 'I've thought long and hard about it. At one point I was going to rent the place out, fully furnished, too. However, not all tenants are honourable, and I didn't like the idea of someone slopping drink over the furniture, or leaving stains on the rugs, or white rings on the wood-topped tables. I've put a lot of love into that house. Much of the furniture was sourced second-hand, but Charlotte upcycled everything as a gift. I'm sure you've seen some of her stuff in the local magazine. It's awesome. I couldn't bear to risk the house and its contents being treated shabbily by a possibly inconsiderate tenant, so I stalled on the rental. However, now that Jack and I are married with a baby on the way, I won't be living there again. Also, I'm still throwing money at the place, like the outstanding mortgage for starters. So, after much consideration, I've had the cottage valued.'

Suddenly my heart was beating far too quickly.

'Clover Cottage saw me through a very dark period of my life,' Sadie continued. 'It was my sanctuary. I felt safe there. I'd like to think that whoever buys it might look upon it as their own haven.’

Now my heart was threatening to squeeze through a couple of ribs and leap right across Sadie’s beautiful kitchen.

‘Although’ – she added – ‘it’s going to be a problem emptying the cottage out. Putting all its furniture into storage is going to be expensive. I suppose I could get one of those house clearance places to take it all away.’

‘Um…’ I croaked, fiddling like mad with the handle on my mug. ‘Would you be prepared to sell it fully furnished?’

Sadie looked at me quizzically.

‘Why? Do you know someone who might be interested?’

‘Er…’ My voice was now no more than a strangled whisper. ‘Yes. Me.’

# Chapter Six

Sadie regarded me in surprise.

'I think you'll find Clover Cottage to be a bit on the small side. I mean, if you're looking to downsize, then it would be okay for you and Derek, but don't you still have Ruby and Mo at home?'

'I do.' I licked my lips nervously. 'But…' I closed my eyes for a moment and then took a deep breath. 'I have a mad idea rampaging through my skull.'

I put my fingers to my temples and gave them a savage rub. Dropping my hands into my lap, I looked at Sadie's kind face which was etched with concern.

'I-I'm thinking about leaving Derek,' I stuttered. There. The words were out in the open. 'Let me correct that.' I cleared my throat, straightening my spine at the same time. 'I *am* leaving Derek. So, I'll be wanting my own place – my own safe haven.'

My heart, unused to such frantic activity while the body was static, felt like it was going berserk. Was I having a panic attack?

'You've gone very pale,' said Sadie gently. 'Take some deep breaths.'

I did as she said, doing my best not to hyperventilate.

'Sorry,' I gasped, trying not to sound like I was in the midst of single-handedly blowing up an airbed.

'It's okay. That's better. You have some colour returning to your cheeks.' Sadie gave a reassuring smile as my breathing steadied. 'My goodness. That's quite an announcement you've just made.'

'I meant every word,' I said, still wrestling a tad with the breathing.

'Wow.' Sadie blew out her cheeks.

'You're the first to officially know.'

'You mean, Derek has no idea?'

'He's currently oblivious.' I briefly studied my hands before looking at her again. 'Does that make me sound like a complete bitch?'

'Hey, I'm not judging you, Wendy. Your body's reaction a moment ago tells me that you're a very stressed lady. And, you know, stress isn't good for the body. It can play havoc if you're not careful.'

'I expect you're right.'

'There's no *expect* about it. The last thing you want is to end up taking to your bed, like I did. Apart from missing out on life's big adventure – for every day is exactly that – the downside is feeling lousy *and* causing your family worry.'

I gave her a rueful smile.

'I guess you're a lady who speaks from experience.'

'Yes, and if I could put back the clock, I would. There's nothing worse than sticking a plaster on a failing relationship. It's like a sore that keeps getting bigger and bigger until the plaster falls off revealing a stinking mess. It's much better to act early on. Self-preservation is all when it comes to matters of the heart.'

'I did hear about…' – I chose my words carefully – 'your situation with Felix.'

'Of course you did. Everyone heard. As I said, you can't live in Little Waterlow without being the subject of gossip at some point. At the time, I thought I'd never get over Felix and' – she sighed – 'well, you know the rest of the tale. I won't bore you regurgitating it. But life goes on, Wendy. I never thought I'd love again, but now I know I have the real deal.'

'I'm so pleased for you.' My words were sincere. 'You deserve it.'

'Everyone deserves it, and one day you'll meet Mr Right too.'

I instantly recoiled.

'Don't even go there,' I shuddered. 'What, *another* man to look after? *Another* bloke who can't be bothered to pick up his socks? Who clears off to the driving range at the weekend leaving you to struggle, alone, with all the heavy shopping? Or lets you get a backache as you singlehandedly weed all the flowerbeds and mow the lawn? Why are men so useless?'

'Some are, and some aren't. Felix let me wait on him and totally took me for granted. Thankfully Jack is kind, considerate and always willing to help.'

'He's lovely, your Jack, and handsome with it. You both make a very striking couple.'

'Thank you,' Sadie smiled. 'And when you leave Derek,

I get the feeling you won't be alone for long. Call it female intuition.'

'I think your female intuition might have lost its compass,' I said, giving a rueful grin.

'You should ask Jack to give you a reading,' Sadie chuckled.

'A reading?' I frowned. 'What, you mean like tarot cards, or something?'

'Kind of, but with tea leaves instead. Jack's gran taught him, and he's rather good at it.'

'I'm not sure I believe in that sort of thing.' I pulled a face. 'Anyway, I haven't even started the separation process yet, although telling you has been a starting point. The subject is becoming more real by the second.'

'Really? You're absolutely sure about wanting to leave Derek?'

'Yes,' I said, this time without hesitation. 'A hundred per cent. This weekend I shall pick my moment to tell him. However, if you could keep it to yourself for now, I'd be very grateful.'

'Oh your secret is safe with me,' Sadie assured. 'I promise not to tell a soul. Not even Jack. You have my word.'

'That's very sweet of you, Sadie. And I really do mean it. I want to buy Clover Cottage. Can you give me a few days' grace to set the necessary wheels in motion?'

'Look, how about you properly view Clover Cottage first? That way, you can be sure it's what you want. I'm happy to show you right now if it's convenient for you.'

'But what about your accounts?' I protested. 'If you take me to the cottage, I'll be holding you up.'

'Listen, the accounts will still be here when I get back. Anyway, if you're serious, I'll have to tell Lenny – he's the estate agent – that the property is as good as sold.'

'I'm deadly serious,' I promised.

Sadie scooped up her keys.

'Come on, then.' She flashed a mischievous grin that said we were in this together. 'I feel like a naughty schoolgirl playing hooky, hoping the headmistress doesn't catch me out. Let's go.'

I stood up with sudden alacrity. Heavens, could this really be happening? Me, Wendy Walker, forty-eight years old, a grandmother no less, on the threshold of a brand-new future? As I trotted after Sadie, I mentally punched the air, adding a silent shriek of *yippeeeeeeee!*

God knows what Derek would say.

# Chapter Seven

I followed Sadie's car back to Little Waterlow, breathing in sharply as our respective vehicles squeezed past a tractor coming in the opposite direction.

In that moment I was grateful not to have a flashy car. As my vehicle hugged a thorny hedgerow that bordered the lane where Clover Cottage was located, for a few seconds the only sounds that could be heard was that of twigs scraping Betty's paintwork.

This side of the village was very rural with fields full of grazing cows and sheep. It was stunningly pretty in summer when the sun shone down on meadows dotted with brightly coloured wildflowers.

In winter it was a different place. Stripped of leaves, the trees would stretch their branches against a bleak, milk-white sky. I also knew that the wind could howl across those same fields that were so open to the elements. Gusts would rattle the rafters and letterboxes of the cottages crouched over the North Downs.

Sadie parked directly outside Clover Cottage. I was pleased to note there were spaces for two vehicles. This meant there would be no issue for Ruby parking the little Fiat 500 my parents had so generously bought for her recent birthday.

I shoe-horned Betty into the space beside Sadie's car, belatedly realising there wasn't quite enough room to open any of the car's doors. My Picasso was much bigger than Ruby's Fiat so, right now, I was well and truly hemmed in by Sadie's vehicle on one side and a vast hedge on the other.

Sadie tapped on Betty's rear window, making me jump.

'How are you going to get out?' she called.

I pointed and mimed by way of answer. *The boot.* Thank goodness I was dressed in my scruffy dog-walking trousers and wouldn't have to hitch up the hemline of a skirt.

Sadie watched in disbelief as I reared up from Betty's front seat, twisted round, bashed my privates on the gearstick, clambered over the brake, fell awkwardly into the rear passenger area, hit my knee on Mo's rigid car seat, then wrestled with the rear-folding seat's lever, before finally crawling into the cargo area. I knocked on the window for Sadie to let me out. She released the catch and the rear door swung upwards.

'My goodness,' she declared, as I scrambled out. 'You're bendy.'

'Yes,' I agreed, panting slightly. 'That was one of my nicknames at school. Bendy Wendy. The other being Wendy House. Not very original, eh?' I locked the boot. 'I remember, as a stroppy teenager, getting very cross with my mother for giving me the name. The class bully taunted me all the time.'

When I'd met Derek, he'd also called me Bendy Wendy on account of how I'd managed to fold up my body for sex in the back of his Ford Escort. At the time, we'd had nowhere else to go for shenanigans.

For a moment I found myself wondering what had happened to those two giggling youngsters… the carefree blonde who thought herself sassy and daring, and the slightly gangly boy who had laughed aloud and larked along. At what point had that young couple grown into a tight-lipped man and a resentful woman with little in common other than the genes of their daughter and granddaughter?

'Being a teenager isn't easy,' said Sadie, dragging my mind back to the present. 'I was teased mercilessly for having red hair.'

'Probably jealousy.' I followed her between our respective vehicles, moving towards the garden gate. 'Your hair is beautiful. It's your crowning glory.'

'Thanks,' she smiled. Her attention immediately fragmented at the sight of an elderly lady who'd appeared on the doorstep of the cottage next door. 'Oh dear,' she said, under her breath.

I followed her gaze, and my heart sank at the sight of Mabel Plaistow. The old girl hovered, making a show of deadheading flowers from a pot of long-withered geraniums. Mabel looked up as we approached. Her expression was cool.

'I saw you this mornin',' she said, eyes narrowing.

'You did,' I agreed pleasantly. I stood alongside Sadie as she paused by the front door. 'How are you?' I politely enquired. After all, it might be a good idea to ingratiate myself to Mabel. Especially as I was hoping that we'd soon be neighbours.

'I'm the same as this mornin',' she said dourly. 'Me ears are still ringin' from the racket William Beagle made – all over a slice of cake. I've never known a dog like it. I 'ope yer 'aven't brought 'im with yer.'

'No, Mabel,' Sadie soothed. 'He's at home having a nap, but on his behalf, I convey sincere apologies. Anyway, we won't hold you up.'

Sadie stuck her key in the lock and pushed against the door.

'I saw Lenny 'ere earlier,' said Mabel, not yet willing to let Sadie go. 'Are yer already showin' people around then?'

Sadie gave the tiniest of sighs as she turned back to face Mabel.

'This is Wendy, my friend. She's looking at some of the furniture that would otherwise go into storage. But you're right, Mabel. I am thinking about selling. That said, I haven't yet made a firm decision.'

'I see.' Mabel gathered her cardigan across her matronly bosom. The gesture indicated that she was offended by Sadie redirecting the conversation away from the local estate agent and any confirmation of selling. 'I know of *you*,' she said, addressing me again. 'I've seen yer 'usband out and about, and so 'as my Sharon.'

'Yes, well, I suppose Little Waterlow isn't exactly a big place. We all know most of the faces here, if not always the names.'

'I know the name of the woman yer 'usband was with,' said Mabel, eyes glinting behind her wire-rimmed spectacles. 'She calls 'erself Coco.'

I raised my eyebrows in surprise.

'I don't think either of us know any lady by that name.'

'I don't suppose *you* do,' Mabel sniffed. 'But yer 'usband does, and I don't mind tellin' yer that she's no lady. She's trouble, that's what she is. My Sharon knows all about it because she rents the 'ouse next door. She's brought shame ter the village.'

'Er' – my brows knitted in confusion – 'Sharon or Coco?'

Mabel instantly bristled.

'Coco,' she snapped. 'My Sharon is sixty years old. She's done with all that nonsense. Unlike yer 'usband. I suppose 'e found Coco on one of those new-fangled dating baps.'

'You mean a dating app,' Sadie corrected. 'I think I know the one you're talking about. It's called *The Butter Half*.'

'I see,' I said, not really seeing at all. 'I don't think my husband is into dating apps, Mabel, being that he's married to me.'

'Is that so,' she said darkly.

'Sorry, Mabel,' Sadie interrupted. 'But I have an appointment with my accountant in half an hour. I need to crack on showing Wendy this furniture I'm looking to get rid of.'

'Oh, right, love. Well, don't mind me.' Mabel sniffed again. 'You two carry on. I'm not one ter gossip, as yer know.'

She turned on her slippered heel and went back into her own home, all pretence about deadheading flowers now forgotten.

'Sorry about that,' said Sadie, as we stepped into the tiny hall. 'At least you know what you're letting yourself in for if you move here.' She shut the door behind us. 'Heaven knows what Mabel was yakking on about. Perhaps she's losing her marbles. She is eighty-something, after all.'

'It's fine,' I laughed. 'What would the world be like if we didn't have the likes of Mabel telling us what our husbands are supposedly up to.'

'Well, quite,' Sadie agreed.

'Now if your neighbour had told me that she'd spotted Derek at the driving range or on the golf course, or even in the club's bar indulging in a sneaky pint and a ploughman's, then I'd have agreed with her.'

'Ah, you're a golf widow.' Sadie smiled sympathetically. 'Do you know, I have a solicitor friend who told me that the single biggest factor in divorces for the over sixties – not that you're anywhere near that age' – she added hastily – 'is down to golf.'

'I can believe it,' I nodded, following Sadie into a delightfully quaint sitting room. 'Oh, this is gorgeous.'

I gazed about in delight at the small but cosy lounge. Cut logs were neatly stacked in an alcove which also housed a sizeable woodburning stove. I could imagine it burning brightly on a cold winter evening as I sat, legs curled under my bottom, on that lusciously thick rug. I'd be holding a plate of hot buttery toast in one hand and a cuppa in the other while a cheesy romance played out on the telly. The remote control would rest on the hearth, untouched. There would be no husband snatching it up to flick the channel to a bunch of footballers running back and forth, or a famous golfer – whose name meant nothing to me – doing a record-breaking hole-in-one. Bliss!

'Do you like it?' asked Sadie, straightening jewel-coloured cushions on a squashy looking sofa.

'I love it,' I breathed, taking in the small sideboard and coffee table that looked like they had once been pallets. 'Did your friend really revamp these pieces?'

'Yup,' said Sadie happily. 'Charlotte is one of those people who could turn a removal company's packing crate into something spectacular. Let me show you the kitchen.'

By the time I'd wandered through the rest of the cottage, I was enchanted. I was pleased to note that both bedrooms were a decent enough size and wouldn't present any space problems for Ruby sharing with Mo. Outside, there was a pocket-sized garden with a small outbuilding. This was where Sadie had founded her pottery business.

'It shouldn't be hard to connect running water,' she said, as I voiced aloud the possibility of turning the outbuilding into a mini hair salon. 'The biggest factor with the local council is parking for clients. They want to be sure it doesn't impact on the road. I didn't have that problem as I delivered to clients. I'd suggest extending the current parking area by getting rid of the hedge, which is thoroughly overgrown. The boundary line belongs to Clover Cottage, so taking it down won't be a problem.'

'That's good to know,' I said.

My mind was racing with possibilities.

'So' – Sadie led me back inside – 'are you still up for buying the place along with everything within?'

'Absolutely,' I replied, eyes shining. 'Obviously there's a few things to sort out first.' My tone was deliberately blasé. 'Nothing major.' Just a small matter of ending a twenty-seven-year-old marriage.

I had no idea how or when to broach the subject with Derek. While he was shouting at a referee? "You PILLOCK! Are you BLIND? That should have been a RED CARD. Why are you hovering, Wendy? What did you say? A divorce? Yes, yes, fine. Whatever. Have we any crisps? I fancy some nibbles." I'd have to pick my moment.

'There's absolutely no rush,' Sadie assured. 'But it would be nice to have a completion date marked in our respective diaries for, say, six months' time. How does that sound?'

'Marvellous,' I breathed, hiding my hands behind my back in case Sadie noticed my crossed fingers.

# Chapter Eight

Sadie pushed Betty's boot lid down as I repeated the assault course back to the steering wheel.

Landing in the driving seat, I looked up to see a shadow fall across the net curtains of Mabel's lounge window. Ah ha! The old lady was spying. The nets began to twitch like a shoal of fish out of water. As I started Betty up, I flashed a cheeky grin and waved. The curtains instantly stopped moving.

Despite Sadie giving the excuse about me being interested in furniture, I knew that, right now, Mabel's brain was whirring. The rumour mill was about to go into action. It would begin with Mabel immediately gossiping to Fred. "That Wendy woman was lookin' around next door. What's the bettin' she'll be back but without that 'usband of 'ers? Somethin's afoot, Fred, and it's not my fluffy slippers."

As I set off, I knew there would be a reaction. Village gossip. And if I didn't box clever, it would only be a matter of time before Derek overheard something and then challenged me.

As I shunted Betty into third gear, my mind set a scene; me, peeling sprouts in the kitchen while Derek looked on suspiciously. Would he hem me in against the cupboards? If so, escape would be impossible. I could see him now, angrily demanding to know why I'd been viewing a cottage before it was even on the market. "Are you mad, woman? I'm not moving from our comfortable semi." Then me carefully setting down the paring knife, turning to him, stuttering, "W-Well, actually, D-Derek, I'm off." How would he react? "You're leaving me? And what are you going to survive on, Wendy? The sprouts that you're peeling? Because you'll not be able to afford much else on your piddly income."

I'd definitely have to pick my moment, and preferably without Ruby and Mo around. Or should I tell Ruby first? Or might she be horrified? "Omigod. I'm going to be a child from a broken home. Isn't it bad enough that my baby girl has no father figure? Are you *really* going to deprive Mo of the one man in her life?"

But then again, Ruby could always live with her father. Couldn't she? I had a fleeting vision of my daughter and husband squaring up to each other. He, outraged over her refusal to cook his dinner. She, incensed at him saying no to babysitting Mo.

Or should I not say anything to either of them until I'd sought the advice of a solicitor? Suddenly I felt overwhelmed about which way to turn.

I pressed down on Betty's brake pedal and rolled to a stop by a red traffic light. I was only a couple of minutes away from Mo's crèche but still had half an hour to kill before the collection deadline. I dithered. Should I pop into the local Costcutter grocery store? I'd run out of time to do the usual cusp-of-the-weekend big shop at King's Hill, but –

if I hurried – I could chuck a few things in a wire basket from this little store.

I mentally ran through my shopping list: milk, bread, and something for dinner tonight, other than fishfingers and alphabet spaghetti. The latter would guarantee Derek having a hissy fit. "Do you honestly think this is a meal fit for a hungry man after working his socks off? I mean, what *is* this, Wendy?" he'd likely splutter, while his fork stabbed a pasta-shaped A. Me replying, "Why, Derek, I do believe it's an A for Arsehole."

The traffic light changed to green, and I once again set off. I wanted two things this evening. First, Derek not ranting about the meal put in front of him. Second, a peaceful shop without Mo on my hip screaming blue murder. Especially when Nanna refused to buy twenty packets of *thweeties*.

The thought of Mo's angelic face morphing into apoplectic rage, was enough to have me pushing down on the accelerator. I headed smartly towards the mini supermarket – alone.

Inside, I grabbed a basket and set about chucking things within. First, the loaf. Phew, that was lucky. There were only two remaining on the shelf. Second, a large carton of milk. I trotted to the end of the aisle and wrestled a jumbo jobbie from the refrigerator cabinet.

*Oh, look what you've done,* sighed my inner voice. *You've squashed the bread.*

'Bugger,' I muttered, tugging the sliced white from under the hefty carton. It now looked like it had been stamped on. Did I have the nerve to return it to the bread section and swap it for the very last loaf? Yes.

I retraced my steps then, looking about furtively, retrieved the flattened loaf. I was just about to slide it back from whence it came, when there was a tap on my shoulder.

'And WHAT do you think you're doing?' said a stern female voice.

I squeaked in terror and promptly dropped the wire basket. It landed painfully on my foot.

'*Owww*,' I bleated.

I stooped to pick it up, crimson with embarrassment.

'Sorry.' I put the loaf back in my basket. The milk carton was now battered too. 'I was–'

I broke off and stared at my interrogator. Far from it being a Costcutter security employee, it was my bestie.

'Kelly!' I croaked in relief.

'Sorry, Wends,' she roared, creasing up with laughter. 'I didn't mean for you to hurt your foot, but I couldn't resist making you feel guilty about that knackered bread.' She peered into my basket. 'Look at the state of it! You're not going to buy it, are you?'

'I suppose I'd better,' I shrugged. 'After all, I'm the one who wrecked it.'

'Don't be ridiculous.' She quickly looked from left to right, then deftly swapped it for the one that didn't look like it had been flattened by a steamroller. 'At the prices they charge in here, they can afford to miss out on the sale of one loaf. Anyway, Mrs Patel will simply *whoops* it and someone will make a bread-and-butter pudding with the squashed loaf. No harm done.'

'Thanks,' I said, exhaling with relief.

'I'm glad I've bumped into you because it saves me ringing later.'

'Oh?'

Kelly gave me an expectant look. Her eyes were shining.

'So tell me!' she urged.

'Tell you what?' I frowned.

'You know. About–'

'*Excuse* me,' said a pained male voice.

I turned to see a very attractive middle-aged man trying to manoeuvre his shopping trolley past us. However, his good looks were marred by the irritation etched into his features. Shame. He reminded me of Paul Newman in his heyday, but right now the piercing blue eyes boring into mine were like two chips of ice.

'Why do women always block shopping aisles?' he snapped. Kelly and I immediately stepped aside, but he didn't pass us. 'Can't you both gossip somewhere else? In a coffee shop? Over the garden fence? Outside the school gates? I mean why, specifically, here?'

'Sorry,' I quickly apologised. Best to nip any argument in the bud, especially as Kelly was likely to retort, "Because we want to."

The man's eyes flashed with annoyance.

'I suppose you're also the type of woman who thoughtlessly parks her car on pavements or blocks folks' driveways.'

'What if I am?' I said, bristling slightly at his words of truth.

'Because it's annoying and inconsiderate,' he retorted. 'Now if you don't mind, I'd like to get to that shelf you're obstructing. I want a loaf of bread.'

'A loaf of bread?' I repeated stupidly.

'Is there an echo in here?'

Kelly edged away, suddenly very interested in the Jaffa cakes further down the aisle. Meanwhile, the man's gaze had dropped to the contents of my wire basket.

'Your milk carton is battered, almost as if it's been dropped. So how come your bread isn't squashed?'

I straightened myself up to my full five foot four inches.

'I'm afraid I can't hang around making conversation with you. You see, we're blocking this aisle.'

And with that I moved smartly after Kelly, who had already disappeared into the next aisle.

'Gordon Bennett,' she muttered, as I caught up with her. 'Let's get out of here before he discovers that the last remaining loaf of bread is now flatter than a pancake.'

'But I need something for dinner,' I said, pausing by a chiller cabinet. 'Oh look. Minced beef.'

I had plenty of passata in the larder at home. I could easily knock up a spaghetti bolognese. Kelly grabbed a packet for me.

'Here you are,' she said, tossing the meat into my basket.

'Mind my bread,' I squawked, half expecting Paul Newman to be lurking nearby.

'Never mind the bread,' Kelly hissed. 'Hurry up and tell me your news.'

'What are you on about?'

'Clover Cottage, of course! You *are* buying it, aren't you?'

My eyes widened in surprise.

'How on earth did you know–'

'I bumped into Fred Plaistow as I was coming in here. He was just on his way out. He looked at me and said, "Oh, you again. You were at Trosley Park earlier." And then he went on to say that Mabel had rung his mobile. She told him you'd been over at Clover Cottage measuring up before moving in.' Kelly clocked the giveaway expression on my face. 'Oh, my goodness.' Her eyes widened. 'I'm reading you like an open book. It's true, right?'

I took a deep breath.

'Yes, I am buying it, but–'

'*Excuse* me,' said a horribly familiar voice. Paul Newman had materialised behind us. 'Not only are you once again blocking the aisle, but I wondered' – he held up a squashed loaf – 'if you'd like to trade your bread for this one? After all, it would match your milk carton perfectly.'

# Chapter Nine

'Wretched man,' I said to Kelly as we stood outside the Costcutter.

My cheeks were still flaming with embarrassment – not that I'd owned up to knowing anything about the flattened bread. Paul Newman had flashed us a telling look before trundling off with his trolley.

'He knew,' I added.

'Yes,' she agreed, as we walked to the small carpark at the rear. 'He looked livid. By comparison, he made Roger Hargreaves' Mister Angry look positively orgasmic.'

'Kelly!' I hissed, glancing around lest young ears be listening.

'Well it's true,' she tutted. 'Shame, because he was a bit of all right.'

'If you like that sort of thing,' I sniffed.

'He's certainly miles better looking than my current beau.'

'Well go back in there and chat him up. Offer to unsquash his loaf, or something.'

'You mean invite him to look at my baps?' she snorted.

I rolled my eyes. Kelly loved to resort to smut.

'Anyway' – she continued – 'I think I'd be wasting my

breath. He didn't even seem to notice me.'

'That's because you sidled off,' I pointed out.

'Before that,' she countered. 'When he caught up with us for the second time, he didn't so much as glance at me. Those amazing eyes were firmly fixed on you.'

'Yeah, because I had the loaf he wanted. Anyway, I'd better get a wiggle on and collect Mo. If you're more than ten minutes late, the nursery fines you twenty quid.'

'That's outrageous.'

'Yes,' I agreed. 'Unfortunately, they're private and can make up their rules as they go along.'

'Don't forget' – she added, pointing the zapper at her car – 'to keep me in the loop about Clover Cottage *and* your marital status.'

'Will do,' I squeaked, noticing the effect her last two words had on my body.

Butterflies were suddenly dancing in my belly. A nervous reaction. Blimey, and I hadn't yet even broached the subject of separation with Derek. This heightened feeling of anxiety didn't bode well for my chat with him.

I hopped into Betty and started the engine. As the car inched forward, I spotted Paul Newman exiting the shop. Horrible man. I hadn't seen him around these parts before. Was he new to Little Waterlow? His bright blue eyes suddenly snagged on mine. I quickly looked away, pretending I hadn't seen him.

Fred and Mabel Plaistow might be the biggest village gossips, but at least I knew where I was with them as future neighbours. I momentarily recoiled at the thought of having someone like Paul Newman as a neighbour. I had a mental picture of pegging laundry on the line in the tiny garden, and then Paul Newman's face appearing on the other side of the fence. "Ah, Mrs Walker. Wouldn't you agree that *this* is the best place for an informal chat? How uplifting to know that Costcutter's aisles are now free from one more gossiping woman."

But then again, Paul Newman was a man and unlikely to partake in exchanging pleasantries over a garden fence. He probably had a wife who did that on his behalf. Or maybe his wife was just like him. Perhaps she had matching eyes that froze your soul at ten paces.

I joined the main road and headed off in the direction of Mo's nursery, dismissing Paul Newman and his eyes that were colder than a North Pole ice floe. Instead, I thought about Derek's eyes. Dark brown. Mocking. Who had said that a person's eyes were the doorway to their soul? I couldn't remember. Nonetheless, I was inclined to agree with that pearl of wisdom.

Derek's eyes had never been merry, although they must have once held some warmth. I couldn't remember when the inner light had died but, just like a blown-out candle, the fun had been extinguished. How long had his eyes been devoid of joy? Two years? Five? My mind stretched back to find the answer. I was shocked to realise that it was more like a decade ago. Ten years of just going through the motions with each other. I'd been too busy to realise. Too caught up in the juggle of raising my daughter, virtually singlehandedly, while running a home and holding down a job in London as a legal secretary, knackered from keeping all those balls in the air.

I couldn't remember how many times Ruby had shaken me awake over the years, either not feeling well or lamenting about a forgotten piece of homework. Midnight was usually the appointed time for her bursting into our bedroom. Not forgetting, of course, the absolute favourite: "Muuummmmmm! I completely forgot to tell you that I'm a shepherd in the school play and need an outfit." Cue me peering blearily at her in the gloom. "It's okay, darling. We'll make one together this weekend." Her sobbing. "No, I need it tomorrow." Me looking at the bedside clock and realising that today was already tomorrow. Derek snoring peacefully by my side, ear buds in, eye mask on, undisturbed as I reared up from the covers like a squinty-eyed sea monster, before rushing downstairs with a distraught daughter at my heel.

At this witching hour, a fifteen-minute frenzy of activity would then take place. I would raid the tea towel drawer. Flop the cloth over Ruby's head. Secure it *just so* with an Alice band. Then rummage within the hot cupboard for a spare flat sheet and hack it to bits. "A hole here, for your head. See, darling?" The kitchen scissors would then flash under the overhead lighting as a crude hemline would be quickly fashioned. "Don't worry, sweetheart. Nobody had Wonder Web when Joseph and Mary were around." Next, swiping one of Derek's ties to use as a fastener around Ruby's waist. "Look at you, Rubes! You're going to be the best dressed shepherd in the school play!" And then – after hurriedly wangling an afternoon off work – crashing into the school hall thirty seconds before curtain-up only to discover kids wearing flashy costumes that their parents had bought online. I cringed at the memory. Poor Ruby's attire had seemed to shout, "MY MUM AND DAD DON'T CARE!"

Derek had never once made the effort to attend such events. "Do you really expect me to watch a bunch of kids re-enact a scene from some long-ago event that hardly anyone truly believes in? I'd rather watch grass grow."

Nor had Derek ever attended Ruby's parents' evenings. He'd cited stress as the reason. I'd never quite understood how being a self-employed painter and decorator had sent his adrenalin levels soaring. Unlike me, he'd never had to deal with cancelled trains, or an irate boss demanding coffee for six in the boardroom while you were still shrugging off your coat. "Now, please, Wendy. And by the way, there's a thirty-two-page contract on your desk for amendment which I'd like in the next five minutes."

However, three years ago, my boss had delivered unexpected news. The firm was merging with another, and I was one of several to be made redundant. I hadn't exactly wept, but noticing the twenty-somethings who had kept their jobs while the forty-somethings were let go had made me feel like a has-been.

My spluttering hormone system had compounded this feeling. It reminded me that I could no longer have children – not that I'd wanted another baby – but it would have been nice if my body had consulted me instead of just doing its own thing without me having any say-so.

At the time, Derek had made it quite clear that, beyond paying the bills, he wasn't sharing his wages. "No, Wendy. If you want a hairdo, you'll have to earn the money yourself. I'm not letting you fritter my hard-earned dosh on fancy highlights." But he'd had no truck blowing money at The Angel before coming home. When I'd once dared to voice my thoughts, he'd been outraged. "You begrudge a working man half a shandy at the end of a day's graft? Shame on you, Wendy. *Shame* on you." I'd never told him how Cathy, the landlady, had once telephoned me to say that Derek had drunk six pints of bitter before getting in his van. She'd also threatened not to serve him again as she didn't condone drink-driving. She must've said something to Derek because he stopped going there. Instead, he took to buying extra strong lager from the supermarket. He'd drink it in front of the telly before retiring to bed, and then snoring like a pen full of farrowing pigs.

Finding another job in London had been tough but not impossible. I went on to reach the third stage of an interview process. I was feeling wildly optimistic, too, but then Ruby had sprung her surprise pregnancy news. And the rest, as they say, is history.

The clouds of the past cleared as Betty chugged into the carpark of my granddaughter's nursery.

I hastened towards the pick-up point. These days my stress levels still went up and down, but usually over minor matters. Like Mabel Plaistow moaning about William Beagle's bark. Or Paul Newman complaining about women who blocked shopping aisles after they'd murdered an innocent loaf of bread.

'Hello, Mrs Walker,' greeted Sophie, one of the crèche

assistants.

'Hi.' I smiled at her over the security gate. 'How's my little granddaughter been today?'

'Still causing bedlam when it comes to sharing things,' Sophie laughed. She lowered her gaze to observe the approach of a small person. 'Look, Mo. Nanna's here.' Sophie's tone was cajoling. It instantly told me that Mo was in a fractious mood. 'I'm afraid she refused to nap today, so she's a little grumpy.'

'Not to worry,' I said, as Sophie opened the gate.

I crouched down and opened my arms wide. Mo toddled towards me, a scowl on her pretty face.

'Oh, and just to let you know, Mrs Walker' – Sophie dropped her voice – 'we've had another case of nits in the nursery. It might be wise to check Mo's hair once home.'

# Chapter Ten

I staggered into the hallway, granddaughter and handbag on one arm, shopping dangling off the other, whilst holding myself at an unnatural angle. The strange posture was due to, first, avoiding my eardrums taking a direct battering from Mo's screams and, second, to avoid her head touching mine.

'Don't pull Nanna's hair, darling,' I pleaded, as fingers starfished into my tresses and yanked. It was probably psychological, but my scalp already felt as if it were crawling.

I let my handbag drop to the floor. The shopping swiftly followed. My new loaf of bread possibly now matched Paul Newman's.

Balancing on one foot, I kicked the front door shut, then set down my furious granddaughter.

'Nooooo,' she protested. 'Want pick up.'

'Nanna needs to put you down.'

'Nanna PICK UP!' she bellowed.

'I think my little Mo is a tired girlie.'

'No bed,' she objected.

'No bed,' I agreed.

The trick now was to keep Mo awake until bedtime. With a bit of luck, she'd crash out and sleep all the way through the night. Hopefully peace would then reign until the morning.

'What about Mo and Nanna having a nice cup of tea together?' I suggested. I then played my trump card. 'With a piece of cake.'

The bawling instantly ceased.

'Cakey,' she agreed.

Mo slid down my torso and landed on the floor before toddling off to the kitchen. She knew that this was the room where a worktop wasn't just for prepping food or storing the kettle. It also was also home to the Tin of Nice Things. I gathered everything up from the hall floor and followed after her.

Five minutes later, Mo was in her highchair enjoying a beaker of lukewarm tea. It was mainly heated milk. She was also making a spectacular mess with some Victoria sponge. I sat down at the kitchen table with my own cuppa and slice of cake.

'Well isn't this nice,' I said chattily.

'Nice,' Mo agreed.

'Nanna is having tea with one of her most favourite people in the whole wide world. That's you. Nanna loves you very much.'

Mo beamed at me, her smile all jammy, and her cheeks full of endearing dimples.

'After we've had our snack, Nanna will need to check your hair to make sure there's no unwanted visitors. I don't know where they all come from, do you?'

'Dunno,' Mo replied, picking up her beaker and glugging.

'Nanna will find some tea tree oil and mix it up with hair conditioner.' I took another sip of tea. 'That will kill the little buggers,' I muttered to myself.

'Buggers,' Mo repeated.

'Oh… no, Mo. You mustn't repeat that word. Nanna is very naughty for saying it. I meant to say *baddies*. I'm going to kill the baddies, right?'

'Buggers,' Mo nodded.

Oh God. I could remember Ruby picking up the odd ripe word in the school playground, but that was when she was about six. Mo was only *two*.

The sound of a key in the door diverted my attention.

'Yoo-hoo,' Ruby called.

'In here,' I answered. 'The kettle has just boiled.'

A moment later and my daughter appeared in the kitchen doorway, college bag hanging from her shoulder.

'Hiya,' she grinned, moving over to kiss the top of Mo's head. She dumped the bag on the floor, then collapsed into the chair next to me. 'God, I'm knackered.'

Ruby's elfin features were perfectly set off by a candy-floss-pink pixie crop. The colour highlighted her stunning blue eyes. I was suddenly reminded of another pair of blue eyes that had bored into mine less than an hour ago.

'Good thing you have short hair,' I said.

'Why? Oh no.' Ruby gave me a horrified look. 'Not nits again?'

'Buggers,' said Mo sagely.

'I beg your pardon?' said Ruby, looking horrified.

I cringed, but didn't say anything. Ruby tutted with

annoyance.

'Mummy is delighted her little Mo is learning new words every day, but that one needs to go.' She stood up again and went to the kettle. Satisfied with the water level, she flicked the switch. 'Honestly, that nursery is something else. Nearly every day Mo comes home saying something inappropriate. Blimey!' She broke off to inspect the bread sitting on the worktop. 'What did you buy this for? Looks like it's been run over.' She paused to gather her thoughts and pick up from where she'd left off. 'Sometimes I think the nursery staff are deliberately indiscreet. Bloomin' twits.'

'Blimmin twats,' Mo agreed.

Ruby regarded me in horror, teabag momentarily suspended mid-air. I shook my head imperceptibly. Least said, soonest mended. Hopefully.

She returned to her chair with the tea and a slice of cake.

'I need to crack on with an assignment. Can I spread out on the kitchen table? It's easier to work here rather than the surface of my dressing table, what with Mo's cot taking up nearly all my elbow space.'

'Of course you can,' I said, getting up. I took my empty plate and cup to the sink. Reaching for a handy packet of wet wipes, I peeled off a couple, then wiped Mo's hands, face, and the highchair's tray. 'Just ensure there's enough room to lay up when dinner is ready. You know how your dad will otherwise moan. If I give him a telly dinner, eating off his lap, he complains about indigestion. He likes to sit at the table.'

'Yes, I know what Dad likes,' said Ruby under her

breath.

Her tone held a vitriol that had me glancing at her curiously, but she made no further comment and instead set about spreading textbooks, paper and neon marker pens over the tabletop. The tea and cake instantly became islands in a sea of homework.

I lobbed the used wet wipes at the bin, missed, took care not to explete out loud, then stooped to pick them up.

Mo leant forward in her highchair. A small hand shot out and tried to intercept the marker pen Ruby was holding.

'Dwarr,' said Mo.

Ruby snatched the pen away, so Mo instead grabbed some of her mother's notepaper.

'No, darling,' said Ruby, retrieving the pad. 'Mummy isn't drawing. She's working.'

'DWARR!' Mo insisted.

'Oh God,' said Ruby, getting exasperated. 'Mum, can you do something?'

I reached into a kitchen drawer. It was stuffed with emergency supplies specifically for Mo. Couldn't get her to eat? "Look at the aeroplane!" I would cry, pretending the fork was a plane zooming towards her mouth. Couldn't get her to sit still? "Look at Percy!" Ruby would coax, while Percy – a hand puppet with googly eyes – distracted Mo from an epic tantrum. Couldn't keep her quiet when overtired? "Draw Nanna a beautiful picture to show all her friends," I now said, doling out paper and crayons. Mo immediately settled down.

For a while the kitchen was a peaceful hive of activity.

Ruby was writing, Mo was scribbling, and I was chopping veg for the spag bol, with broccoli on the side.

The atmosphere shifted when the front door banged shut. Ruby's mouth pursed, Mo stopped drawing, and my tummy contracted.

Derek was home.

# Chapter Eleven

Derek's hands were deliberately tucked behind his back, as if to hide something. Which he was. As he stomped into the kitchen, it was immediately apparent he wasn't in a sunny mood. That was nothing new. He glared at Ruby.

'Why do you always take up half the table with your college crap?'

'Crap,' repeated Mo.

'Hello, Dad,' said Ruby.

Our daughter's cool tone made the point that he hadn't greeted any of us.

Derek sat down opposite Ruby. Whatever had been behind his back was deftly transferred to the floor, right under the table and therefore out of sight.

'Are you being narky?' Derek demanded.

Ruby looked at her father with wide eyes.

'Me?' she said innocently, while gathering up her things. 'No.'

Derek's eyes narrowed, but he didn't reply. Ruby ignored him.

'Mum, I'm going to check Mo's hair, then pop her in the bath with me. Keep my dinner warm in the oven, please. We'll be down again in a little while.'

'Okay, sweetie,' I said, opening the cutlery drawer.

'Why does Ruby need to check Mo's hair?' asked Derek.

'She might have nits.'

Derek looked appalled.

'I hope she doesn't give them to me.'

'I don't think you'd be a nit's first choice for a new home,' I laughed, as I set about laying the table.

'Are you insinuating that I'm going bald?' he said, looking affronted.

I immediately dropped the banter.

'Good heavens, no.'

Yes.

Derek eyed me suspiciously.

'You're in a very punchy mood this evening, Wendy. Have you been associating with that Kelly woman?'

'*That Kelly woman*' – I said evenly whilst dishing up – 'is one of my closest friends. Hungry?' I asked, diverting the conversation away from my bestie.

'Starving.'

'Good, because I've made plenty.'

'Spag bol,' he said, and the scowl momentarily disappeared. 'That's a big improvement on fishfingers and alphabet spaghetti.'

'It is,' I agreed, setting down a steaming plate before him. 'Unfortunately, I didn't get time to do a full shop today.'

'Oh? Where did this mincemeat come from?'

'The local mini supermarket,' I said, serving myself and then sitting down alongside him.

'Wendy,' Derek spluttered. 'For heaven's sake, do you

know how much that place charges? Next time you want to buy the groceries, make some effort to go to the main store at King's Hill. There are far more economical places to splurge the housekeeping I give you.'

'I only bought a few things,' I reassured. 'Tomorrow I'll do a full shop at Asda.'

'Make sure you do,' he growled as one arm momentarily disappeared under the table.

There was a rustling sound. A second later, his hand reappeared with a can of lager.

So that's what he'd been hiding. Likely a Costcutter carrier bag with six tins straight from the chiller cabinet. I refrained from saying anything. There was always money for booze, but God help me for spending a few pennies more on Costcutter's minced meat.

'Are you going to the driving range tomorrow?' I enquired, endeavouring to make normal husband-and-wife conversation.

'Tomorrow is Saturday, so yes.' Derek wound a huge amount of spaghetti around his fork, then shovelled it into his mouth. 'You know perfectly well' – he chided, spitting food everywhere – 'that I like to unwind after a hellish week's work. We can't all amble around the countryside walking dogs for a living, all the while gassing with friends. Some of us must climb ladders and risk life and limb.' He waggled his fork at me. 'It's dangerous work being a decorator.'

'I know,' I soothed.

Prat.

'I'm seriously thinking about billing clients a surcharge.

Danger money.'

'Absolutely,' I said mildly.

Double prat. I put down my fork and looked at him properly.

'You should write to the Prime Minister about it.'

'That's a very good idea, Wendy.'

Derek masticated thoughtfully, no doubt mentally drafting a letter.

*Dear Prime Minister*

*I'm a decorator. I might not have climbed the giddy career path that you have, but nonetheless I consider myself to also be a VIP (Very Important Painter) who clambers up and down a ladder every single day. It's a risky business. Talking of risks, I'm not particularly impressed about the recent shambles at Number 10. Hopefully you'll be better than Liz and Boris. He took a big risk having parties between 2020 and 2021 when the rest of us were in lockdown. That was bang out of order. However, I thought cancelling Christmas was quite inspired. Just think of all the family rows that never took place with the in-laws. Anyway, I digress. People like you have taxpayers like me paying for security bods to look out for you. But who looks out for decorators precariously perched upon their ladders? No one. So I'm writing to suggest that you include danger money for decorators in your next manifesto.*

*Yours sincerely*

*Derek Walker, PaD BBm (Painter and Decorator) (Bachelor Before Married)*

*PS My rates are very reasonable if you want to revamp*

*Mrs Johnson's previous handiwork at Downing Street.*

'Do you know' – Derek stabbed his knife in the air to emphasise the point he was about to make – 'that today's client didn't so much as offer me a cup of tea?'

'Shocking,' I murmured.

I forked up my own food while Derek ranted on about the injustice of his working lot, and how he'd taken revenge on his client by watering down the paint.

I zoned out and let my thoughts wander elsewhere. Fields. A leafy lane. The prettiest cottage in Little Waterlow. Inside, the new owner was sitting at the kitchen table talking companionably to a girl with shocking pink cropped hair while a sweet little tot played with her toys at their feet. Was now a good time to bring up the subject of divorce?

'…and I said to him, "Bill, if you want my advice, it's a totally unnecessary expense. All you have to do is keep the missus happy. Just like I do with Wendy." I must admit I was slightly smug when I told him that.'

'Sorry, what?' I said, tuning back in.

'Divorce,' said Derek.

'Divorce?' I croaked.

Had my husband somehow read my thoughts?

'Don't look so worried,' Derek chuckled. 'Bill can't make up his mind whether to leave Jackie. But you don't need to be alarmed, Wendy. There's no chance of that ever happening to us.'

'Really?' I ventured.

Surely this was the perfect moment to discuss the topic.

'Absolutely not. For one thing' – Derek gave me a look

that dared to suggest otherwise – 'I'd never agree to it. Divorce is an utter waste of money. Anyway, I look after you very well financially. And you' – he pointed to the dirty pots and pans – 'keep the house nice in return. At our time of life, it's a very civilised arrangement.'

*Our* time of life? Derek made us sound like a couple of octogenarians. My mind instantly conjured up a picture of Fred and Mabel Plaistow. I gulped. There was another three decades to go before getting anywhere near that age.

'I-I see,' I stammered.

Evidently, I wasn't going to get that Decree Absolute without a battle.

Derek put his knife and fork together. He got to his feet, picking up the carrier bag from under the table.

'I'll be in the lounge relaxing.'

'Okay.'

*And I'll be in the kitchen, clearing up after you.*

But hopefully it wouldn't be for much longer.

# Chapter Twelve

The following morning, Saturday, saw me gazing blearily at my reflection in the bathroom mirror. My eyebags looked worse than usual.

Last night Mo had interrupted Ruby's sleep three times. Consequently, my daughter was shattered. What Ruby didn't realise was that Mo's cries had also disturbed me. However, Derek had continued sleeping. Ear buds in. Eye mask on.

'Can you look after her, Mum,' Ruby had pleaded, appearing in my bedroom doorway just before the alarm went off. 'I'm desperate to catch up on some sleep.'

This wasn't an unusual scenario. I'd mastered the art of one-minute showers pretty much the moment Mo had been born. Ruby was a good mother to Mo. She'd had to quickly grow up, but the reality was my daughter was still a teenager. And teenagers were always tired.

'You're too soft on her,' Derek frequently grumbled.

But then Derek was never happy unless he was moaning, and Ruby's sleep requirements were on his Top Ten List of Complaints.

I could still remember my own teenage years. The exhaustion. Struggling to get up in the mornings for school. Was it any wonder? All that growing. All that morphing from child to adult in such a short period. Going to bed as a twelve-year-old child, only to wake up the following morning and find straggly pubic hairs that had seemingly grown overnight.

I relieved a grateful Ruby of Mo and took my granddaughter into the bathroom with me.

'Shower with Nanna,' said Mo, peeling off her pyjamas.

I turned the tap's diverter valve, waiting for the water jet to warm up. Mo toddled across the bathroom floor towards the cubicle.

'Nanna will shower with you another time,' I said, whipping my nightdress over my head. I hopped smartly into the cubicle, shutting Mo out. 'Nanna is in a hurry.'

'Why?'

'Because she has to go shopping.'

'Why?'

'To buy food for us all.'

'Why?'

'So we aren't hungry.'

'W–?'

I cut her off before she could ask the same question again.

'Would you like to come shopping with me?' I asked, squirting shower gel over my body.

Mo considered.

'Toys?' she asked hopefully.

'Lots of toys,' I agreed, hurriedly rinsing off foam.

'Cuddlies?'

'Oh yes. Cuddly unicorns. Cuddly teddies. Lots of

cuddly things.'

I stepped out and, dripping, reached for a towel.

'Poo,' said Mo, frowning.

'Wait!' I cried. The frown indicated that pushing was imminent. 'Quick. Potty.'

Potty training was still a work in progress. To be fair, Mo rarely had an accident. But when she announced the need to go, generally there was only a five second window to park her bot on the pot.

Ten minutes later we were both dressed. Mo's hair had happily been devoid of visitors. That said, I wasn't taking chances and had scooped my blonde hair into a ponytail. I slicked on some lippy, lifted Mo onto my hip, then went downstairs.

Derek wandered into the kitchen just as I was juggling Weetabix for Mo, toast for me and replying to a text from Sadie Farrell.

'Grumpa,' said Mo, pointing at Derek with a stubby finger.

'*Grand*pa,' Derek corrected.

Mo looked momentarily shocked. As well she might. Derek didn't usually acknowledge his granddaughter. As far as he was concerned, she was a small person who caused several minor inconveniences. Proper conversation would take place when Mo had started secondary school or, better still, graduated from university.

'I don't know why you're feeding that child,' he grumbled.

*That* child. *That* Kelly woman. I felt like turning round

and saying, "I don't know why I married that Derek person."

'You should let her feed herself,' he continued. 'You'll stunt her growth, or something.'

'By that, I presume you think I'm interfering with her hand-and-eye coordination. I'm in a hurry, Derek. I don't have time this morning to clean Mo up. I need to get that big shop done. Also, Sadie has just texted asking if I can walk William and Sylvie this afternoon. She's had a family emergency and been called away. William Beagle is a complete nightmare if he doesn't get his daily exercise.'

'Why, what does William do?'

'Chews furniture. Raids cupboards. Upends bins. He's obsessed with food. Oh, and squirrels. He spends his entire time, when off-lead at the woods, galloping through the undergrowth in search of fluffies. Basically, he's the canine equivalent of a juvenile delinquent.'

'I don't know why people have dogs if they can't control them.'

'He's a sweet pup, just unruly. It's the breed, apparently. Very loving, but unpredictable. A prospective owner never knows if they're taking home a *character* or a four-legged lunatic.'

'Hmph,' said Derek, by way of response. He went to the larder and reached for a box of Crunchy Nuts. 'I'm spending the whole day at the golf club.'

Didn't he always?

'Yes, that's fine.'

'I wasn't seeking your permission, Wendy.'

'I know, I was just saying' – why did he always try to

wrong-foot me? – 'that I'm happy for you. Enjoy.'

'I'll try,' he sighed wearily, as if going to the club was now a hardship. He shook the cereal into a bowl, added milk, then sat down at the table. 'After I've finished at the driving range, I'll meet Bill in the bar for a sandwich and then we'll have a round of golf together.'

'Give Bill my regards,' I said, turning my attention back to the text I'd started to tap out to Sadie.

*William and Sylvie – not a problem. Have house key. Hope your dad is okay xx*

The temperature in the room suddenly dropped a couple of degrees.

'It's rude to text when you're meant to be having a conversation,' said Derek petulantly.

'Sorry, but Sadie–'

'You have time for everyone, Wendy, but me. Are you aware of that?'

'What? I–'

'Are you aware you haven't been a proper wife to me for months?'

A spoonful of Mo's Weetabix hovered mid-air as I stared at Derek in disbelief. Was this what his endless griping boiled down to? A lack of leg over? That said, I didn't particularly feel romantically inclined towards a man who endlessly picked his nose, was the master of the silent putrid fart, who *still* hadn't learnt how to pick up his clothes, and who put down everyone I liked or loved. The weekly duty bunk-up had long ago changed to fortnightly, then monthly, then quarterly and yes, if I'm absolutely honest, I'd privately hoped it might become an annual arrangement. And if Derek could see his way to agreeing to once every century, then that would certainly get me out of the next encounter.

'I'll just leave that thought with you, Wendy,' said Derek piously.

'Well, I, well, really, I–'

'Please stop spluttering. It's most unattractive. And as for that ponytail you're sporting. One word comes to mind. Mutton. You know, you're not sixteen anymore. Right, I'll be off.' His spoon clattered into the empty cereal bowl. 'See you later.'

'Later,' said Mo, snatching the spoon from my hand and lobbing it after Derek. A second later and her bowl followed. The sloppy Weetabix only narrowly missed the back of Derek's polo shirt. Shame.

He spun round, his face contorted with rage.

'You need to teach that child some table manners. And clear up that mess.'

'Yes, of course, I-'

But I was talking to the air. The front door slammed shut so hard, the internal letterbox flap was dislodged and clattered to the floor.

*Breathe*, I told myself. *Just breathe. You'll be shot of him soon. Patience is a virtue.*

'Pick up,' said Mo, letting me know she wanted to be released from the highchair.

'Yes, darling,'

'Darling,' she repeated, instantly melting my heart.

I reached for the ever-handy wet wipes. Cleaning her

face, I then removed the plastic bib with its inbuilt kangaroo pouch designed to catch spilt food. Whoever had invented that had been a genius.

'Come on, Miss Mo,' I said, lifting her into my arms. 'Let's go and spend Grumpa's money on some toys.'

'Yeth,' she squealed with delight.

Needless to say, the Asda store at King's Hill was packed. Much to Mo's delight, an awful lot of trolley bashing took place. My granddaughter seemed to regard the experience as a supermarket dodgem ride.

Walking away from the checkout, I was just heading towards the automatic exit door, when there was a tap on my shoulder.

'I thought it was you,' said a familiar voice.

'Bill!' I exclaimed. 'Hello. Whatever are you doing here?'

'Jackie's got me doing chores. I came here to buy some bits.' He pointed to the contents of his wire basket. It was full of window cleaning products and soft cloths. 'I'm not allowed to go out and play until I've obliged. It's better to keep the peace than argue. That's what your Derek advised anyway.'

Ah yes. Derek had mentioned that in Bill and Jackie's household the divorce word had reared its head. What a strange parallel. Perhaps I should be more like Jackie and metaphorically kick some husband-arse. "You want to play golf? Okay, you can, but only if you repair the lock on the bathroom door, sort out the leaky guttering, wash the cars and mow the lawn. Oh, and if you could put the vacuum around afterwards while I go and get my nails done, that would be splendid."

'Will you get your chores finished in time for later?'

Bill looked puzzled.

'Why, what's happening later?'

'Your round of golf with Derek.'

Bill's eyebrows nearly shot off his face.

'Heavens, no. Not a chance. I'm under the thumb today. Maybe next week if I've been a very good boy.' He gave a hearty laugh. 'Talking of which, I'd better get a wiggle on. Lovely to see you, Wendy.' He gave my cheek a friendly peck. 'And your little granddaughter is a smasher.' He beamed at Mo, who dimpled back. 'Catch you later, love.'

And with that he headed off leaving me wondering why my husband had lied and – without Bill's knowledge – used his friend as an alibi for the afternoon.

# Chapter Thirteen

By the time I arrived home with half a dozen bags of shopping, Mo was fast asleep.

Ruby greeted me at the door.

'Hiya, Mum. Thanks for taking Mo with you so I could catch up on some shuteye.'

'That's okay,' I said, puffing into the hallway. Two bulging bags were threatening to split. 'Your daughter is sparko in her car seat. Can you bring her in while I start putting this little lot away.'

'Of course.'

I was in the kitchen, rearranging the larder cupboard, when Ruby reappeared.

'Mo is now in her cot, still asleep, and clutching a lurid pink monkey.'

'Yes, she was very smitten,' I laughed. 'Thankfully, it kept her quiet whilst in a horrendously long check-out queue.'

Ruby opened the fridge and checked its replenished contents.

'What are we having for din-dins tonight, or do you think Dad might take you out?'

Derek? Take me out? I boggled silently at the larder's

contents before shutting its door.

'No, we're not going out. I thought I'd do cheeseburgers with some chips and a big salad. Fancy that?'

Ruby helped herself to some fresh orange juice before replying.

'Yeah, sounds good.'

Her tone was flat.

'What's up?' I asked, immediately picking up on the moroseness.'

'I just feel a bit, you know, out of sorts.'

'Time of the month?' I asked sympathetically.

In the old days our menstrual cycles had been in tune with one another, but then mine had gone haywire. Consequently, I didn't know whether her dip in mood was hormonal, or something else.

'No, it's nothing like that.'

'So what's wrong?'

She took a swig of her orange and scuffed one toe of her slipper back and forth.

'Ah, never mind.'

A thought occurred to me.

'Is someone having a party tonight?'

'Yeah,' she sighed. 'It's Callie's eighteenth.'

'Weren't you invited?'

She drained her glass and placed it on the worktop.

'Yeah, I was invited, but I'm not going.'

'Why not?'

'Oh, come on, Mum. I can hardly take Mo with me. What? Park her in the corner of the club and say, "Be a good girl for Mummy," while I do some dance moves and laugh the night away. I know there's a few underage kids who try to get in the club, but it's rather pushing it hoping to get a two-year-old in without questions being asked.' She gave a mirthless laugh.

'Darling, you should have told me about the invitation. Babysitting isn't an issue. I'll look after Mo while you go and have a nice time.'

'No.' She shook her head vehemently. 'You do enough for the two of us as it is. It's not fair on you.'

'Don't be silly.'

'I'm being realistic,' she said sadly.

'What do you mean?' I frowned.

'It's really kind of you to offer, Mum, but there are other factors.'

'Like?'

'A lack of readies for starters.' She blew out her cheeks. 'I can't wait to qualify and earn my own money.'

'Erm,' I warbled, as my mind flitted to the little outbuilding at Clover Cottage. 'Earlier, I had a bit of a lightbulb moment. It was regarding your intended career. We'll have a proper chat about it when, er, the timing is right. Meanwhile, I think I have twenty quid, if that helps?'

I reached for my handbag, but Ruby's hand instantly came down on mine.

'Stop. No, Mum. It's very nice of you, but I'm not taking your money. Anyway, I think it costs that just to get inside the club.'

My shoulders drooped.

'Oh dear.'

'Going out is hideously expensive. All my mates will be drinking, and I couldn't begin to offer to buy a round. Even if I stuck to lemonade, it's not much fun being the sober one. Everyone else larks about, either pretending they're French or asking the barman for six diet waters. I bought Callie a cream egg as her birthday present. It was all I could afford, but she understood. Even so, I felt embarrassed when she later unwrapped blingy stuff from the others, along with top brands of make-up.'

'If money were no object, would you reconsider going out?'

Ruby shook her head again.

'Nope.'

'Why ever not?' I said in surprise.

'Because' – this time her sigh was heavier – 'I'd only suffer for it the following day. I love Mo to bits. However, clubbing and motherhood don't really go hand in hand.'

'No, I guess not.'

'I have no regrets about having Mo, but sometimes I wish I'd been more sensible, and not tried to rush into adulthood. Plus, I still miss Simon,' she added with a gulp. 'That's the other thing. All my friends have boyfriends. It's all new and exciting for them. They talk about their dates and going out to the cinema. Or just, well, a walk in the park. Holding hands and grinning gormlessly at each other. But who wants to hold my hand when I have a small child in tow?'

'Someone will. One day. You'll see.'

Ruby reached for the kitchen towel on the worktop, and tore off a sheet before noisily blowing her nose.

'Ignore me. I'm just feeling sorry for myself.'

'It's allowed,' I said, giving her a fierce hug. 'Have you tried getting in touch with Simon? I'm not talking about when his parents whisked him off to Scotland and barred communication. I'm talking about lately. After all, he's now eighteen. Strictly speaking, he doesn't have to do his parents' bidding anymore because he's no longer a minor.'

Ruby was silent for a moment.

'I've had moments of wondering whether to try and track him down. After all, it wouldn't be hard. But whenever I've started to type his name into Instagram or Twitter, I've stopped.'

'Why?'

'Because if he really cared about me and Mo, he'd have sought us out by now.'

'Maybe he will, one day.'

'When the moon turns blue?' said Ruby sadly.

'Yes,' I said staunchly, releasing her. 'Listen, I'm going to have a quick sandwich and then pop over to Sadie's place. Her dogs need walking. Would you and Mo like to keep me company?'

Ruby was about to reply when her mobile rang. She glanced at the screen before answering.

'Hey, Meg. Oh, right. Yeah, I'm up for it.' She visibly perked up. 'Cool. Come on over whenever you're ready. Only thing is, my daughter will probably want to join in. Okay, brill. See ya!' She tucked the phone into the back pocket of her jeans. 'If you don't mind, Mum, I'll say no to the dog walk. Meg has bought a load of half price nail polish. She's suggested we give each other a manicure. I've said yes. Is it okay if she comes over?'

'Of course,' I said, glad that her doldrums had so swiftly lifted. Thank goodness there were still some teenage things she could do with a mate. 'I'll give Kelly a ring and see if she fancies coming along with me instead. Alfie gets on well with William and Sylvie.'

'Okay. Actually, it will be quite nice to have the house to myself for a bit. Especially with Dad out the way. He's so embarrassing sometimes.'

'Aren't all parents embarrassing?' I grinned.

'No, thankfully not you, Mum.' She plucked an apple from the fruit bowl, threw it up in the air and then caught it. 'If it's all right with you, I'm going to watch some telly before Mo wakes up and Meg gets here. Make the most of having the remote control.'

'You do that, darling,' I said.

I reached for my mobile, and rang Kelly's number, hoping to chat while, at the same time, rustling up a hasty sandwich. She answered almost immediately.

'Hello, Wends.'

She sounded cagey. Piped music played in the background.

'Can you talk?' I asked.

'Very quickly.'

'I'm walking William and Sylvie this afternoon. Fancy bringing Alfie along and the two of us having a good old natter?'

'I can't. I'm waiting for Steve.'

'Ah, okay. How's it going?'

'Too thrilling for words. Guess where I'm meeting him!'

Heavens. Had Steve gone all upmarket? Had this flirtation moved from Waitrose to Harrod's food hall?

'No idea,' I said. 'Spill the beans.'

'I'm in Boots.'

'O-*kayyy*.'

I couldn't see what all the excitement was about.

'Steve told me to meet him in *Cameras and Accessories*. And guess what, guess what?' she squeaked.

'Tell me, tell me,' I squeaked back.

'Only a stone's throw away from where I'm standing, there are shelves FULL of condoms. Loads of 'em. Perhaps Steve is going to give me a few nod-nod-wink-winks and say, "My goodness! Whatever have we got here? It looks like the universe is telling us to take things further."'

'Maybe,' I said, trying not to giggle. Kelly sounded thoroughly overexcited.

'Bit odd though,' she mused. 'Why would Boots put contraceptives in the same aisle as photography?'

'I suppose it's because they both capture that special moment.'

'Eh? Oh heck, he's here. I must go,' Kelly hissed urgently. 'Steve!' I heard her coo, just before the line went dead.

I swallowed down the last of my sandwich, wondering what it was like to have a guy give you some knee-tremble.

My daydreaming about Brad Pitt, Bruce Willis and George Clooney was very limiting. Sighing, I picked up my car keys.

'Laters,' I called out to Ruby.

As I swung through the front door and headed towards Betty, a deep baritone voice stopped me in my tracks.

'Hi, Wendy.'

I turned to see the divine Ben emerging from the house next door. My knees instantly went weak. This man slept mere feet from my bed, albeit on the other side of the party wall. A case of *so near, but so far.*

'Hello,' I gasped, trying to appear unflustered.

'Going anywhere nice?' Ben enquired with a friendly smile.

'Walkies,' I nodded foolishly. 'I mean. Dog walking.'

'Enjoy,' he said, heading towards his own car.

'Thanks,' I said, trying not to hyperventilate.

*God, get a grip, Wendy.*

I was aware of him giving me a curious look as I started Betty up and, knees now trembling violently, failed to properly engage the gear causing my Citroen to initially kangaroo down the road.

# Chapter Fourteen

It was pouring with rain when I arrived at the Farrells' house. As I got out the car and attempted dodging the raindrops, I mentally cursed myself for not checking my weather app before setting off earlier.

The wool coat I'd hastily flung on before leaving home wasn't remotely suitable. First, the rain would soak through the fabric. Second, it would whiff like a sheep while later drying.

'Typical,' I muttered, letting myself into Sadie's house.

I hastened over to the coat cupboard where the alarm was housed. Disappearing within, I punched out the code to stop the ominous bleeping.

William and Sylvie greeted me, the former boisterously, the latter courteously. Sadie's cats, Rosemary and Thyme, bounced down the stairs, loudly meowing. No doubt the moggies were hoping my visit heralded a top-up to their feeding bowls.

I reversed out of the cupboard and then paused. Sadie's all-weather coat dangled from a peg. I pulled my mobile from my back pocket and sent her a quick text.

*Can I be cheeky and borrow your waterproof? My walking boots are in the back of the car, but I left home with my thoughts elsewhere and, stupidly, am wearing an inappropriate coat! Xx*

Her reply came back almost instantly.

*Help yourself xx*

Relieved, I swapped the coats over, shut the cupboard and then regarded the animals at my feet.

'I could say it's raining cats and dogs outside, but the same seems to be the case in here too.'

William barked joyfully. He knew what my visit heralded. Walkies. And walkies meant squirrel chasing. Yippee!

Five minutes later we were off. As I was walking without Kelly today, instead of putting William and Sylvie within Betty's boot, I opted to take the dogs to nearby Manor Country Park.

Once part of an eighteenth-century country estate, the park was made up of beautiful meadows, peaceful woodland copses and a tranquil lake. The place was popular with visitors, particularly in summer. But today it appeared to be empty.

Once away from the road, I let both dogs off their leads. William instantly shot off down tree-lined pathways in hot pursuit of fluffy rodents. Sylvie trotted along at my heel. She was a sweet girl who never strayed far.

I stuffed my hands deep into the waterproof's pockets and tried not to shiver. Right now, November seemed to be hellbent on impersonating December. It was decidedly cold.

I huddled into the coat's collar and stepped up the pace, knowing that some powerwalking would soon get the blood pumping.

As I bowled along, my mind wandered. I thought about Ruby. It wasn't great having money worries at her tender age. I knew she was impatient to qualify and turn her business ideas into reality. When the time came, I'd give her every encouragement. Inevitably my thoughts turned to Derek. He'd succinctly let me know that he'd never agree to a divorce. That left two options.

Number One: get proper advice from a solicitor, although heaven only knew how I'd pay any legal bill. Could Mum and Dad help me out? I could repay them from the proceeds of the house sale. That said, I didn't really want to involve them. They'd only worry. I could almost hear their squawks of anguish from their retirement villa in Spain. Mum, fretting away. "Wendy! Oh, darling. Are you *sure* you're doing the right thing? I know Derek was never our choice as a son-in-law, but in another couple of years you'll be fifty. FIFTY! Isn't it better to resign yourself to making the best of things? After all, thousands of couples do the same at your time of life. If nothing else, at least you'd have companionship." Except Derek wasn't a companion. We never did anything together except share table space when eating and bed space when sleeping.

Number Two: pray.

*Hello, God. My name is Wendy Walker, although you already know that. I suppose you also know how many hairs I have on my head – which is quite incredible, because even I don't know the answer to that and they're MY hairs! Anyway. I need to have a chat with you, because I have a big favour to ask.*

William suddenly appeared from nowhere, swerving in front of my legs and almost tripping me up.

'For heaven's sake, mister,' I grumbled.

William took no notice. He bounced along, head up, eyes firmly pinned on an overhead squirrel. The creature was leaping from branch to branch, tree to tree, just like an acrobat. A second later and both squirrel and dog had disappeared again.

*Sorry, God. Where was I? Oh, yes. A favour. It's about Derek. My husband. Look, I'm not going to beat about the burning bush. I no longer want to be with him, and I don't know how to end our marriage. You see, Derek has made it quite plain that the D word is out of the question. He thinks it's a waste of money. And when it comes to money, my husband is tighter than Mabel Plaistow's mouth when she's radiating disapproval. I know marriage is sacred and you're not meant to break your vows, but I simply can't do this anymore. So, if you could, you know, have a Holy word in Derek's ear, or something.*

My mind wandered further. Hmm. *Or something.*

*Um, listen. I've had an idea. I know Derek is only fifty, but if you could see your way to calling him home – and I don't mean our semi-detached – then... well, it would just be between us, wouldn't it? A private arrangement. Nothing gory or awful. No murder. Maybe... a biscuit crumb going down the wrong way. Then a quick coughing fit before gently expiring. Or falling off his ladder, landing on his head and – BAM! – waking up at the Pearly Gates rather than in*

*Accident & Emergency.*

I wandered on, lost in thought. The rain had stopped, and the ground was wet and slippery. Every now and again I slid on a bit of mud but, on autopilot, corrected my balance and walked on.

*Oh, hang on a minute, God. I've just had a horrible thought. Karma. Oh, my goodness. Have I now inadvertently invited the law of cause and effect to visit me? In which case, I'm very sorry. The last thing I want is to find MYSELF choking on that biscuit or – in the absence of not going up ladders – falling down a flight of stairs. You see, I have two dependents who I love and adore, and I couldn't POSSIBLY leave them – even though it would get me out of being with Derek. I'd be devastated to find myself at the Pearly Gates and having to leave Ruby and Mo behind. So, um, sorry to mess you about, God. Cancel that last bit, eh? You know, the choking thing. Oh, and the ladder business too. But if you could instead ask an angel to visit Derek while he's asleep with the suggestion that divorce would be the best thing for both of us, then I'd be HUGELY grateful.*

I had a sudden vision of Derek waking me up in the middle of the night. "Wendy. WENDY! Oh, my goodness, you'll never guess what. An angel appeared to me. Over there. Right by the dressing table. He told me that I was to be the spokesperson for painters and decorators all over the land… nay, the world… and that I must go forth and round up my brethren, lobby governments, and demand danger money for each and every one of them." And with that Derek would fling back the duvet, pull his suitcase from under the bed and say, "Not a minute to lose. I'm off. Please divorce me for desertion. Toodle-oo." And I'd regard him with wide eyes and briefly protest – just to show willing. "Oh, Derek. How sad. But I'm so glad you've found your mission. Bye-eee!" And then, despite the hour, I'd ring up Kelly and excitedly say, "You'll never guess what's hap–"

My thoughts fragmented as a tri-coloured missile shot out from the undergrowth straight in front of a cyclist who'd appeared from nowhere. The man was peddling at great speed. William was oblivious, but the cyclist looked horrified. Dog and bike were on a collision course if the man didn't take immediate evasive action.

I froze, physically paralysed by fear. My eyes widened in horror at the situation that was surely about to unfold, and my vocal cords instantly shrivelled and died. The cyclist slammed on his brakes causing the bike to wobble violently. A second later and the machine pitched sideways. The back wheel bucked like a wild stallion, catapulting the cyclist over the handlebars.

For a moment all I could see was a man sailing through the air, arms and legs windmilling, before he crash-landed at my feet with a sickening thud.

I stared down at him, appalled. Oh God. He wasn't moving. Even worse, he didn't appear to be breathing.

# Chapter Fifteen

William, unaware of the havoc he'd caused, simply shot off again into the undergrowth. I was left looking on in shock and disbelief at the aftermath of this horrendous accident.

The bicycle lay on its side. The front wheel was spinning eerily, as if a ghost rider was working the pedals. The cyclist continued to lay motionless on the ground. I felt like the park had transformed into a graveyard where nothing moved. Unwelcoming thoughts invaded my brain, whirring like the bike's wheel. The reason nothing moved in graveyards was because… was because… everyone was dead. Shit! This cyclist was dead. I was staring at a body.

I suddenly felt a bit peculiar. A *body*. Omigod. A BODY! I gulped hard and tried to get my voice to work.

'Help,' I croaked.

Sylvie looked at me, head on one side.

'Help,' I repeated, my larynx loosening up. Suddenly, I was violently shaking. 'HELP!' I bellowed. 'SOMEONE, PLEASE HELP.'

My legs chose that moment to buckle, and I sank to the ground. Oh God. Nooooo. Get me away from the body. This couldn't be happening. Let this be fantasy. From somewhere in my mind the soundtrack to Queen's

*Bohemian Rhapsody* began to play.

'What's happened?' said a lone jogger, puffing over.

'*Just killed a man*,' I warbled, as Freddie Mercury's grand piano reverberated through my head.

'You killed him?' said the jogger, nervously backing away.

'*There was a beagle in the wayyy, lost his balance and I began to swayyy, mamaaa…*'

'Bloody hell. A nutter,' muttered the jogger. 'I'm calling the police.'

'*Mama, oooh, didn't mean to make you dieeee…*ARGHHH,' I screeched.

The body was moving.

'For God's sake stop that caterwauling,' said the corpse.

'Ooooh, I feel so sick,' I whispered, as the entire band began to sing in a falsetto voice.

'I think you're in shock,' said the jogger.

He stepped closer, deciding that perhaps I wasn't a murdering lunatic after all.

Beneath me, the ground was cold and hard but oddly welcoming. I closed my eyes and pressed my cheek into the damp earth. It felt good. Calming. Perhaps I could just lay here until this whole nightmare had somehow gone away. Maybe this had happened because God was annoyed with me. Yes, that must be it. My prayer requesting Derek to be called home had invoked karma. Meanwhile, the cyclist was making a miraculous recovery. A resurrection no less! But a spiritual debt needed to be repaid, so now it was my turn to expire. I could imagine a coroner's verdict: *The deceased died from shock.* My eyes shuttered down.

In the blackness, I heard thumpity-thump sounds. Lifting my heavy eyelids – a herculean task – four canine legs swam into view. William. Oh God, *William.* Sadie would kill me for being such an irresponsible dog walker. Actually, no she wouldn't, because I'd saved her the bother by unwittingly doing it myself in this park.

Something soft and fluffy was gently placed upon my head. How nice. It was still warm. Perhaps it was a hot water bottle, albeit a faintly smelly one.

'Jesus,' said a man's voice. Not the jogger.

'Is that you, Lord?' I mumbled.

'Is she delirious?' asked the jogger. 'I was going to ring the police, but maybe I should call for an ambulance.'

'She's in shock,' said Jesus.

'Can you heal me?' I mumbled.

'I've a good mind to sue the pants off you,' said Jesus, sounding most unlike a saviour. 'I hope you're insured.'

My eyes snapped open. *Concentrate, Wendy.* I stared at the cyclist. I couldn't work out what he looked like. His helmet was thankfully in one piece and still in place on his head, so that meant his skull was intact. Good to know. However, I couldn't see his hair, nor the upper part of his face. Large wraparounds completely covered his eyes. The lower part of his face was unshaven and covered in mud.

'I thought you were dead,' I whispered.

'Thankfully not. Just badly winded, no thanks to that crazy hound of yours.'

The man snatched up my hot water bottle and flung it

into the bushes.

'Give that back,' I demanded.

'It was a dead squirrel,' he said scathingly.

'Wha–?'

I gagged and clamped a hand over my mouth. How awful.

'Look, do you two need me or can I go?' said the jogger, clearly anxious to be off.

'Go,' said the cyclist irritably. He turned his attention back to me. 'Are you going to get up or are you planning on making this park your bed?'

Pushing myself up into a sitting position, I paused. Nausea washed over me. Trying to ignore the queasiness, I squinted up at him.

'I'm so sorry but I was worried about karma because, you see, I asked Him' – I jerked my head skywards – 'to kill Derek, but then I thought God had killed *you,* yet you've come back to life and it's nothing short of a miracle because, omigod, don't you see? You're now a Born-Again Cyclist.'

'I haven't the faintest idea what you're burbling about but, yes, I'm alive, and it's a miracle I haven't broken anything.' The man flexed his shoulders and neck. 'That said, I suspect my body will later feel like it's been in a boxing ring.'

I got to my feet, staggering slightly, and sucked in a lungful of cool air. That was better. I did a few more greedy inhales. Yes, definitely feeling better by the moment.

'I'm terribly sorry,' I said again. 'You're the one who has been injured and yet I'm the one behaving like a dying swan.

Thank goodness you're okay and, yes, of *course* I'm insured. If you want to make a claim, I'll quite understand. Is your bike terribly damaged? I'm happy to put it in the back of my car and run you home.'

The man didn't reply. Instead, he was staring at me with an uncomfortable intensity.

'Haven't we met before?' he asked.

'I don't think so.'

'Yes, we have.' His tone hardened. 'Yesterday you were squashing loaves of bread. Today you're flattening cyclists.'

'W-What?' I stuttered, taking a step back in alarm.

The man whipped off his wraparounds revealing a pair of icy blue eyes.

I paled. It was Paul Newman.

# Chapter Sixteen

I stared in horror at the cyclist. Of all the people to knock off a bike, it was Sod's Law that William had chosen this one.

'For your information' – I squeaked, finding my voice – 'I do not go around wrecking bread and I am *not* in the habit of causing people to topple off their bicycles or... WILLIAM!' I bellowed. The little beagle had re-emerged from the undergrowth with – oh good heavens – a dead mouse in his mouth. 'HEEL!'

William gave me a naughty look before taking off in the opposite direction.

'Great dog,' said Paul Newman sourly. 'Not only does he murder wildlife, he's also completely out of control.'

'William Beagle is a poppet,' I said furiously.

'Oh, you're one of those,' he scoffed, folding muddy arms over his chest. 'The type who insists their dog wouldn't hurt a fly seconds before it mauls a child.'

'William wouldn't *touch* a child,' I protested.

'The evidence tells me otherwise. Can I remind you that your beagle has caught and *slaughtered* both a squirrel *and* a mouse in a matter of minutes? He's a serial killer. What if his next target is someone's beloved cat?'

'William lives with two cats and, if anything, they

terrorise *him*. He has the deepest respect for moggies and–'

'I don't agree,' Paul Newman interrupted. 'He's a killing machine in every sense of the word. It's damn lucky he didn't cause me to break my neck! You know, I can't stand sanctimonious dog owners like you who permit their pets to cause havoc.' He glared at Sylvie who was still obediently sitting by my side.

'Leave Sylvie out of it,' I said heatedly, folding my own arms across my chest. My temper was rising faster than a gearless traction elevator. 'It was *one* dog that caused a problem and, quite frankly, maybe *you* should've been looking where you were going, because if *you* hadn't been belting along at a million miles per hour, then *you* wouldn't have had to brake sharply, and *you* wouldn't have parted company from your bike.'

'Oh, so it's all *my* fault?' he said incredulously.

'YES!' I shouted, chin jutting out.

Well, why not? It could've been a swan or a duck that had stepped into this idiot's path. Okay, not right here. But maybe further down, by the lake.

'You really are quite incredible,' said Paul Newman, shaking his head in disbelief.

'And *you* are a pompous, arrogant, rude, sarcastic, condescending…'

'Keep going. What's the matter? Have you run out of adjectives?'

'… fretentious PART,' I spluttered, glaring at him.

That hadn't come out quite the way I'd wanted, but no matter. He'd got the gist of it.

'Are you done?' he hissed.

'Yes, I think so, and as fascinating as this conversation has been, I'm now going home.'

'Don't forget to take your murdering pet with you,' he spat, as William reappeared and cantered towards me.

Thankfully, the only thing now hanging out of William's mouth was his tongue. I grabbed the beagle's collar before he could cause any more problems with Paul Newman. What a horrible person. Any previous sympathy I'd had for the guy had completely evaporated. The self-righteous pillock. Okay, William had played a part in the guy taking a tumble. That said, Mr Newman had been whipping along at a furious speed. Never mind the ducks and swans, what if someone's tot had happened to be in his way? What if Mo had been with me? My heart clattered wildly at the thought of my granddaughter toddling joyfully along and suddenly being in the wrong place at the wrong time.

By the time I'd walked back to Sadie's house, I'd totally convinced myself that William Beagle was completely in the clear and Paul Newman was nothing more than a thoroughly irresponsible cyclist.

Once inside the house, I sponged down Sadie's waterproof, then returned it to the coat cupboard. All I wanted to do now was go home, get in the shower, and wash my hair.

As I started up Betty, I savagely scratched my scalp. First a concern about nits from the nursery. Now the possibility of fleas from a squirrel.

Fifteen minutes later, I was home.

'Hi, Mum.' Ruby greeted me in the hallway. Mo was on her hip. 'Like my nails?' Fingers were waggled at me.

'An' me, Nanna,' Mo beamed, waving her own tiny Barbie-pink fingernails.

'Gorgeous, my darlings,' I said, mustering up a smile.

'You missed Meg, but she said to say hello and' – Ruby abruptly broke off and stared at me – 'what on earth has happened to you?'

'How do you mean?' I said, slipping off my wool coat.

'Your hair and face are covered in mud and, *ewww*, you have a bogie.'

'It's a long story,' I sighed, heading for the downstairs toilet.

I pulled a ribbon of paper off the toilet roll, then caught sight of myself in the mirror over the washbasin. Ruby was right. I wondered if Paul Newman had seen that hanging out of my nostril. How embarrassing. Oh, what did it matter? It wasn't like I was ever going to see him again. I blew my nose, flushed the tissue down the loo and then washed my hands.

'I'm all ears,' said Ruby, practically tripping me up outside the loo.

'Ears,' repeated Mo, pointing to her own.

'Basically, William ran in front of a speeding cyclist and there was a bit of a row.'

'Full on mudslinging by the looks of it,' Ruby guffawed.

'The man was a total dick… I mean, pinhead,' I said, quickly changing my initial word.

'Dickhead,' Mo echoed.

# Chapter Seventeen

By the time Derek had returned from his long day of golf, I was out of the shower, hair washed – thoroughly checked for any further nasties – and in my pyjamas.

The nights were drawing in. Outside, light was rapidly fading and the temperature sharply dropping. Comfort food was required.

Sprinkling oven chips over a baking tray, I then placed some beef quarter-pounders in a separate dish. A quick forage in the fridge had me locating some blue cheese to later melt over the burgers. That done, I set about putting together a salad.

Derek strolled into the kitchen. He looked exuberant.

'What a day,' he declared.

I looked up from tossing the salad.

'Good round?' I ventured.

'The best,' he chirped.

My goodness, he was in a cheerful mood. What a pleasant change.

'So you didn't get put off by the rain?' I said, adding some chopped tomatoes to the bowl. 'That was quite a shower. I was out in it for a little while.'

'I didn't see any rain,' said Derek in surprise. He watched

me for a moment as I sliced some cucumber. 'Must've got lucky and dodged a cloud burst. Anyway, rain is for wimps. It wouldn't stop an enthusiastic player like me.'

'Of course it wouldn't,' I said loyally.

I grated some carrot over the peppery rocket leaves, then set the bowl down on the table.

'And Bill didn't mind the rain either?'

'Bill?' said Derek blankly.

I kept my expression neutral as I walked over to the oven to check on the chips and burgers.

'Yes, Bill.' I set the oven's timer for another ten minutes. 'I thought you said something about meeting him for lunch before hitting the fairway together. Didn't he turn up?'

'Oh, *that* Bill.'

How many Bills were there?

'Yes, of course he showed up,' said Derek, not quite able to meet my eyes. 'Bill loves golf as much as I do. We had a terrific round. Put the world to rights at the same time. Worked out exactly what we'd do if we were running this country. Fire the entire cabinet for starters.'

Okay. I'd given Derek the opportunity to say that Bill hadn't been able to make it. Instead, my husband had opted to lie. I pondered where he'd really gone. I also wondered what he'd say if I revealed that I'd bumped into Bill at the supermarket, and listened to his mate's itinerary which had left no time for swinging a wood or driver through the air.

The words were on the tip of my tongue, but I quickly reeled them in. If I challenged Derek, what would it achieve? Well, a row, that's what. And did I want a quarrel? No, not really. I was still smarting from the argument with Paul Newman. No, it was best, for now, to keep my own counsel – and crack on with getting that legal advice.

An hour later, meal finished, I cleared up, switched on the dishwasher, and then took myself off upstairs. Derek remained in the lounge, sprawled out on the sofa, and watching television. Ruby was now in the bathroom, sharing a bath with Mo. As I walked along the landing, I could hear the two of them chatting away.

''plash, Mummy, 'plash,' said Mo, shrieking with delight.

Seconds later I could hear splashing sounds as mum and daughter slapped their hands down on the water. I could imagine hundreds of droplets being propelled upwards, before raining down again, soaking their upturned faces. I smiled to myself as I pictured Mo, cheeks dimpling as she laughed, her curls stuck damply to her head. Such joy to be had from such a simple pastime.

Inexplicably my eyes filled with tears. I didn't want my granddaughter to ever experience falling out of love or suffer heartache or grief. But she would. At some point we all did. But then again, there were other "taster" lessons that started so early in life. Whether it was breaking one's heart over not having *thweeties*, or grieving because another tot at nursery had snatched your beloved teddy, the heartache and grief were still there – just on a scale proportionate to one's height and age.

My thoughts switched to Ruby. My daughter had fallen madly in love with her first crush, only to have him whipped away by panicking parents fearful about police, social services, and the consequences of underage sexual activity.

At the time I'd felt as if we'd all fallen into an emotional minefield. Ultimately my heart had squeezed for Ruby who – whether at fault or not – had learnt some tough lessons at a tender age.

I sighed. No parent ever wanted their precious offspring to have unhappy experiences. Regrettably it was unavoidable. Sometimes many times over. Such was life.

My eyes momentarily brimmed. Hastily I blinked away the tears. Closing my bedroom door, I settled down in a small armchair that occupied one corner of the marital bedroom.

The chair was winged and classic in style. It had once belonged to my maternal grandmother. Whenever I'd stayed with her as a child, I'd perched upon her lap as she'd read stories from this chair.

When Grandma had passed away, the chair – along with all her furniture – had been taken by a house clearance company. I'd rescued this item just as two men had been lifting it into their van. Since then, the chair had been completely reupholstered. The new fabric was a thick damask covered in a riot of blue roses. Blue because that had been Grandma's favourite colour. Roses because they'd been her favourite flower. Whenever I sat here, it made me feel close to her.

I now sank within its depths. This was where I came when I needed to think straight. To ponder. Closing my ears to the background sound of seasonal fireworks going off at the local park, I concentrated on my mobile's screen.

Moments later I was on the internet. Carefully, I tapped into Google what I was looking for.

*Matrimonial solicitors within a five-mile radius of Little Waterlow.*

# Chapter Eighteen

By the time Monday morning rolled around, I had a plan. I also had a piece of paper in my back pocket. Written upon it was the name and telephone number of a firm of solicitors not too close to home, but not too far away either.

I waved Derek off to work. He didn't wave back. An hour later Ruby left for college dropping Mo at nursery enroute. Then it was my turn to leave the house. This morning's client was Freddie the bulldog.

Of all my canine customers, Freddie was the most stubborn. Walking was not his thing. On an exceptionally good day, he managed half an hour. At worst, only five minutes.

As we set off together, I felt quite optimistic. However, after one hundred yards, Freddie sat down and refused to budge. Rather than argue with him, I let him have his way. While Freddie rested, I retrieved my secret piece of paper and nervously tapped out the number.

'Gardener and Stewart Solicitors, good morning,' said a friendly voice.

I instantly warmed to the female at the other end of the line. She sounded just like my mum. Cosy. Someone in whom you could confide.

‘Oh, er, hello.’

‘How can I help?’

I cleared my throat.

‘I found your firm on the internet and understand you offer, erm, matrimonial advice.’

‘That’s right. Gabrielle Stewart specialises in family law.’

‘I’m… well, after some assistance with…’

I trailed off as a sudden lump in my throat caught me by surprise.

‘Are you thinking about getting divorced, dear?’ she asked gently.

‘Yes,’ I croaked.

‘I understand. When would you like to come in and have a chat?’

‘As soon as possible,’ I whispered.

Freddie glanced up at me, unused to my compliance with his obstinacy.

‘Okay, let’s look at the diary,’ said the telephonist. There was a pause as her fingers moved over a keyboard. ‘As it happens, Gabrielle has had a cancellation this morning. Would half past eleven be too short notice?’

‘N-No,’ I stammered. Just so long as Freddie obliged and didn’t refuse to get up for ages. There was no hope of scooping him up and tucking his solid body under one arm. He weighed at least fifty pounds. ‘I’ll take it, please. That would be great.’

*Great, Wendy?*

I wasn’t sure that was the right word to use about divorce. “Ah, Mrs Walker. Having a good Monday?

Excellent! And I understand you want a divorce, is that right? *Great*!"

'Okay, let's get that booked for you. What's your name, dear?'

'Wendy Walker,' I quavered.

Oh, my goodness. I was really doing this. Derek would have an absolute hissy fit. I'd tell the solicitor about my husband's potential reaction. Ask if she had any good old-fashioned advice on how to deal with a spouse who wouldn't so much as spit feathers as foam from the mouth.

'That's all booked in for you, Wendy,' said the telephonist, her voice both kind and efficient.

'Thank you,' I said. 'Um, before you go, can I ask' – oh heck, why was it so difficult to talk about money? – 'how much will the appointment cost?'

'Absolutely nothing, dear. The first hour is free.'

'Really?' I breathed out a huge sigh of relief, thankful that my credit card had escaped an initial bashing. 'That's marvellous.'

'If you wish to proceed after the initial consultation, Gabrielle will then discuss the firm's fee structure.'

'Fabulous,' I said, beaming at Freddie. Again, probably not the best word in the circumstances. "So, Mrs Walker. Your final divorce bill totals sixty-four squillion pounds and five pence. Is that okay with you?" "Yes, *fabulous*!"

'See you soon, dear,' said the telephonist.

'Bye.'

I hung up feeling slightly breathless. I also had a pressing need to share my news.

'I'm seeing a solicitor,' I said to Freddie.

He responded by putting his head on his paws. I gave the lead a gentle tug. Freddie sighed heavily but didn't move. Terrific. Okay, let him have his way for a few more minutes. I took advantage and tapped out a second number. Kelly answered almost immediately.

'Hey, Wends,' she said. 'I was about to call you, but you beat me to it. I have BIG news!'

'Me too,' I gasped.

'Oooh-er, you sound tense. What's up?'

'I'm seeing a solicitor.'

There was a pause while Kelly digested this.

'As in, you're having a clandestine tryst with a guy who happens to be a legal bod?'

'No, you wally. I'm *seeing* a solicitor. For advice.'

I glanced furtively about in case Derek suddenly stepped out from behind a nearby wheelie bin.

'Omigod,' she squawked. 'Do you mean legal advice about getting a *divorce*?'

'Yes,' I said, my heart immediately doing a swoop worthy of a Red Arrows dive.

'Cripes. How are you feeling?'

'Nervous,' I admitted, immediately rubbing my palms down my jeans. 'Which possibly isn't a great start because I haven't even set off yet. Heaven knows what I'll be like when I get to the solicitor's office. My hands are already sweating profusely.' I gave them another vigorous wipe. 'It's like they're leaking, or something. Hell, now my pits have gone all gushy.'

'Take some deep breaths to calm you. So, does Derek know what you're up to?'

'Of *course* not!'

'Er, isn't it best to prepare him?'

'Yes, well, I guess so. But Kelly, this is *Derek*. I mean, he's not your average man.'

'Isn't he?' said Kelly, sounding confused.

'No! He'll go barmy. Bonkers. Doo-bleedin'-lally. Over the weekend he told me that he talked a mate out of filing for divorce, claiming it was a waste of money. He ever-so-succinctly let me know that he'd never agree to us going our separate ways.'

'In that case he must have had an inkling of your thought processes. You should have seized the moment and been honest.'

'Unfortunately, I didn't.'

'So, let me get this straight. You're going to start proceedings but carry on as normal at home. And then one morning, while Derek is enjoying his cuppa, the postie will deliver a large white envelope. You'll watch him open it. Observe his eyes bulge. Note how the vein in his forehead starts pulsing. Then you'll calmly ask, "Another brew, darling?"'

'Something like that,' I agreed.

'Wends, don't be daft. You can't just spring it on him.'

'No, I know. Oh, heck. Why am I so wet?'

'You're not wet. You're just…'

'Yes?'

'A big scaredy-cat.'

'In other words, a coward.'

'Yes,' she agreed. 'Look, do you want me to go with you? I can tell the solicitor that you're afraid of Derek. Make out he's a bit of a headcase, or something. It might even speed things along.'

Despite my mounting anxiety, I laughed.

'No, you don't need to do that. After all, Derek isn't a nutter. Just a…'

'Git?'

'Yeah, he's that all right. Anyway, I'm only getting advice. I don't have to do anything about it.'

'Is there any point in going if you don't follow it through?'

'I need to pace myself. One step at a time. Get some guidance. Sleep on it. Weigh it all up.'

'In other words, procrastinate.'

'No,' I protested. 'I simply don't want to rush in like a French gendarme, whistles blowing and arms waving.'

'Hmm. Well let me know how you get on. Who are you seeing?'

'A lady called Gabrielle Stewart. Apparently, she's the matrimonial specialist.'

'Ask her if she'll do a two-for-one price, in which case I'll be right behind you. What time are you going?'

'Soon. I'm currently out walking Freddie, except he's stationary. Anyway, enough about me. What's your big news?'

'Too thrilling for words,' she purred.

'Progress with Steve?'

She gave a throaty laugh.

'And some.'

'Oooh,' I squealed. 'Tell me.'

'Okay! So, obviously you know that Steve and I usually meet each other in shops.'

'Yes,' I said impatiently.

'For the first time ever, we're going to meet in Costa,' she shrieked. 'Isn't that exciting!'

'Er, thrilling. I guess.'

'Of *course* it's thrilling. It's amazing. Exhilarating. This is taking our meetups to a whole new level.'

'From standing up to sitting down.'

'No, Wends,' Kelly sighed. 'I mean it will be more like a proper date rather than lurking in shopping aisles. This will be, you know, more daring.'

'You're right.' Best to agree. Kelly sounded so happy. 'And which Costa are you going to? The one at Meopham?'

'Yes.'

'I presume Steve isn't worried about Caroline unexpectedly turning up and catching you both holding hands over your cappuccinos.'

'Not at all. Apparently, Caroline is a raging snob and only ever frequents the food hall at John Lewis for her coffee.'

'Right. And what if Henry walks in?'

'Henry?' said Kelly incredulously. 'Do Costa sell beer?'

'No,' I said, seeing her point. 'So, when is this cosy coffeetime experience taking place?'

'Saturday. Meanwhile I have the whole week to get

through. How on earth will I survive until the weekend?'

'You will. Meanwhile, I'd better get a move on. Freddie looks like he's gone to sleep.'

'Why does he loathe going for walks?'

'I don't know. None of my other doggy clients are like him. Still, at least he's had some fresh air and watered a couple of lampposts.'

'Give me a text later.'

'Okay, will do.'

'And seriously, if I were you, get a stiff gin in you before that talk with Derek.'

'Maybe,' I said, as my tummy contracted with anxiety. 'By the way, Derek told me he was playing golf on Saturday with his mate, Bill.'

'And?'

'He wasn't. I bumped into Bill in Asda. Derek lied.'

'Why would Derek lie?' said Kelly, puzzled.

'No idea. I mean, for a fleeting moment I wondered if he was having an affair.'

'Oh *bleurgh*. Who'd want a fling with Derek? Sorry, Wends. That was tactless. I didn't mean to be disrespectful, but frankly I'm amazed Derek hasn't started plaiting his nostril hair. Such a major turn off. Apart from anything else, it's not like he even has a sparkling personality.'

'I know, and thank you for your honesty,' I said, albeit a little tartly.

It was never nice having someone else point out your husband's faults, even if they were true.

'I've offended you.'

'It's fine,' I shrugged.

'No, it's not. I'm sorry. I'm always putting my size sevens in it.'

I grinned, instantly forgiving Kelly.

'It's okay, honest. And now I really am going to have to get a wiggle on and drag Freddie home.'

'Okay, and don't forget to text me.'

'I won't.'

We rang off, and I looked down at Freddie in dismay. He was now lying on his side, snoring. I reached inside my pocket and extracted a packet of dog treats, then wafted one in front of his nose. He opened one eye and then, jowls quivering with excitement, hauled himself upright.

'Good boy,' I beamed, holding the treat out and making him take a step forward. Then another. And another. 'You're going to have to work for this, Fred.' I gave him the biscuit, then withdrew a second from the packet. 'Twenty more steps before you get the next chew-chew.'

# Chapter Nineteen

Thanks to Freddie's stubbornness, I was ten minutes late in arriving at Gardener and Stewart Solicitors. I crashed into reception feeling hot, bothered, and flustered.

'Mrs Walker?' enquired the receptionist.

'Yes! Sorry I'm late but–'

I was all set to come up with an excuse about appalling traffic, roadworks, and temporary lights that weren't working, when she interrupted me.

'Gabrielle is behind schedule, so take a deep breath, and also a seat,' she smiled, pointing to one of the sumptuous leather chairs in the waiting area.

'Thanks.'

Feeling anxious, I perched on a chair. The furniture looked hideously expensive, which made me wonder what the hourly charges were in this establishment.

'If you fancy a tea or coffee, help yourself from the machine,' said the receptionist.

She nodded at a nearby sideboard. Upon it rested a contraption that looked so hi-tech it was a wonder one didn't need a manual to operate it.

'I'm good, thank you.'

No way was I going near that thing and making a fool of

myself. Apart from anything else, my hands seemed to have developed the shakes. The last thing I wanted was to slop coffee everywhere.

With fluttering fingers, I instead leant forward and plucked a glossy magazine from a glass-topped table. The mag was stuffed with celebrity photographs, so I settled down for some vacant flicking. On page six an ex-glamour model was, despite many problems, looking fabulous and talking about her latest beau. On page twenty a footballer and his wife, both sporting teeth whiter and brighter than a new moon, were showing off their first child. On page thirty an English actress, fragile and beautiful, was being photographed for the first time since her stressful divorce. The byline caught my eye.

*Why my two-million-pound settlement isn't enough.*

Blimey. Perhaps I should take a leaf out of her book and tell Gabrielle Stewart that I wasn't prepared to settle for anything less than three mill. That would take Derek's anticipated foaming-at-the-mouth to a whole new level. "How dare you! I'll give you three hundred quid and throw in our broken CD player as a gesture of goodwill."

'Mrs Walker?' said a voice, startling me out of my reverie.

I glanced up to see a fresh-faced girl looking at me. Heavens, this must be Gabrielle. Surely, she'd only just left Sixth Form.

'Hello,' I said nervously.

'Would you like to follow me?'

I abandoned the magazine and sprang to my feet.

Moments later we were swinging through some double doors and padding along a thickly carpeted corridor. We walked in silence, my shoes sinking into the rich plush. I eyed the quality of the pile uneasily, once again pondering what the hourly charges were in this place.

Perhaps I should have Googled information about a do-it-yourself divorce. Yes, of *course* I should have done. Why hadn't I properly thought about that option before rushing into this appointment? There were probably all sorts of packages available to suit one's purse.

BASIC:
Expert advice.
Drafting the application.
Please make your own arrangements upon leaving the court.

MIDDLE OF THE ROAD:
Everything handled for you.
Courtesy taxi from court with a celebratory stop at McDonalds.

ALL THE BELLS AND WHISTLES:
Sit back while we do everything.
Complimentary stretch limo and triumphant lap around town before taking you home.

'Here we are,' said the girl, stopping by a door. 'He'll see you now.'

'He?' I said in surprise. 'Aren't you Gabrielle?'

'No,' she laughed. 'I'm, Annabelle, the temporary secretary. His last one is currently off with stress, which is no wonder. The guy is a nightmare to work for. I'm driving him potty because I have no legal experience plus I'm a rotten typist, but the agency can't find anyone else willing to work for him, so he's stymied.'

My brow puckered with confusion.

'But Gabrielle is a female name.'

I wasn't sure if I wanted to air my dirty laundry with a male divorce lawyer.

'Rosie on reception is always mispronouncing his name, which doesn't help our Mr Stewart's temper. His name is Gabriel. Like the angel,' Annabelle added. 'Except he's definitely not one of those.'

She pushed against the door, and suddenly I was in a room that was all chrome and black, and monopolised by a vast state-of-the-art desk. As my eyes rested on Gabriel Stewart, I blanched.

Oh, please. Not again. It was Paul Newman.

## Chapter Twenty

I stared at Gabriel Stewart, appalled.

'I thought you were a woman,' I said foolishly.

The ice-blue eyes bored into mine.

'My favourite skirt and blouse are currently at the drycleaner's,' he parried. 'So I had no choice but to come to work in a man's suit.'

I reddened.

'Your name confused me.'

'It's no different to Lesley and Leslie. Or Peter and Peta. Anyway, I prefer to be called Gabe.'

He stood up and extended a hand across the desk. I looked at it, then mentally sighed with relief. He didn't recognise me. Thank goodness for small mercies.

Politely, I leant in for a handshake but, as Gabe's palms touched mine, an unexpected jolt of electricity shot up my arm causing my entire body to physically jerk.

'Pleased to meet you,' I gasped.

'Really?' He released my hand, indicating that I sit down. 'That surprises me. The last time we met, you called me a pretentious fart. At least, I think that's what you were trying to say.'

Hell. He *did* recognise me.

There was a snigger and Gabe's eyes flicked to the hovering temp.

'Annabelle, can you make yourself useful, please? Go and make two coffees while Mrs Walker and I get on with our meeting.'

'Of course,' Annabelle demurred, slipping away.

'Look' – I began – 'when I made this appointment, I didn't realise you were the same man as–'

'Shall we draw a line under the topic of "Delinquent Beagle" and instead talk about why you're here in my office?'

I took a deep breath. Oh, for goodness' sake. I'd taken time out to be here. Any advice was going to be free. I might as well get on with it.

'I'd like to divorce my husband, but I don't know how to go about it, or even if it's possible given that Derek will refuse to co-operate.'

'Why?'

I laughed mirthlessly.

'There are loads of reasons why. He's rude. Unpleasant. Spiteful. Mean. Tight. Everything he says is a putdown or sneer. After years of enduring his behaviour, I feel completely demoralised. All that aside, he doesn't take the rubbish out. Or mow the lawn. He doesn't clean the toilet after… well, you know. He doesn't *do* anything.' I put my hands up in a gesture of helplessness. 'And saying all this out loud might sound trite and simply the moans of just another depressed housewife, but the truth is, Mr Stewart, I'm lonely.' I gulped as my eyes unexpectedly pricked with tears. '*Really* lonely. And I'd rather be lonely on my own eating a telly dinner in front of Coronation Street than be banished to the kitchen to get on with the ironing while Derek holds the remote hostage. I'm also aware that you divorce lawyers want to know all the ins and outs of *everything*' – I gave Gabe a meaningful look – 'so before you ask about our sex life, I can confirm that there isn't one. That side of the marriage ceased months ago, although Derek did complain only last weekend that I wasn't fulfilling my wifely duties.' I gave an involuntary shudder. 'It's possible that he might be hoping to reignite things sexually, but it's not an activity I wish to partake in, especially after my best friend enquired if Derek was planning on plaiting his nostril hair any time soon. Please don't think I'm shallow because I'm not. Our marriage problems go way beyond excessive nasal hair and not taking the bins out. Do you understand?'

The blue gaze didn't waver. There was a moment's silence before Gabe cleared his throat.

'Thank you for all that information, Mrs Walker.' His mouth twitched. 'I was actually asking why you thought your husband wouldn't agree to a divorce.'

I briefly closed my eyes and wished the plush carpet would tear apart and consume me.

'Derek told me at the weekend – when discussing an acquaintance's marriage – that if we were ever in the same situation, he'd block a divorce for financial reasons.'

'I see. So, right now, your husband hasn't a clue that you're unhappy and wanting to end your marriage?'

'No,' I whispered. 'I was hoping you might, er, tell him for me.'

I squirmed in my seat. Maybe coming here today hadn't been such a great idea. What was I doing with a head full of pipedreams? And as for buying Clover Cottage, I probably had more chance of winning the National Lottery.

The temp returned with a tray of coffee and biscuits. My eyes landed on the plate of chocolate digestives, and my belly growled with hunger. For a moment no one spoke, and the only sound was that of my empty stomach rumbling like approaching thunder.

'Thank you, Annabelle,' said Gabe, over the gurgling. 'That will be all for now.' He turned to me, and his face was a smidgen kinder. Only a smidgen, mind. 'Please, have a biscuit.' He pushed the plate towards me. 'I don't want you expiring in my office.'

'Thank you,' I mumbled, taking one.

'Now then.' He reached for his coffee. A regrouping gesture. 'If you're hoping for this firm to write a letter to Derek saying something along the lines of, "We represent your wife who would like to have a *Very Important Conversation* with you," then I'm afraid that isn't something we do. The starting point in this situation is to sit him down, share your feelings and let him know you've not been very happy. After all, talking might resolve the situation. Sometimes this can involve a third party, like a marriage guidance counsellor.'

I shook my head and hastily swallowed down the biscuit.

'I've made up my mind. I no longer want to be with him.'

'What if Derek said, "Please, give me a second chance. I

promise to mow the lawn, take the bins out, give you the remote control and remove my nasal hair." How would you feel then?'

'Exactly the same,' I said firmly. 'Those grievances are minor. The breakdown of our marriage goes way beyond that, and the result is that I no longer love him. If the truth be told, I suspect he feels the same way about me. I mean, if you love someone, you treat them with kindness. Respect. I know that's a two-way street. I'm not saying I'm disrespectful to him – because I don't believe I am – but he's just' – I fought to sum up what I was trying to say – 'so emotionally retarded. There's no joy. No fun. No togetherness. Not properly. There hasn't been for years. We've simply been going through the motions.'

I rattled to a stop and, with a shaking hand, picked up my coffee cup. The trembling caused me to slurp noisily.

'Then you must tell him that. Share your feelings. Express your desire for a separation. Say that you've made up your mind. That you will be filing for a divorce, and he will be served with papers. Then politely excuse yourself from the conversation.'

'You mean, before he starts hurling gin bottles,' I said wryly.

'Is he violent?' asked Gabe.

'No.' I shook my head slowly. 'But he'll definitely go apeshit.'

'Define apeshit.'

'Oh, you know,' I sighed. 'Rant and rave. Turn purple. Refuse to comply.'

Gabe put down his cup.

'Look, a civil divorce starts with the right words. Your husband might not like the initial conversation, but if you keep it short, sweet, and calm, it's the first step to an amicable split. Ultimately that will save time, money, and an awful lot of emotional energy. Meanwhile, the law recently changed. You no longer need to tell a judge *why* you want a divorce. Instead, the marriage ends on the basis that both parties agree their relationship has broken down. Once the legal ball is rolling, it will take a minimum of six months to achieve Decree Absolute. Can I ask how long you've both been married?'

'Twenty-seven years.'

'After that length of time it will be a straightforward split. Fifty-fifty.'

'I can't see Derek agreeing to that. You see, after my redundancy I couldn't financially contribute much towards–'

'Doesn't matter,' Gabe interrupted. '*Everything* is straight down the middle. That includes any savings your husband might have. Also, his pension.'

'Right,' I croaked, trying not to wince at Derek's reaction once he knew all this.

'So, shall I leave you to have that conversation with your husband? Then we can go from there.'

'Um, yes, okay.' The meeting was over. I quickly threw the dregs of my coffee down my neck and clattered the cup back in its saucer.

'Good. Meanwhile' – he reached into a drawer and extracted a laminated leaflet – 'should you wish to go ahead, here's a list of my firm's charges.'

'Thank you, Mr Stewart.'

'Gabe,' he corrected, as I took the leaflet from him.

'Wendy,' I muttered.

Once again, he proffered his hand. As I shook it, another unexpected zinger shot up my fingers, straight into my armpit and exited somewhere round my left ear. What the heck was *that* all about?

My arm was still tingling when I started up Betty and headed back to Little Waterlow.

# Chapter Twenty-One

I rang Kelly as soon as I was home.

'You'll never guess who my solicitor is,' I said breathlessly, flopping down on the bottom stair and pulling off my shoes.

'Don't tell me. Some bitch in a power suit who oversees celebrity divorces and will milk Derek dry on your behalf.'

'Ha! Not even close. First, the solicitor turned out to be a guy. The receptionist kept referring to him as Gabrielle, but in fact his name is Gabriel. Or Gabe, as he prefers to be called. Second, you've met him.'

There was a pause as Kelly digested this.

'Really? I don't know anyone by that name.'

'It was the same guy in the mini supermarket.' I stood up and walked into the kitchen. 'You know. Mr Squashed Loaf Man.'

'No way!'

'Yes.' I reached for the kettle and stuck it under the tap. 'It was all rather embarrassing, especially as I recently had a second encounter with him. William caused Gabe to part company from his racing bike at the park.'

'Flaming Nora,' said Kelly. 'I'm amazed you didn't do a U-turn straight out of the man's office.'

'The thought did cross my mind.' I stuck the kettle back on its electric base and flicked the switch. 'I seem to be bumping into this guy everywhere, but never expected him to turn up at a law firm.'

'You can say that again.' At the other end of the line, I could hear Kelly blowing out her cheeks. 'So how did you manage to get over the initial awkwardness?'

'He graciously suggested we draw a line under the topic of a certain beagle dog.'

Kelly giggled.

'Yes, William is a bit of a liability, but from what I recall of your solicitor, he's something of a babe.'

'He's not really my type,' I said, reluctantly remembering those starbursts whizzing up and down my arm.

I suddenly froze. Could that have been some sort of chemistry? *Oh, don't be so ridiculous, Wendy.* No, I did *not* fancy Gabe Stewart. The guy had probably touched a tiny nerve, or something. Like when you hit your funny bone and got a weird reaction.

'Do you think you'll go ahead with the divorce?' asked Kelly.

'Yes,' I nodded, dropping a teabag in a mug, and adding the boiled water. 'I might as well crack on with it.' I added a dash of milk, then sat down at the kitchen table. Sunshine was streaming in through the window, warming the back of my neck. 'However, Gabe suggests that first I have a conversation with Derek. You know, to give him fair warning of what the postman will be delivering.'

'So will you chat about it tonight?'

My stomach immediately fluttered at the very thought. Anxiety. I swatted the feeling away.

'No time like the present,' I chirped, taking a sip of tea. 'Can't say I'm looking forward to it.'

'Does Ruby know?'

'No,' I sighed. 'I'll have to have a chat with her too. Do you think I'm a bad person, Kelly?'

'What do you mean?'

'Well, I'm rocking the boat here, aren't I? I mean, it's not just Derek's life I'm turning upside down. This will affect Ruby and Mo, too.'

'For the better, Wends. Remember that. And anyway, Ruby is a young woman, not a kid.'

'I know, I know. But she's still under the marital roof and won't be immune to an unpleasant atmosphere.'

'Focus on buying Clover Cottage.'

'Yes,' I said, relaxing slightly. 'It will all work out, won't it.'

'Course it will,' Kelly soothed. 'So, what did this Gabe chappie say about finances?'

'He said everything will be divided straight down the middle. Derek won't be able to refuse me half the house or any of the savings he's squirrelled away.'

'That's good to know.' I could almost hear the cogs whirring in Kelly's brain as she mentally calculated her own potential settlement. 'You know, I should take a leaf out of your book, Wends. This flirtation with Steve is all well and good, but it's not healthy, is it? It's just putting a plaster over a sore.'

'Yes,' I agreed sadly. 'I can't remember what it was like when I was happily married, can you?'

'No,' Kelly sighed. 'Although we must have been once.'

'Now I'm starting to feel depressed,' I said gloomily.

'Sorry, Wends. I didn't mean to make you feel rubbish. Let's catch up in the morning with some fresh air and a dog walk. We'll put the world to rights.'

'Okay. Laters.'

I hung up and took another sip of my tea, then mentally began to rehearse what I was going to say to Derek.

## Chapter Twenty-Two

I don't know how long I sat there, running through various conversation scenarios with Derek, but in the end, I decided to wing it.

I spent the rest of the Monday afternoon stripping beds and getting on with laundry. I was in the middle of gathering up duvet covers fresh from the tumble dryer when the front door slammed, making me jump. Seconds later, Ruby stomped into the kitchen with Mo hanging off her.

'What a flipping day,' she fumed. 'Everything that could go wrong, did.' She chucked her keys and bag down on the table, then let Mo slide down the side of her torso.

'*Weeeee*,' cooed Mo, enjoying the glide down her mum's side. She toddled over to me. 'Nanna pick up. More *weeeee*.'

'Okay, darling,' I said.

Abandoning the bedding, I scooped her up. Unfortunately, my hips were a lot more matronly than Ruby's. Consequently, Mo's glide-and-slide wasn't the same experience. Unimpressed, she began to wail her displeasure.

'Oh no,' Ruby sighed. 'Not more grizzling. She was like it all the way home in the car.'

'I expect she's tired,' I said to Ruby, before turning my

attention back to my granddaughter. 'Would Mo instead like to dance with Nanna?'

I immediately broke into a waltz around the kitchen.

'Yeth,' Mo squealed with delight. 'More,' she grinned, holding on tightly.

I marvelled at how quickly a toddler's mood could shift from discontent to laughter.

'You have the patience of a saint, Mum,' said Ruby.

She went over to the kettle, checked the water level, and switched it on.

'Years of practice from being married to your dad,' I said carelessly, before pirouetting past the oven. 'Sorry,' I quickly added. 'I shouldn't have said that.'

'Go ahead,' Ruby grinned. 'I'm eighteen, Mum. Not a child. As husbands go, I am aware that yours is crap.'

'Crap,' Mo grinned.

Ruby and I exchanged horrified looks. Oh no. We'd done it again.

'Naughty mummy,' said Ruby to Mo. 'She said a bad word. Tell Mummy she can't have any sweeties.'

'Thweeties!' Mo whooped, instantly wriggling to be put down.

'You walked straight into that one,' I laughed.

I went to the fridge and extracted six Smarties from a tube. Transferring them to an eggcup, I handed it to Mo.

'Fank yoo,' she beamed. 'I share with Sally.'

She toddled off to the lounge, in search of her doll.

'I'm sorry you had a bad day, darling,' I said.

Sitting down, I watched Ruby making her cuppa.

'Oh, I suppose it wasn't that awful. Just silly stuff.' She pulled out her own chair and sat down beside me. 'Hair dye going wrong. The tutor being snappy. How was yours?' She glanced around the kitchen. 'Drowning in laundry?'

'Actually' – I said carefully – 'laundry aside, it's been… quite an interesting day.'

'Oh?'

Ruby regarded me over the rim of her cup, waiting for me to enlarge. I took a deep breath.

'Look, Rubes. At some point I'll be having a chat with your dad, but, before I do, perhaps I should talk to you first.'

'Oooh-er. That sounds ominous. Don't tell me. You've met a really hot man, fallen madly in love, and the pair of you are going to run away together.' She guffawed into her cup.

'Er…'

The laughing abruptly stopped, and her eyes widened.

'Geez, have you?'

'There's no easy way to say this. Me and your dad…' I trailed off.

'Go on,' she urged.

'I want to leave him. Our marriage isn't a happy one and, well, it just seems silly living together for the sake of it.'

'I understand.'

'Do you?'

'Mum, of course I do. I don't know how you've stayed with Dad for so long. He treats you like rubbish. Anyway' – her face darkened – 'I wouldn't put up with the way he behaves.' For a moment her face was suffused with anger.

'His disrespect is quite breathtaking.'

'He's not that awful.' I leant forward and patted her hand. 'We just no longer have anything in common.'

'Mum, it goes way beyond that.' Ruby was getting angry, and I wondered why. 'If you knew–' She abruptly broke off.

'Knew what?' I prompted.

'Nothing.' She shook her head, lips pursed. 'Just do it, eh? Leave him.'

I didn't say anything for a moment, and instead studied her face. What had my daughter been about to say? I cleared my throat.

'As it happened, I saw a solicitor today. Only for advice, but it was very positive. He suggested I have a chat with your dad first, so he's not shocked when the papers are served. However, I'm chatting to you now so that you're prepared too.'

'Thank you,' Ruby whispered, her eyes suddenly filling with tears.

'Oh darling, don't get upset.'

I took her hands and squeezed them in mine.

'I'm not,' she promised. 'I'm happy. Truly. It's about time things changed for you, and for the better. You've had years of being miserable with Dad. I'm more than aware that I added to the strain, springing a granddaughter on you when I was still a kid myself. I'm so sorry, Mum.'

And with that she burst into tears.

'Rubes, don't be silly.' I leapt to my feet, looping my arms around her shaking shoulders. 'I wouldn't change anything. It's *you* I feel for. Being a single mum. Juggling motherhood with studying. Missing out on gigs with your kiddie-free pals.'

'You've always been there for me, even when I was behaving like a total cow.'

'That's what mums do, sweetheart. Just like you will be there for Mo when she's older. Anyway, enough of the gloom and doom. I have a plan, and now is as good a time as any to tell you. The solicitor informed me that I'm entitled to half the proceeds of this house, so I'm going to buy Sadie Farell's place. Clover Cottage. It's only small, but it will be perfect for you, Mo, and me. And guess what! There's an outbuilding that can be converted into a tiny hair salon. It will be perfect for when you've qualified.'

Ruby instantly stopped crying. Suddenly her eyes were shining with a light I hadn't seen for a while. Hope.

'Really?' she gasped. 'Oh my God, *really?*'

'Really,' I beamed, squeezing her shoulders.

She leapt to her feet and hugged me hard.

'I can't believe it,' she said, half laughing, half crying. 'It will be a dream come true. We should celebrate. Shall we crack open the rest of Mo's Smarties?'

'Good idea!'

I swung round to go to the fridge but stopped dead in my tracks. The smile on my lips withered and died. Derek was standing in the doorway. A vein was pulsing in his forehead.

Oh crap. Neither of us had heard him come in. How long had he been standing there? When Derek spoke, his voice was like a pistol shot.

'Sorry to interrupt the rejoicing.' His glare was glacial. 'I think I caught the gist of that conversation.'

# Chapter Twenty-Three

Slowly, Derek advanced towards me. Ruby was on her feet in a trice.

'You stay away from Mum,' she quavered, planting herself between the two of us.

'*You* keep out of it,' Derek snapped. 'And show some respect.'

'Respect?' Ruby hissed. 'One word. Coco.'

Derek visibly paled. I wondered why. What was going on here? Why was cocoa such a touchy subject?

'Mind your own business,' he snarled.

'I would, but unfortunately news travels fast in a place like Little Waterlow.'

'What about cocoa?' I asked.

Mo chose that moment to toddle into the kitchen dragging her doll by one arm. She paused to regard the tense faces within.

'Want cocoa,' she announced.

'I don't think so,' said Ruby grimly, pushing past her father. 'Come on, Mo. Mummy will take you to McDonald's for a special treat. Nanna and Grandpa need to be alone for a little while.'

I turned my back on Derek and began busying myself

again with the abandoned bed linen. It seemed vital to concentrate on smoothing out those creases before folding up yards of cotton. My ears registered the sound of the front door closing. Ruby and Mo had left.

'So,' said Derek. His tone was ominous. It was amazing how one small word could carry such foreboding. He sat down on Ruby's vacated chair. 'Now that you've told everyone else around here that you want a divorce, how about you discuss it with me? Or am I just the husband and therefore the last to know?'

I carried on with the folding, mentally scrabbling to recall the earlier conversation with Gabe.

*A civil divorce starts with the right words. Your husband might not like the initial conversation, but if you keep it short, sweet, and calm, it's the first step to an amicable split. Ultimately that will save time, money, and an awful lot of emotional energy.*

'STOP FOLDING THE FUCKING SHEETS AND TALK TO ME,' Derek roared.

I nearly dropped them in fright.

'Okay,' I said, digging deep for courage. 'I'm not happy.'

'NEITHER AM I!' he boomed. His fist banged down on the table as if to emphasise the point. 'But when I walk out of this house and go to work, I cheer up. When the weekend rolls around and I play golf, I'm deliriously happy. In other words, I entertain myself and find my own pleasure.'

'W-Well isn't that rather sad?' I quavered. 'I mean, wouldn't you like to be cheerful *all* the time?'

'But you don't make me cheerful,' he said shrilly.

'S-So maybe it's time to do something about it,' I ventured. 'Life's too short to be miserable with someone who doesn't make you happy.'

'I. Just. Told. You,' he enunciated. 'I'm perfectly happy when I'm not under the same roof as you.'

'Look, Derek.' I hugged the folded laundry to me, as if a shield. 'This is ridiculous. Marriage isn't about only being happy when you're at work or on a golf course. It's about doing things together and–'

'Doing things together?' he hooted. 'You don't know the meaning of the word, Wendy. You choose to do "things" with other people. Not me. You swan off on your silly little dog walks with your silly little *clients*' – he spat the word as if it were a dog turd that William Beagle had sent by courier – 'or you spend hours gossiping with that airhead mate of yours. And then, when you've finished devoting your time and energy to those people, you turn the spotlight on Ruby and Mo. From babysitting, to ferrying Mo about. From helping Ruby if she has a sleepless night, to singing nursery rhymes with Mo. Then there's your projects–'

'What projects?'

'Your ridiculous obsession with cosy domesticity – like almost wallpapering the kitchen with Mo's finger paintings.' His face hardened. 'When do you have any time left for me?'

'But you don't want my company,' I protested. 'The second you've put your knife and fork together, you're up from the table and off to the lounge to watch football. You never hang around in the kitchen to make conversation with me, or suggest we watch a film together on the telly.'

'Some daft bloody romcom?' he yelled, rolling his eyes.

'Okay, forget movies. What about going out on a Saturday evening? Many husbands and wives have a date night.'

'A date night?' Derek scoffed. 'Wendy, date nights are for people who are romantically involved with each other. They go out to dinner. Hold hands across a candlelit table. Gaze deep into each other's eyes. Then they skip dessert and coffee because they can't wait to get home, rip each other's clothes off, and fuck the living daylights out of each other.' I winced at his language. Noticing my reaction, his face darkened. 'What's the matter? Don't you like that word? Does it offend your senses? You're pathetic, Wendy. Utterly pathetic. Look at you. Dressed like a drag as you play the role of downtrodden wife. Supposedly up to your armpits in laundry before making sure the kitchen floor is spotless in case Mo drops a *thweetie* and pops it in her mouth. You're like an ice maiden. Everything about you is cold and frigid.'

My mouth dropped open. It was all coming out now, wasn't it!

'So *you* divorce *me*,' I said, finding my voice. 'Is that what this is about? Not wanting to be the Respondent or the... the Second Applicant, or whatever it's called these days?'

'You really are such a silly little woman,' he laughed, but there was no humour to the sound. 'A divorce costs money. I'm not wasting my hard-earned brass on a team of legal bods.'

'You don't need to,' I cried. 'All that's required is

splitting everything fifty-fifty and Bob is your uncle, as they say. A basic fee for a divorce certificate, and then we go our separate ways.'

Derek leant towards me. Instinctively I shrank away.

'This house' – he hissed – 'is *my* house. Not yours. It's *my* name on the deeds. *Mine* on the mortgage. That's how dense you are, Wendy. You never had the brain cells' – he tapped the side of his head – 'to think about important details like that, did you?'

'Only because you insisted you were head of the house and it was easier for me to be in a traditional role,' I protested. 'I've paid my way throughout this marriage–'

'On a dog walker's earnings?' he ridiculed. 'Ten pounds here. Twenty quid there.'

'I'm talking about when I used to commute to London,' I protested, my voice rising. I was angry now. How *dare* he fail to acknowledge my years of contribution to the mortgage repayments and bills. 'It's only since I was made redundant and–'

'And ended up on the scrapheap' – he pointed out – 'and weren't you the lucky one having a husband who bailed you out. Who kept a roof over your head, instead of booting you out.'

'Booting me out?' I gasped. 'I'm your *wife* for God's sake, not some tenant who failed to cough up the rent. And what about you enjoying the benefits of an unpaid lacky? I've cleaned and cooked for you these past twenty-seven years. Doesn't that count for something?'

'That's just about your one saving grace, Wendy. In fact,

your *only* saving grace. The quid pro quo for me supporting you financially these last few years. So, no. I am not agreeable to any divorce. And if you oppose me, you'll find out just how unreasonable I can really be. I'll see you homeless first, because you won't get a penny out of me. Over my dead body. DO YOU HEAR?' he bellowed. 'OVER MY DEAD BODY!'

And with that Derek scraped back his chair and stalked off.

# Chapter Twenty-Four

'And then Derek said I'd never get a penny out of him. In fact, his exact words were *over my dead body.*'

'What a dickhead,' said Kelly.

We were back at Trosley Country Park on this chilly Tuesday morning, walking under a canopy of trees that had already shed most of their leaves.

Alfie was trotting along at Kelly's heels. Today my client was a pretty border collie called Maid. She was cantering back and forth alongside me. Her owner always visited elderly parents on Tuesdays. Unfortunately, Maid was too lively to be around mobility-compromised oldies. It was my job to give her a good run, so that she'd spend the rest of the day snoozing in her basket.

'So, what are you going to do?' Kelly prompted.

'I've already spoken to Gabe Stewart.'

'Ah, yes, the hot solicitor.' Kelly waggled her eyebrows.

'I rang him this morning, after Derek had left for work. I have an appointment this afternoon at three o'clock. Gabe was very reassuring. Apparently, it's quite normal to have one's spouse go into a verbal meltdown and let rip with ugly histrionics.'

'Even so' – Kelly pulled a face – 'it's not nice being told

you're on the scrapheap, or that you'll be made homeless. What a bastard.' Her cheeks flushed with anger. 'If Henry spoke to me like that, I'd stick my hands under the waistband of his trousers, grab the side of his underpants, and pull hard.' She gave a satisfied nod. 'A violent wedgie, ensuring the instant transferral of the front appendage to the rear.'

I winced at her description.

'I didn't realise Derek hated me so much.'

'He doesn't hate you.'

'Oh, he does,' I sighed. 'I think it's safe to say he totally despises me.'

'His reaction is simply down to you rebelling against being his personal doormat. Did he sleep on the sofa last night?'

'Don't be daft. I did.'

'That's going to do your back the world of good. Not,' she tutted.

'It's fine,' I shrugged. 'I stayed awake for ages last night, listening to the sounds of the house. The hum of the fridge. The tap dripping in the kitchen. In a weird sort of way, it was quite relaxing. It also gave me a chance to make tentative plans.'

'Oh?'

'I'm going to ring my parents later.'

'Omigod, are you bolting off to Spain?' Kelly squawked.

I gave her a wry smile.

'It's tempting, but no. I'm toying with the idea of seeing if they could give me a loan, just until the marital home is sold. I was thinking about asking Sadie Farrell if I could rent

Clover Cottage in the interim – until I'm financially in a position to buy it.'

'That's a brilliant idea,' Kelly agreed. 'Do your parents have the readies to fund you renting?'

'I think so,' I said. Mum and Dad were, financially speaking, sitting pretty after selling up their UK home and buying abroad at a fraction of the cost. 'That said, I won't rush into anything. I mean, Derek might calm down. He might decide that getting divorced is a terrific idea and insist we crack on with it.'

'And pigs might fly,' said Kelly. 'Oh look!' she pointed. 'How very romantic.'

I glanced ahead and instantly felt all warm and fuzzy. A young guy was down on one knee, evidently proposing to his girlfriend. He was holding something in the palm of his hand. A ring? Yes, it must be judging from the shocked and delighted reaction of the girl standing before him. From this distance I couldn't see her face, but her body language indicated she was thrilled. Her hands had flown to her face, suggesting she was overcome with emotion. The man was now reaching for her left hand and slipping the band over the knuckle of her third finger, and–

Oh God.

'Maid!' I yelped.

The border collie had also spotted the couple ahead. She was suddenly very keen to check out what the man had passed to the woman. A squeaky toy? Or was it some sort of delicious treat? There was only one way to find out.

'MAID!' I bellowed.

The collie took off like a rocket, then launched herself at the guy, completely knocking him off balance. As he toppled sideways and landed squarely in thick mud, Kelly gave me a horrified look.

'Why are all your doggy clients total headcases?'

'Maid isn't a–'

The guy's head swivelled in our direction.

'OY!' he yelled.

'I'm *so* sorry,' I called. 'She just wanted to say congratulations.'

'FUCK THAT. IF I GET HOLD OF YOUR DOG, I'M GOING TO KICK IT. DO YOU HEAR ME?'

'I think the whole of Trosley just heard him,' Kelly muttered. 'Blimey, he's livid.'

'On second thoughts' – said the girl, her words floating our way – 'I could never marry a man who threatened to hurt an animal. Here, you can have this back.'

And with that, she tossed the ring at his feet and stalked off, just as Maid galloped back to me.

'NOW LOOK WHAT YOU'VE DONE,' roared the man.

'What shall we do?' I hissed to Kelly.

'Bugger off smartly,' she advised.

She immediately turned on her heel and took off like a gazelle. I followed, legs whirring like an adrenalised daddy longlegs. As I belted after Kelly, I wondered how something as simple as dog walking could sometimes be so stressful.

# Chapter Twenty-Five

As I drove into Gardener and Stewart Solicitors' private carpark, my stomach gave an unexpected lurch that left me feeling a bit peculiar.

One part of my mind focussed on carefully reversing Betty into a space, lining up the wheels between the bay's white lines, while the other wondered why I was suddenly feeling so nervous.

I tried to reassure myself. It was simply pre-match nerves about starting divorce proceedings.

*More like seeing a pair of ice-blue eyes that play havoc with your blood pressure*, piped up the little voice in my head.

Don't be ridiculous, I countered. There's nothing wrong with my blood pressure. If anything, my GP has always said it's a little on the low side.

*Hmm. Well let's see if Gabe's handshake has you gasping again, eh?*

I unbuckled and, hugging my handbag to my chest, hastened round to the front of the building. Moments later I was in the waiting area being greeted again by Rosie, the sweet receptionist.

'Hello, Mrs Walker,' she beamed. 'You're here to see

Gabrielle, aren't you.'

I smiled at her mispronunciation.

'That's right.'

'How are you, dear?' she asked, looking concerned.

'Oh, you know,' I shrugged.

How was anyone when they sat in a place like this? In a depression? Or looking forward to the moment they could pop champagne corks?

'It will all be fine,' she assured. 'Remind yourself that you're in very good hands.'

A sudden mental picture of Gabe's hands all over my body nearly had me hyperventilating. I stared at Rosie in horror.

'Take a seat, dear,' she said, looking at me with consternation.

I collapsed down on the leather sofa. Oh no. No, no, no. This couldn't be happening. I did *not* fancy Gabe Stewart.

*Yes, you do.*

I really don't.

'Hi,' said Gabe's temp, interrupting my inner voice. 'Gabe will see you now.'

'Thanks,' I muttered.

Once again I followed her through the double doors and along the plushly carpeted corridor.

'Um, Annabelle?' I said tentatively.

She paused and swung round to face me.

'Are you okay? You look awfully pale.'

'I'm fine,' I assured, dredging up a smile. 'I just wondered if… er… Mr Stewart is the right solicitor for me.'

'How do you mean?'

'Well, I'd like a lawyer who has some empathy. Who, perhaps, has been in a similar situation and–'

'Oh, he has,' she interrupted. 'He's been married and divorced six times. He's Henry VIII reincarnated, but this time around he doesn't behead his exes.'

I stared at her, appalled.

'He's been married *six* times?'

'Only kidding,' she hooted. 'I do believe he's had his own personal heartbreak. Well, from what I once heard on the office grapevine. I promise Gabe has sympathy for all his clients.'

'That's… good to know,' I said, nonetheless still feeling anxious.

'Maybe he's too kind, because many of his clients end up developing thumping great crushes on him. They ring him up over anything. *Everything*. "Oh, Gabe, I'm *sooo* sorry to bother you, but my ex-husband is arguing about custody of the cat. I wondered if we could discuss it over a drink after work." They make it so obvious that they want to get into his Calvin Kleins. Why, only yesterday a previous client turned up without any announcement. "Gabe, darling, I happened to be passing and, as I never got around to personally thanking you for handling my affairs" – cue a throaty chuckle because she had a ton of affairs under her Gucci belt – "I absolutely insist on taking you out for a drinkypoo. *Right now*."' Annabelle shook her head. 'He has a terrible time seeing them off without causing offence. However, I can see why women love him. I mean, you must agree that he's a bit of a stunner.' She gave me a cheeky look. 'Gabe might be forty-five to my twenty-five, but I wouldn't say no.'

Forty-five. Gabe was three years younger than me.

*What does it matter what age he is?* said my inner voice suspiciously.

It doesn't, I hastily retorted.

'And did he?' I asked.

'Did he what?' Annabelle frowned.

'Go for a drink with Ms Gucci Belt.'

'Doubt it,' she said cheerfully. 'He already has a girlfriend.'

'Oh,' I said, feeling inexplicably deflated.

'Mind you, I think she's on her way out.'

'Really?' I said, perking up.

*Why should that please you?*

Stop flipping mithering me.

'Yeah,' said Annabelle. 'Her name is Lisa. I've met her a couple of times. She's a right stroppy cow, but gorgeous with it.'

Of course Lisa was gorgeous. With Gabe's film star looks, his pulling power must be phenomenal.

'However' – Annabelle continued – 'I think Lisa was pushing to move into his place, but Gabe said no. Obviously, that caused a bit of friction between the two of them. You see, he doesn't like getting too close to anyone. Probably because of his own emotional scars.'

'I see,' I said, wondering what – or who – had caused him such pain.

‘So don’t you worry, Mrs Walker,’ said Annabelle cheerfully. ‘Gabe totally empathises with what his clients are going through.’

‘That’s good to know.’

‘Thanks for the glowing reference,’ said a clipped voice. Annabelle and I jumped guiltily. ‘However, I’d quite like to get on with my meeting instead of listening to the two of you yakking in the corridor.’

Oh no. How much had he heard?

# Chapter Twenty-Six

My cheeks flamed as Gabe looked from Annabelle to me, then back to Annabelle again.

'And for your information' – he was now looking faintly amused – 'Lisa and I are no longer together, but I'd be grateful if you didn't pass that information on to Ms Gucci Belt.'

Okay, he'd heard everything.

'Wendy, shall we?'

Gabe held open the door. As I moved past him, his arm briefly brushed against mine. A shockwave ricocheted through me with such velocity I was surprised there wasn't an earthquake in the epicentre of Gardener and Stewarts' offices. Gabe gave me a concerned look.

'Everything okay?' he asked, moving round to his side of the huge desk.

'Yes,' I nodded, collapsing weakly in the chair opposite.

His eyes bored into mine.

'You seem a bit out of breath.'

'Just nervous,' I squeaked.

I felt like a rabbit trapped in the light of those bright blue headlamps.

'Take a breath, Wendy. Just relax. Annabelle, two

coffees, please. Now then.' The eyes once again rested upon me, but I noticed they held kindness. 'Following our earlier telephone conversation, I take it the chat you subsequently had with your husband wasn't well received.'

'Correct. It was awful. Derek told me he'd see me homeless before I got a penny out of him.'

'That isn't going to happen, and I will make that quite clear in my correspondence to him. Did you bring your marriage certificate?'

'Yes,' I said, reaching into my handbag.

'Thanks.' He took the piece of paper from me and set it to one side. 'So, as previously discussed, I'll be applying for a Conditional Order – formerly known as a Decree Nisi – then submit a Consent Order and then apply for a Final Order – formerly known as a Decree Absolute. I strongly recommend that we make all financial agreements legally binding.'

'Okay. I'll be advised by you,' I said.

Annabelle returned with a tray of coffee and biscuits. Oooh, yummy, custard creams and chocolate bourbons. My stomach instantly rumbled in anticipation.

'Are you always hungry when you come to my office?' asked Gabe in amusement.

'I forgot to eat earlier,' I confessed, reaching for a custard cream. 'Also, I was a bit stressed, so didn't fancy anything.'

*Apart from you.*

Omigod, where had that thought come from?

I crammed the custard cream into my mouth and concentrated hard on chewing.

'Try not to let your emotions run high,' said Gabe.

'Although I know that's easier said than done.'

'Oh, I'm not upset about Derek,' I said, trying not to spray crumbs everywhere. 'It's something else entirely. Earlier, one of my dogs, Maid, wrecked a guy's marriage proposal.'

'I've heard of crazy cat ladies. Are you the mad dog woman of Little Waterlow?'

'Maid isn't mine,' I said quickly.

'I see. It's just the delinquent beagle that belongs to you.'

'No! William isn't mine either. I walk dogs for a living.'

Gabe looked astonished.

'Have you thought about a career change?'

'After this morning, the idea did occur to me,' I admitted. 'Unfortunately, there's not much call for women of my age in the workplace.'

'Rubbish,' said Gabe dismissively. 'Can you type?'

'Yes,' I nodded. 'I used to be a legal secretary in the City until I was made redundant.'

Gabe raised his eyebrows.

'Why on earth haven't you applied for work locally? I've been looking for a secretary for ages. Annabelle is a sweet girl, but her typing is atrocious, and I don't always catch the bloopers she makes.' He gave me a frank look. 'I'm happy to interview you.'

'That's very kind' – I reached for a chocolate bourbon – 'but my personal circumstances have changed. Holding down a full-time job went out the window a couple of years ago.'

*Apart from anything else* – I added to myself – *I don't think I could cope being around you every day.*

Even sitting here, I was very aware of the churning going on in my stomach. It was nothing to do with the digestion of the biscuits and everything to do with the effect those extraordinary eyes seemed to be having on me.

'What happened to change things?' Gabe asked.

'My daughter unexpectedly made me a Nanna.'

'You don't look old enough to be a grandma.'

'Thank you,' I smiled. 'Ruby – my daughter – embarked on motherhood while very young. She was still at secondary school and a typical know-it-all teenager.'

'Ah, so you had to give her lots of support.'

'Yes, and I still do. Even though Mo recently started crèche, I like to know I'm available to look after her, especially if she isn't well.'

'Shame,' he said lightly, before taking a sip of coffee. Placing the cup back on its saucer, he glanced at the paperwork before him. 'I now have enough details to put together the divorce application. Your husband will hear from this firm shortly. He will be urged to appoint his own legal adviser. After that, it's a case of sitting tight until we receive his official response.'

Instantly an image popped into my head of Derek's written reply, namely an illustrated two-finger salute followed by a double-underlined *yours sincerely* sign off.

I sighed.

'What if he ignores your letter and doesn't reply?'

'This firm will point out to him that it isn't in either party's best interests not to comply. There will be a reminder that any resistance to cooperation runs up costs. Usually that's enough to galvanise the most reluctant spouse.'

I took this as my cue that our meeting was over and drained my cup.

'Thank you for your time.'

'A pleasure,' said Gabe. He stood up and moved around his desk to open the door for me. 'Any questions, I'm always at the end of the phone.'

I sidled past him, almost bashing myself on the door frame to avoid any part of us accidentally touching. Even the space around Gabe Stewart seemed to quiver as I scuttled into the corridor.

'And Wendy?' he called after me.

'Yes?'

'Try and stay out of trouble with your canine clients,' he grinned.

The smile was like a blowtorch and completely transformed him. I noticed how very white his teeth were, making the blue eyes even more piercing. The effect wasn't lost on me either. As I walked along the corridor towards reception, I wondered if Gabe Stewart's aura hadn't somehow singed my eyelashes and eyebrows.

# Chapter Twenty-Seven

Once home and alone with my thoughts, I fretted about what would happen next.

In my mind's eye I saw Derek coming home, then opening his mail. "What the heck's this?" he'd say, while opening the sizeable envelope. "Correspondence from my solicitor" – I would reply – "because I'm divorcing you." Derek then smirking as he ripped the paperwork into tiny pieces and threw it up into the air like wedding confetti.

I put the kettle on, wringing my hands together as that water slowly heated. Had I done the right thing seeking advice from a solicitor? Surely it would be cheaper and easier to hire a hit man?

I instantly felt guilty for entertaining murderous thoughts. How many times did a spouse bump off their partner? Quite often, according to the national newspapers. The motive was usually money, like a hefty life insurance policy. Years ago, Derek had been insistent about us taking out such a policy. He'd also been meticulous about keeping up the payments. I seemed to recall the pay-out figure being as much as two hundred thousand pounds. Way back then, it had been a stonking sum of money. These days, whilst being nowhere near the stinking rich category, it was still a comfortable sum to fall back upon.

I made the tea, added the milk and stirred thoughtfully. It wasn't lost on me that sometimes I'd caught Derek giving me peculiar looks, especially once, when I'd wielded the electric knife over the Sunday joint. He'd gone so far as saying, "Just think, Wendy. If you accidentally fell on that blade and sliced a main artery, I'd be quite a wealthy widower."

His comment had prompted me to have several dark fantasies myself. What if I instead delegated Derek to do the carving? I'd visualised him carelessly dropping fat on the kitchen floor. Then slipping. Then the knife accidentally slicing through his wrist. Oh dear. A total bleed-out before I'd even finished basting the roast potatoes and been able to call 999.

And why stop at the electric carving knife? What about upscaling to a mini chainsaw? I took a sip of the hot tea, my gaze going out of focus for a minute as I contemplated.

There was Derek on a ladder, chainsaw whirring as he attacked the garden hedge. Now a swooping pigeon was startling him and – oops – the ladder was wobbling violently. Derek was tumbling backwards. The chainsaw was arcing through the air. Gravity was pulling the machine down. Down, down, down. Straight through my husband's neck and – oops again – there was Derek's head bouncing right over the fence and rolling to a standstill in Ben's garden.

Repulsed by my homicidal imagination, I promptly tipped the tea down the sink and gave myself a stern talking to. Enough of this mental torture. Settle down and wait for

Gabe's correspondence to arrive.

The next couple of days were fairly humdrum. On the Wednesday, I bumped into neighbour Ben who usually had the power to make me blush and flush. However, I was somewhat bemused to discover that Ben's chit-chat had zero effect on making me trip over fresh air, or in any way make a berk of myself. As I gave him a friendly wave, I wondered why that should be.

*Something to do with a Paul Newman look-a-like taking up the attraction baton?* said my inner voice, slyly.

I ignored the taunt.

On the Thursday I walked a couple of other canine clients, thankfully without any mishaps or drama.

At home, the vibe with Derek wasn't so much chilly as freezing. But other than the sub-zero atmosphere, the pair of us went through the usual motions – like him leaving a daily pile of clothes on the floor outside the bathroom, so it looked as though someone had melted, and me scooping them up.

On more than one occasion I picked up the phone to ring my parents. However, the thought of asking them for a loan instantly had me replacing the handset. Shame played a part.

*Forty-eight years old and running to Mummy and Daddy for financial help*, my inner voice mocked.

The sneer had me backing away from the phone faster than a high-speed train in reverse. I couldn't do it. Not yet anyway. I told myself that it was better to wait and see how Derek responded to Gabe's correspondence. After all, by the time the copy application arrived, Derek might have tired from impersonating Frosty the Snowman and instead surprised me by saying, "I've had an epiphany, Wendy. Getting divorced is a *brilliant* idea. After all, the one thing we both have in common is our mutual dislike of each other. This is a superb opportunity to move on and go our separate ways." Cue an instant sigh of relief from me that I'd never tapped Mum and Dad for that loan.

Nonetheless, I was aware that I needed to have some sort of conversation with my parents, if only to keep them informed of what was happening in my life. That said, I was anxious about them worrying. Eventually, feeling a little more decisive, I once again picked up the handset.

'Darling!' Mum screeched down the line. 'How's England?'

'Cold,' I said. 'Some things never change, and the British weather is one of them.'

'You should book yourself on a plane and come over here. It might be the middle of November but we're still having a healthy dose of sunshine and sangria,' she chortled.

I could tell from her jolly tone that she and Dad were likely halfway through a jug of red wine, brandy, and fresh oranges. I could see them now, sitting on their terracotta terrace with a direct view over a sparkling sea.

'It sounds tempting,' I sighed.

'Then do it,' Mum asserted, slurring slightly. 'Bring Ruby and Mo. But leave that husband of yours behind, darling. Last time Derek was here, he ate and drank us out of house and home and didn't once offer to put his hand in his pocket. We love to be hospitable to our guests, but your hubby is tighter than my pelvic floor muscles – and that's saying something for a woman in her seventies.'

'Yes, he's, er, very careful,' I agreed.

'Careful?' Mum scoffed. 'More like downright stingy. Your dad and I were saying only this morning that we don't know what you see in the man.' There was a loud gasp at the other end of the line. 'Sorry, darling. That was remarkably indiscreet of me. I shouldn't have said that. Slip of the tongue and too much of the sauce in the sunshine.'

'It's okay,' I said, feeling momentarily mortified that Derek had so thoroughly abused my folks' hospitality. 'Actually, Derek is the main reason for my call.'

'Oh?'

'I've filed for divorce.'

There was a pause.

'Are you serious?' my mother finally spluttered.

'Never more so.'

'Omigod,' Mum squawked. 'WOOHOO! Oh, sorry, darling. I don't mean to be ecstatic but' – she let out another great whoop of joy – 'Nigel! NIGE!' she boomed to my father. 'Guess what. Our Wendy is divorcing Derek.'

'About bloody time,' I heard my father rumble.

I boggled at the handset. First Kelly. Now Mum and Dad. Was there anybody in my circle of friends and family who had ever liked my husband?

'Have you met someone else?' Mum breathed. 'You can tell me. I won't tell a soul. Discretion is my middle name. Nigel – NIGE – I think our Wendy has met someone else. Hang on, let me put the phone on loudspeaker so your father can hear. That's it. So, tell us all about your new fella.'

'Mum, stop! I haven't met anyone else.' A pair of ice-blue eyes swooped through my brain. I swatted the image away. No, I wasn't going to be distracted by Gabe Stewart and mimic Ms Gucci Belt with a schoolgirl crush. 'I've simply come to my senses, that's all.'

'It won't be long before you find someone else,' Mum assured. 'You're like a rose in full bloom. You still have your figure and looks. However, if you want to meet someone else, don't muck about wasting time. You need to act smartly, before you wilt, and all your petals fall off. Do you understand?'

'Mum, for goodness' sake, another husband is the last thing I want.'

'Ah, you say that now. Give it time and you'll feel differently. You should come over to us – and pronto. Our neighbours' divorced son is currently staying with them and' – I sensed Mum looking furtively around lest he was lurking – 'Barry seems like a good sort. He offered to help your dad with the pool pump when it went on the blink yesterday, *and*' – she added triumphantly – 'he still has all his own teeth and hair.'

'How thrilling,' I said sarcastically.

'Isn't it,' said my mother excitedly. 'That said, he's a little on the short side, so you'd be wise to wear ballet pumps on your first date.'

Okay, she was getting way ahead of herself.

'I'll bear that in mind,' I said dryly. 'Meanwhile, I'm glad you're not lamenting the imminent loss of your son-in-law.'

‘Oh, not at all, darling. Keep us posted on how the divorce goes. And if you need anything, do shout. Dad and I know that these things cost money. In fact, hang on a mo. Nigel… NIGE! Put that stray cat down, you don’t know where it’s been. Can we send Wendy some money?’

‘Oh Mum, really, you don’t-’

‘Dad’s giving the thumbs up. Is five thousand enough?’

‘Five thou–?’ I spluttered.

‘I’m going to have to dash. The stray cat has raked your dad’s forearm.’ I sensed my mother hastily rising from her sunchair. ‘He needs disinfectant on it. Lovely talking, darling. Keep us posted. Toodle-oo!’

I stood there slack jawed, holding a disconnected handset. A tidal wave of relief flooded through me. Five thousand pounds! Now I’d be able to approach Sadie Farrell about that interim rental of Clover Cottage.

# Chapter Twenty-Eight

On Friday, the postman pushed a white A4 envelope through the letterbox. It was franked with the business stamp of Gardener and Stewart Solicitors and addressed to one Mr Derek Walker.

Derek had left for work prior to the postie's visit. I stared at the large white oblong lying on the doormat as if it were an unexploded bomb. How on earth was Derek going to react when he read the contents within?

I stooped and picked it up, then turned it round and round in my hands, looking for clues as to what Gabe might have written. I was half-tempted to steam the envelope open, but instead left it in the kitchen, propped up against the kettle.

Nervously, I tapped out a message to Ruby.

*Sorry to interrupt your day, darling. Just a quick heads-up. My solicitor's correspondence to your father has arrived. Not sure what Dad's reaction is going to be. You might want to keep a low profile, once home. So sorry about all this. Don't want you stressing. Love you xx*

Ruby's reply was almost immediate.

*Don't be silly, Mum. I'm fine with it. It's you I'm worried about. By the way, forgot to mention that Mo and I will be home a little late. She's been invited to a birthday tea. Someone in her crèche group has turned two. My daughter's social life is currently better than mine! Love you too xx*

I smiled at Ruby's last three words then, grimacing slightly, pocketed my phone. It was important to spend the rest of the day keeping busy and staying calm. However, all calmness did a bunk the moment my husband's key turned in the lock.

Derek stomped into the kitchen not even attempting to hide the eight tins of lager tucked under one arm. *Eight.* He wasn't planning on drinking that little lot in one evening, was he? Alcohol always made him extra punchy. As he wasn't in the best of moods anyway, I wasn't looking forward to his temper getting shorter as the evening wore on.

Wisely I said nothing, instead keeping my head down as I peeled carrots and potatoes at the sink. Derek dumped his beers on the table then, spotting the A4 envelope, snatched it up.

'What's this?' he growled.

I didn't dare say anything as he ripped the seal apart.

My hands momentarily trembled causing the tip of the vegetable knife to nick my thumb. Damn. I turned on the tap, rinsing away the thin trail of blood. Behind me came the sound of rustling paper as Derek skim-read the application.

'Is this some sort of fucking joke?' he demanded.

I turned off the tap and grabbed a sheet of kitchen towel to stem the still-bleeding thumb. A second later, the tissue paper was snatched away from me, and Derek yanked my arm.

'Face me when I'm talking to you,' he shouted.

I had a sudden overwhelming urge to open a kitchen cupboard, climb within and curl up amongst the pots and pans. Derek's face was contorted with rage.

'I suppose you think this is funny, eh?'

'Of course it's not funny, Derek.' I was amazed how steady my voice sounded. Encouraged, I ploughed on. 'There is nothing amusing about ending a twenty-seven-year-old marriage.'

'I'm not talking about that,' he seethed.

He slapped the application down on the worktop. A stubby finger jabbed at the document's heading. I glanced at where he was pointing, then gasped aloud. Oh Lord. Gabe's temp had warned me that she was a rubbish typist, but on this occasion, Annabelle had excelled herself. It was likely an innocent typo. After all, the L on a keyboard is quite close to the N, but it was most unfortunate that Applicant Two had been named as Derek Wanker.

'Well?' My husband's chin jutted belligerently. 'What do you have to say about that?'

'I say' – my tone was deliberately neutral – 'that it's a sign from the universe I'm doing the right thing.'

'DON'T BE SO FUCKING FLIP,' Derek roared. 'We've already had this conversation, Wendy. The answer then was no, and the answer now is no. No, I am not ending our marriage. No, I am not appointing my own *counsel*' – he spat – 'and no you will not be getting half of all my worldly goods. DO YOU HEAR?'

If the cosmos had a special word for *I'll never agree to a divorce, you greedy, grasping, cow of a wife*, then right now Derek had it with bells on. And with that he picked up one of his precious tinnies and hurled it across the kitchen.

# Chapter Twenty-Nine

Suffice to say that the vibe in the Walker household wasn't just freezing, it now also held an air of menace.

Ruby arrived home with Mo and, sensing the atmosphere, immediately disappeared into her bedroom with Mo hastily trundling after her. My granddaughter, perhaps also detecting the tension, refrained from her usual end-of-day grizzle. Instead, she clutched her doll with one hand and hung onto her mother's coattails with the other.

Much later, I curled up for the night on the sofa with a couple of throws for warmth. My phone, tucked into my slippers on the floor, unexpectedly beeped with a text message. I sat up and peered at the screen's bright glow. Who was texting at this time of night? I made a long arm and reached for the mobile.

*Are you awake? Xx*

It was Kelly.

*Yes. What's up? Xx*

There was a brief pause while she typed.

**Groan*. I'm out of sorts. Steve has cancelled our Costa date tomorrow. He says that Caroline hacked his phone, read our flirty messages, and then she cried like a baby. She has since repeatedly apologised for being a control freak and* *wants the two of them to start afresh.*

Oh dear.

*How does Steve feel about that?* I asked.

*He was very frank. He said that Caroline showed him a side he hadn't seen for a long time, and it made him remember why he fell in love with her.*

Oh double dear. I quickly tapped out my reply.

*Control freaks' egos have a tendency to shove their way back to the surface. A case of as long as everything is exactly the way they want it, then they're totally flexible.*

I should know. After all, Derek was one.

*Not sure about that,* Kelly replied. *It transpires that Caroline is – get this – prepared to forego John Lewis' café and go to Costa with Steve herself. That's MASSIVE for her.*

I sighed.

*Sweetheart, he's married. You're married. Isn't it best to concentrate on your relationship with Henry?*

There was a short pause as Kelly tapped out her next reply.

*Funny you should say that. Earlier on, Henry caught me looking miserable. He said he knew he wasn't making me happy and that he'd been married to work. He also confessed that he'd been using alcohol to destress. He then said he's binning the booze. Mineral water from now on. He's also suggested we go away for a romantic break before the boys break up for the Christmas holidays. I was gobsmacked.*

Blimey. Good on Henry.

*Well, there you go! He obviously still loves you and wants to make things right.*

Kelly replied with a tearful emoji.

*Now I'm crying. I guess I do still love the big lump. Do you fancy meeting up tomorrow morning for a coffee and putting the world to rights?*

I sent her a smiley emoji.

*Sounds good. Could use some fresh air. I've had a tense evening with Derek. The divorce papers arrived. Mr Walker was unimpressed.*

I could almost hear the squawk in Kelly's next message.

*Omigod! I completely forgot to ask you about that. Do you have any doggy clients that need walking tomorrow?*

Thankfully not. I wasn't in the mood to have the likes of Maid or William Beagle getting me into trouble with any more members of the public.

*No doggy clients, but very happy to walk Alfie with you.*

Her reply was immediate.

*Good. See you at Trosley tomorrow. Elevenish xx*

I signed off with another smiley face and then a second emoji that was blowing a kiss.

Chucking the phone down on the floor, I snuggled down, bringing my knees up to my chest and hugging them tightly. Hopefully tomorrow would be a better day.

# Chapter Thirty

I was awoken the following morning by Derek banging around in the kitchen.

Swinging my legs over the side of the sofa, I folded up the throws. Ignoring my burgeoning bladder, I went to see what all the noise was about. No doubt it was Derek's way of conveying he was unimpressed that his rebellious wife wasn't cooking a fry-up before his ritualistic Saturday trip to the golf club.

'Morning,' I said pleasantly. 'Would you like some breakfast?'

'If it's not too much trouble.' His voice dripped with sarcasm.

'Of course not,' I said lightly. 'One egg or two with your rashers?'

'Two.'

'Would you like toast with that?'

'Yes.'

*You're welcome.*

I busied myself heating oil in the pan. Leaving everything to gently fry, I then filled the kettle. I left the packet of bacon on the worktop, intending to cook the lot. Ruby and Mo were partial. The smell would soon drive the two of them out of bed and down the stairs.

'Seeing Bill today?' I asked casually.

'Don't I always?' Derek growled.

'Of course,' I murmured, placing a cup of tea before him. However, I couldn't resist winding him up. 'It's odd though.' I paused. Frowned theatrically. 'I could've sworn I saw him in the supermarket last week.'

Derek's eyes momentarily bulged but he made no comment. Instead, he took a noisy slurp of tea before busying himself with his mobile.

I returned to the stove, making sure the bacon was crispy, the eggs flipped, and then buttered a small mountain of toast.

'Enjoy,' I said, setting his plate down.

He made a grunting noise before picking up his knife and fork.

'Anything else?' I enquired. 'If not, I'll go upstairs and use the bathroom.'

'Actually, yes, there is.'

'Oh?'

Derek gestured at the worktop, where he'd left Gabe's correspondence.

'Those divorce papers.'

'Er, yes?'

'Put them in the pedal bin on your way out.'

I inhaled sharply but didn't engage. Instead, I turned and walked away. Derek's voice followed me up the staircase.

'That's where the application will be. In with the rubbish. Make sure you inform your pathetic solicitor of the same.'

I locked myself in the bathroom and exhaled gustily. As soon as Monday rolled around, I'd have to inform Gabe that Derek wouldn't be playing ball. Gabe had told me not to panic and that the matter would simply go to court. However, he'd also warned this would be time-consuming, add to the costs, and further sour relations between Derek and me. I sighed as I emptied my bladder. So be it.

Squeezing out some toothpaste, I heard the front door slam. Derek had gone. Relief flooded through me. For the remainder of the day, blessed peace would reign.

'Mum?' Ruby knocked on the bathroom door. 'Are you going to be long? I'm busting for a wee.'

With a foaming mouth, I moved across the bathroom and unlocked the door.

'Thanks,' said Ruby, hitching up her nightie and sitting down on the loo. We had no hang-ups about doing such things in front of each other. Girls together, and all that.

I spat and rinsed, then wiped my mouth.

'I've plated you and Mo some breakfast. It's keeping warm in the oven.'

'Thanks, Mum.' Ruby gave me a grateful smile. 'I'll enjoy it all the more now that Dad's left the house.'

'Off to play his precious golf,' I said, rolling my eyes.

Ruby's face momentarily darkened but she didn't say anything.

'I'll be down in a minute, after I've had a quick shower,' I added.

'*Muuuuuummy*,' wailed Mo from across the landing.

'Out! Out cot.'

'Oh Lord,' said Ruby, flushing the loo and hastily washing her hands. 'She keeps trying to climb out. Can we look at getting Mo a junior bed?'

'Yes,' I said.

But I was speaking to Ruby's back. She charged out of the bathroom before her livewire daughter could escape the cot's confines.

I opened the shower cubicle and stepped inside, then gasped at the initial coldness of the water jet before it had properly warmed up. As I quickly soaped myself, my stomach growled with hunger. My tastebuds were priming themselves for the moment I'd join my girls downstairs for family brekkie.

My mobile dinged with a text just as I was wrapping myself in a towel. I grabbed it, half expecting it to be from Kelly. Instead, I was astonished to see a message from Gabe.

# Chapter Thirty-One

Surprised, I read Gabe's text.

*I'm at work. Did the application arrive yesterday? Just checking you've not had a nuclear fallout! Regards, Gabe.*

Good heavens. Were all solicitors so courteous with their clients on a Saturday morning?

*Hi. Yes, and yes. Derek told me to relay that he does not consent xx*

It was only after hitting send that I realised I'd automatically signed off with my habitual two crosses. Hell's bells. This wasn't Kelly or Ruby I was messaging.

*Sooo sorry about the two kisses. Habit! W.*

The phone dinged almost instantly with a reply.

*I gathered. Regards, Gabe.*

Cringing slightly, I continued towelling myself off, but then paused. Hang on. It was all very well being "looked after" by your solicitor over the weekend, but I didn't want this courteous communication being added to my bill. I gulped as another thought occurred. Did solicitors, like electricians or plumbers, charge extra for off-peak services? I picked up the mobile again.

*Do you always message clients at weekends? Xx*

BUGGER. I'd done it again.

*Only when my temp secretary signs off dictation when I'm in meetings and sends out erroneous documentation. I've come into the office to make urgent corrections. Also, if I'm honest, I needed to escape an ex-girlfriend who unexpectedly turned up.* Ah, that would be the lovely Lisa. *Sincere apologies for the howler on your divorce application. Rest assured you won't be billed for any work to date by way of compensation. Are you sure you don't want to reconsider returning to your previous profession? I think my clients might respond very positively to a secretary who signs everything off with two kisses. G.*

I chuckled and tapped out another reply.

*That's very decent of you regarding costs to date. As for the job, I'll stick to causing mayhem with my dogs rather than with your clients. W.*

Smiling to myself, I hung the towel over the hot rail. Clutching my discarded pyjamas to my naked body, I scampered across the landing to my bedroom. Dressing quickly, I then bounced down the stairs to join Ruby and Mo.

'Sorry,' my daughter apologised, putting her knife and fork together. 'I was too hungry to wait for you.'

'That's all right.'

I skipped over to the kettle. There was enough water within, so I flicked the switch.

'Nanna happy,' observed Mo from her highchair.

Ruby gave me a shrewd look.

'What's with the skippy behaviour?'

'Nothing,' I said, reddening.

‘So why are you blushing?’

‘Oh for goodness’ sake, Rubes. Stop giving me the third degree. I’ve had a shower and now I’m having a hot flush.’

Even so, I let my hair fall forward as I dropped a teabag into a mug. I waited for the leaves to stew for a bit, and privately cogitated. It did occur to me that – for the last five minutes or so – I’d felt quite… joyful.

*You mean manic,* my inner voice butted in. *Hmm. Could it have something to do with a good-looking solicitor texting and making light-hearted small talk?*

I ignored the voice. Donning oven gloves, I extracted my plated breakfast from the warm oven and switched the temperature dial to off.

‘What are you up to today?’ I asked Ruby as I sat down.

I was keen to get off the subject of my apparent exuberance. Picking up my knife and fork, I tucked in.

‘What I get up to today depends on whether you’re in agreement to my idea,’ said Ruby conspiratorially.

‘Go on.’

‘Well, now that Dad’s out of the house and not in earshot, how about we go and have a nosy at Clover Cottage? Do you think Sadie might show us around later?’

‘Possibly,’ I said, chewing thoughtfully. ‘You’ve reminded me that there’s something I want to discuss with her.’ I hesitated for a moment. ‘Look, I know I’ve said this before, but I’m going to say it again. You’re my daughter. I don’t want to use you as… well, a *confidante* regarding the situation I’m in with your dad.’

‘And I’ve already told you that I’m no longer kid. I’m

chilled about it. You can tell me anything, Mum.'

For a moment, I balked. Blimey. Not for the first time in recent weeks did I find myself now wondering who the parent was here, and who the child.

'Thank you, sweetheart. However, I don't want to blur the mother-daughter lines. That said, I do want to keep you in the loop. To, you know, tell you the essentials, as it were.'

'Right, Mother.' Ruby gave an exaggerated sigh of patience. 'So cut to the chase.'

'Okay,' I grinned. 'Basically, Nanny and Granddad have very generously transferred me five thousand pounds to give financial support through the initial...' – I chose my words carefully so as not to deliberately badmouth Ruby's father – 'er, difficulties between me and your dad.'

'You mean regarding him behaving like a prat.'

'Prat,' said Mo helpfully.

I closed my eyes for a moment and took a breath.

'If you want to put it that way.'

'I do.'

'So rather than' – I again carefully chose my words – 'the three of us putting up with months of...er, *difficulties*, I thought it might be prudent to rent Clover Cottage immediately, while the divorce formalities take place.'

'Omigod, Mum!' Ruby gave a squawk of joy. 'That's a brilliant idea. Live in Clover Cottage and leave Dad here to rant and rave by himself. Yes, do it. Just *do it*!'

'I need to have that conversation with Sadie first,' I reminded.

'Ring her now,' Ruby urged. 'Where's your phone?'

She glanced wildly around the kitchen, spotted it on the worktop, then pounced upon it like a cat after its prey. 'Here.' Knowing my pass code, she tapped it in. She was just about to hand it over when she paused. 'Oooh, what's this? Text messages from someone called Gabe Stewart. Who's he?'

'You know perfectly well that he is my lawyer. Gabe is one of the partners at Gardener and Stewart Solicitors.'

'Is he now,' murmured Ruby. She arched an eyebrow as she read from the screen. '"Do you always do this at weekends, kiss kiss." My goodness, Mum. Is that why you were all hot and bothered earlier, and bouncing around the kitchen like Tigger?'

'Ruby,' I said sternly. 'It was with reference to me asking why he was working on a Saturday. The kisses were accidental. Also, my texts are private. Now give me the phone.'

'Sorr-*eee*,' she grinned, slapping the mobile into my outstretched palm.

'Thank you,' I said. I shoved the phone into the back pocket of my jeans. 'And for that, I will now make you wait regarding any conversation I have with Sadie.'

'Whatever,' Ruby sighed, picking up her own phone and tapping away.

'Anyway' – I continued – 'I'm seeing Kelly this morning. We're going for a walk at Trosley Woods.'

Ruby no longer appeared to be listening. Instead, she was staring at her phone's screen. She let out a low whistle.

'What?' I said.

'Gabe Stewart. I've just Googled him.' She turned the mobile's screen, so it was facing me. 'He's not bad for an oldie.'

I gazed at the image of Gabe. Ruby had found the law firm's website. Gabe's photograph was under the heading *Meet the Team.*

I looked at the digital image, and it seemed as though Gabe's piercing blue eyes were looking right back at me. I immediately found myself blushing again. Ruby was watching me carefully. She chuckled.

'Go for it, Mum.'

'There's nothing to go for,' I said irritably, putting my knife and fork together. Pushing back my chair, I stood up, then dumped my plate in the sink.

'He's quite a babe,' Ruby commented.

'Babe,' Mo agreed.

# Chapter Thirty-Two

'Let me know about this afternoon,' called Ruby, as I swung out the front door and headed towards Betty.

I was still bristling slightly at my daughter teasing me over Gabe. Her words had touched a nerve.

*Because you fancy him,* said my inner voice.

I swatted the thought away. No. I did not fancy anyone, and certainly not my solicitor.

*Not true. You fancy Ben next door. Or at least you did, until Gabe came along. Are you perhaps simply a frustrated housewife who needs a good sorting out?*

As if. I rolled my eyes and crunched Betty's protesting gears.

*I disagree. You'd probably feel a lot better if you got your leg over.*

Leg over? Seriously? What sort of coarse vocab is that?

*I can say it however I like because nobody can hear me apart from you! Plus, I know everything about your deepest secret thoughts. I know every inch of your brain. The chemicals within. The triggering of the ascending reticular activating system. The wakefulness. The autonomic nervous system. Your endocrine system. Your increased heart rate. Blood pressure. Your sensory alertness and readiness to respond.*

What rubbish are you spouting now?

*In other words* – the inner voice swept on – *I have noted your physical reaction to Gabe Stewart. Basically, every time you see him your pupils dilate to the size of Betty's tyres.*

Okayyy! Hands up. I have a tiny crush on my solicitor. So what?

*So don't make a fool of yourself, Wendy. Don't become another Ms Gucci Belt. Another Lisa. Another – metaphorically speaking – notch on the bedpost.*

You're very contradictory. A moment ago, you suggested I should get my "leg over".

*Inner voices aren't always reasonable.*

Oh sod off.

I gnashed my teeth as Betty's gears once again protested due to iffy clutch deployment. I'd better pay attention. Derek would go bonkers if the car ended up in the local garage's sick bay. At the thought of Derek, I gnashed my teeth some more. At this rate, I'd be grinding them down to the gums and end up looking like an old crone.

'You're looking very punchy today,' was Kelly's opening line when she greeted me.

'Yeah,' I sighed. 'Sorry, I'm feeling a bit…'

'Out of sorts?'

'I wasn't, but then I was,' I finished lamely.

'Hardly surprising,' said Kelly. She linked her arm companionably through mine. 'C'*mon*,' she cajoled. 'Take a few breaths of this bracing November air. That'll sort you out. When I'm feeling off-centre, I like to believe that the first deep inhale is restorative. That it's the universe's love and positivity flowing into my lungs. Then I imagine the exhale contains all the negativity that my body was holding.'

'You sound like a new age guru,' I grumbled.

Kelly laughed good-naturedly as we picked our way around muddy puddles, then headed off along the main track with the lovely Alfie trotting alongside us.

'You seem very chipper,' I said. 'I was half-expecting you to be fretting over Steve now that he's reunited with Captain Caroline.'

Kelly gave a beatific smile. She looked almost Madonna-like this morning – the Virgin Mary, not the popstar. Her long dark hair was tied up in a chaste looking bun, and her eyes seemed to be shining with an inner peace.

'Steve was a moment of madness,' she announced. 'Thank goodness the only things that got touchy-feely between us were our shopping trolleys. You know, I can't believe he ever turned my head.'

'Really?'

'It's true,' she said dreamily.

'You mean, in less than twenty-four hours, you've had an epiphany.'

'I guess so. The lesson is, if you have marriage issues, you both need to address them together, rather than make diversions and avoid reality.'

'Is there a hidden message for me in that little pearl of wisdom?' I asked wryly.

'Not at all' – Kelly shook her head – 'because I know

you're no longer in love with Derek. That's a little bit different from me and Henry. Even when I was flirting with Steve, deep down I still loved Henry – the big oaf. It's just that the love got mixed up with resentment over him wanting to drink every evening. Now he's recognised there's a reason for that behaviour. Work. So, things are changing in that area, thus eliminating the domino effect of a pissed husband incurring a pissed-off wife.

'I see.'

'From now on he's laying down the law at work. No more Mr Headless Chicken. He's going to start delegating. That means less stress. He's also decided to bin the alcohol which means he won't be like a bear with a sore head every morning. Consequently, I'll be a happy bunny rather than a miserable cow.'

'Bears, bunnies and cows,' I observed. 'What a strange language English can be.'

'Indeed, and now Henry is behaving like a tiger with a gleam in his eye' – she gave a husky chuckle – 'and very nice it's been too.'

'I'm pleased for you,' I said, squeezing her arm.

'Enough about me. Give me the low-down on Derek's reaction to the divorce papers.'

'I can sum it up in one word. Vile. He isn't having any of it. I think Gabe Stewart is going to have his work cut out dealing with Derek.'

'As long as you don't give up pursuing your break for freedom.'

'I won't.'

'You never know, Derek might do a U-turn and oblige.'

'I won't hold my breath. Meanwhile, I'm going to push on with my plan of renting Clover Cottage while the divorce gets underway.'

'That's a brilliant idea, Wends. I'll keep my fingers crossed for you. Just think. If Sadie agrees, you'll be in your new home in time for Christmas.'

I gave her a silly grin by way of response. Almost immediately my mind wandered. There was Ruby in the tiny lounge. She'd surprised me and bought a real Christmas tree. It was taking up the entire corner by the wood burner. And there was Mo. My little granddaughter was crouching down, craftily removing one of the chocolate decorations.

Kelly interrupted the rose-tinted image.

'Did you know there are only seventy-one shopping days before Christmas?'

'You're kidding,' I blanched.

'Have you bought any gifts yet?'

'No,' I wailed. 'I can't even get my head around where this year has gone. The hands on the clock turn so fast, I'm amazed Father Time doesn't have motion sickness.'

'At least you'll save a few quid by not having to buy Derek a present.'

'True.'

Little did I know that within the next seventy-one *minutes* there would be a very different reason for Derek not being on my Christmas List.

## Chapter Thirty-Three

An hour later, Kelly and I had finished our chilly walk.

We retired to the nearby Bluebell Café to warm up with hot chocolates and toasted sausage sandwiches. As dogs weren't allowed inside the restaurant area, we made use of one of the trestle tables outside. Alfie immediately leapt onto the bench seat next to Kelly.

'This is going down a treat,' I said, heating my cold hands on the warm mug.

'There's something magical about eating hot food and watching your breath leaving clouds in cold air.' Kelly broke off a bit of her sandwich and shared it with Alfie. 'It makes me feel all glowy inside.'

I was just about to agree when my phone rang. It's shrill tone instantly halted our small talk. Expecting it to be Ruby chivvying me to speak to Sadie about Clover Cottage, I was surprised to see it was Derek calling.

'Hello?'

I was even more taken aback when a woman spoke.

'Is that Wendy?'

'It is,' I said, frowning.

'My name's Coco.' My frown deepened. Where had I heard that name before? 'Er, you don't know me, but I know your husband.'

'Right,' I said, confused. Why was this female using Derek's mobile?

'I'm terribly sorry but–'

The woman gave a strangled sob.

'What is it?' I said, suddenly feeling a frisson of alarm.

Had Derek had a car accident? I might no longer be in love with my spouse, but I didn't wish him any harm – despite all the ridiculous fantasies in dark moments. Perhaps Coco was a paramedic. Was she using my husband's phone to advise he was currently being stretchered into an ambulance? But, no, wait. The woman had said she *knew* Derek. What the hell was going on here?

'Can you just spit out whatever it is that you're trying to say,' I said sharply.

'He's dead.'

Instantly the trestle table and the ground beneath violently rocked. I clung to the table's splintered edge with one hand, while the other gripped the phone.

'Derek is dead?' I gasped.

Kelly – feeding Alfie another bit of sausage – instantly froze. Her hand hovered mid-air as she stared at me in horror.

'Ouch,' she yelped, as Alfie snatched the treat from her fingers.

'*Dead?*' I repeated. 'O-Omigod.' My hand flew to my mouth. I couldn't process this information. It was too shocking. Derek *couldn't* be dead. He was out playing golf with Bill, for heaven's sake. So why hadn't Bill rung me? Or was Bill still banished from the golf course and currently overseeing household chores? Or maybe Bill *had* played golf with Derek, and then this Coco person – another club wielding fanatic – had joined them.

'Were you having a threesome?' I asked tentatively. Was that even a proper golfing term?

'Definitely not. Derek didn't like sharing.'

Didn't like sharing? Surely that must have created all sorts of issues. After all, there were an awful lot of golfers wandering across the fairway on a Saturday. I had a sudden vision of Derek about to tee off before pausing to holler at a small group a little way ahead on the green. "Oy! Sod off because I don't like sharing."

'So where's Bill? Is he phoning for an ambulance?'

'Er, no. Look, Wendy–'

And then another thought occurred to me.

'Was it a golf ball?'

'Sorry?' said Coco.

'Did Derek get hit on the head by a flying golf ball?' I repeated impatiently.

My voice seemed to be coming from far away. This whole situation was surreal. Here I was, sitting in a woodland clearing under a milk white sky, having companionably shared brunch with my bestie while we nattered about Christmas, only to have a stranger call me up and coolly announce that my husband had demised.

'Balls were involved, but not of the golfing kind. Wendy, please listen. You clearly know nothing about me.'

'No, I don't,' I said, beginning to get upset. This whole

situation was utterly absurd.

There was a shaky sigh from the other end of the connection.

'My name is Coco–'

'You've already told me that,' I snapped.

'And I'm a sex worker.'

# Chapter Thirty-Four

'A... *what?* I wheezed.

Opposite me, Kelly was looking as shocked as I felt.

Coco continued.

'Derek is... was... one of my regular clients. I think he must have had a massive heart attack. We were... you know... and then his face contorted, and he went a bit purple. I wasn't initially concerned. After all, he always went that colour when he was about to, er, climax. Anyway, he collapsed down on top of me. I had a lot of trouble getting him to budge. When I said his name, he didn't respond and-'

She paused to break into noisy sobs. I gaped at Kelly, ashen faced.

'What's happening?' she mouthed, eyes wide.

I swallowed hard.

'Coco, could you hold for a moment, please.' I placed my hand over the speaker. Meeting Kelly's gaze, I took a deep breath. 'Derek had a fatal heart attack while shagging a prostitute.'

For a moment Kelly didn't respond. We continued staring at each other, both of us seemingly poleaxed. When she eventually spoke, her voice was barely audible.

'Are you allowed to use that word?'

'What word? Shag?'

'No, prostitute,' she whispered. 'Isn't it… I dunno… not polite, or something?'

'Oh,' I whispered back. 'Possibly. Yeah, you're right. I'd say it's not politically correct.'

'That's it,' Kelly agreed. 'Not PC.'

I leant in closer.

'We probably shouldn't say *prozzie* either.'

'Definitely not,' said Kelly, sotto voce. 'I think the word these days is *escort.*

'Coco introduced herself as a *sex worker.*'

'I suppose that covers all services,' Kelly nodded. 'Wends?'

'Yes?'

'I think we're both in shock.'

'Maybe.'

'No, definitely. Why else would we debate the correct name for this lady's profession when your husband has unexpectedly died?'

'You're right,' I gulped. I put the phone to my ear again. 'Hello?'

'Hello,' Coco squawked. 'I think you should know that I'm starting to feel a bit odd.'

'That makes two of us,' I muttered.

'It's not every day a client dies on me.'

'Well, quite.'

'While you had me on hold, I used my landline to call an ambulance.'

'Thank you, although it might be a bit late for one of

those.'

'Too late to save him, yes, but I need Derek to be taken away. My next client isn't due until this evening, but I can't have your husband sprawled across my bed in the meantime.'

'No, that definitely wouldn't do.'

I was aware that my body was starting to shiver and shake.

'I was genuinely fond of Derek,' Coco wailed. 'He was so funny and had such hidden depths.'

I boggled into my empty mug, and wondered what on earth this woman had found so charming about Derek. Had she, perchance, witnessed the way he would hide behind his newspaper, hook a bogey out of his nose and then flick it across the room? Or the way he sometimes lifted one buttock and made a noise like a squealing trumpet?

'He used to tell me so many jokes it's a wonder our rabbit outfits didn't split at the seams.'

Rabbit outfits?

'Indeed,' I said automatically.

My free hand fluttered to my temple as my trembling body went into juddering overdrive. Was this where I'd gone wrong with Derek? Perhaps our marriage might have been happier if I'd dressed up in the bedroom. Been a doe to his hare. Hopped about declaring, "I say, I say, I say. A priest, a minister and a rabbit walked into a bar, but when the bartender asked the rabbit what he'd like to drink, the rabbit said, 'I dunno, I'm only here because of Autocorrect.'"

Was I losing my mind? Was it normal for one's brain to come up with bizarre jokes whilst making small talk with a sex worker who'd just told you your husband was dead in her boudoir?

'O-O-Oh,' I declared as my teeth began to chatter.

Kelly, who'd been as immobilised by shock as me, was suddenly on her feet and scuttling around the bench. She snatched the phone from my hand.

'Hello, this is Kelly. I'm Wendy's best friend. Wendy has gone into deep shock. Can you tell me where you live so we can follow the ambulance when it comes? I see. Right. Got that. Thanks.' She disconnected the call.

'O-O-Oh,' I wailed again, as my body impersonated a pneumatic drill. Any moment now I was going to vibrate right off this bench.

'Come on, Wends,' said Kelly gently. She rubbed my arms vigorously to quell the shaking. 'It's cold and you've had horrible news. Let's get you in my car.'

'W-What about Betty?' I cried.

'We'll collect Betty later.'

She slipped a hand under my armpit and hauled me upright.

'O-O-Oh,' I bleated again, as we tottered off towards the carpark. A pair of passing joggers gave me a curious look. Then reality hit me.

I was a widow.

# Chapter Thirty-Five

The rest of the day became increasingly dreamlike.

Kelly drove me to Coco's place, which was on the other side of Little Waterlow. Upon arrival, I was dismayed to see Mabel Plaistow framed in the window of the house next door. Whatever was she doing here? I didn't have long to find out. She momentarily disappeared out of sight, then reappeared on the doorstep.

'I told yer, didn't I,' she crowed. 'I told yer about yer 'usband 'angin' out with the likes of 'er next door.'

I stared at Mabel. Her words rang a very distant bell.

'What are you doing here?' said Kelly, none too politely.

'I *told* yer last time. This is our Sharon's 'ouse. She 'eard a lot o' screamin' comin' from next door an' it sent 'er blood pressure through the roof. My Fred was 'avin' a nap an' was absolutely sparko, so I 'ad to get a taxi over 'ere to sort out Sharon's pills.'

'Right,' I said blankly.

It seemed bizarre that a woman in her eighties should be overseeing her daughter's medication, but then again Sharon wasn't exactly in the first flush of youth.

'If you'll excuse us, Mabel,' said Kelly stiffly. 'Wendy's husband has unexpectedly passed away. This is neither the time nor the place to speculate or' – she gave the old lady a stern look – 'gossip.'

Mabel's neck promptly retracted like an indignant tortoise, but she didn't budge from Sharon's doorstep.

We were distracted by Coco's front door suddenly opening. I heard a female speak. The voice invited us inside. Kelly stepped over the threshold, wheeling me after her like a suitcase. I was aware of Mabel in my peripheral vision, standing on her tiptoes and craning to see what was going on within.

'You must be Wendy,' the voice was saying to Kelly.

'No, I'm Kelly,' said Kelly. '*This* lady is Wendy.' She gave me a little prod, pushing me forward. 'Wendy is Derek's wife.'

I noted my friend's emphasis on that last word.

Suddenly I was being embraced in a jingle of bracelets and sweet, cloying perfume.

'Hello, love,' said Coco.

'Hi,' I mumbled, trying not to stare as she released me.

Derek's paramour was nothing like I'd imagined. Coco had a good ten years on me, if not more. She was glamorous in a tarty, full-blown way. With her corkscrew blonde curls, heavy make-up and plastic dangly earrings, she reminded me of a cross between Glenn Close in *Fatal Attraction* and *Corrie's* Bet Lynch.

'I'm ever so sorry' – she apologised – 'but the paramedics have since been and gone. I didn't know the name of Derek's GP and never thought to ask when we spoke earlier. I was in such a state when we spoke, I couldn't think straight.

Consequently, I failed to tell the paramedics you were on your way when the ambulance turned up. Everything happened so quickly, it's now just a blur. They've taken Derek to the hospital mortuary. Do you want to rush off or can I offer you a cup of tea first?'

I licked my lips.

'That's very kind,' I murmured. 'I don't think it would serve any purpose to immediately charge off to the hospital. If you don't mind, I'll have that cup of tea. Apart from anything else, I have some questions.'

'Of course. Take a seat while I put the kettle on. Milk and sugar?'

'Just the milk, please,' I said.

'Make that two,' said Kelly.

As Coco went off to the kitchen, Kelly and I sat down. I glanced around the room. It was small and neat. Framed photographs adorned the walls of, presumably, Coco's children and grandchildren.

I was amazed at how normal everything seemed, from the squashy chintz sofa we had sunk down upon, to the small coffee table before us. The table's surface was littered with magazines about gardening, caravanning, and knitting. Hardly a tart's boudoir.

'Here we are,' said Coco, reappearing with a tray. She pushed the magazines to one side and set everything down in front of us.

'Thanks,' I mumbled.

We all picked up our cups at the same time and sipped. For a moment, nobody spoke, and an awkward silence prevailed. Where to start?

'This room is very cosy,' I said. *Oh, come on, Wendy. You didn't come here to discuss this sex worker's soft furnishings.* 'Your house doesn't, um, look anything like I'd imagined.'

Coco chuckled.

'What were you expecting? Handcuffs dotted about the place. A few whips, and maybe some chains draped over the back of the sofa.' She gave a snort of laughter. 'Hardly. The spare room is my workplace. And yes, it does look a little different to the rest of the house. I cater to clients' desires. In this profession, you need a very broad mind.'

Well, quite – if her story about Derek dressing up as a rabbit bore any truth.

'Some clients have unusual needs,' she continued. 'There are those who simply like to visit and play video games, while others have… let's just say… very *specific* requests.'

'Like what?' said Kelly nosily.

'Grating cheese.'

Kelly did a giggle-snort which she quickly turned into a cough.

'What did you just say?' I gasped.

Coco gave me a defensive look.

'Listen, love. I provide a service and it isn't always about having sex. There are other aspects. Like fulfilling a client's kinks and fantasies. What might seem off to one person is totally normal and sexy for someone else. Anyway, I eventually had to put a stop to that particular client's wishes. I had cheese taking up the entire fridge, which wasn't practical.

Nonetheless I earnt a small fortune just for letting him watch me grate cheddar for the best part of an hour. There are all sorts of folks in this world, you know. I have another client who pays me to throw pies at him.'

'You're kidding,' said Kelly, struggling to keep a straight face.

'Nope. And then there's Mr X who likes me to tie him up and ignore him for two hours. Those are the easiest bucks to be made,' she chuckled.

'And, er, talking of bucks' – I took a deep breath – 'you mentioned that Derek liked to dress up as a rabbit.'

'That's right,' said Coco calmly. 'We'd pretend to graze together. He loved being cuddled and petted. He also liked to keep his costume on and then watch one of my old DVDs. He'd sit right there, where you are.'

I had an immediate urge to leap off the sofa. Dear God, I couldn't get my head around this information. Couldn't process it. I had plenty of images in my head of Derek horizontal on the sofa at home, watching football. But here? Dressed as a giant rabbit?

'What did he watch?' I ventured.

'*Harvey.*'

Kelly let out another strangled snort.

Coco ignored her.

'I keep a huge collection of films especially for my clients.'

'How long was Derek seeing you?' I blurted.

'Let me think.' Coco stared at the ceiling for a moment, chewing her bottom lip as she cogitated. 'Must be a good six months.'

*Six months?* Flaming Nora.

'How long did he stay when he visited?'

'A few hours. I'd block out entire Saturday mornings for him. Afterwards he'd head off to his golf club. However, lately he'd taken to wanting the afternoons with me too. I think it was after a friend – Bill? – wasn't so readily available.'

'That must have cost a bit,' I said, more to myself than to Coco, but she heard.

'I was generous and gave him a fifty per cent discount for the afternoon slot.'

Oh, jolly good. Derek had always loved a bargain.

'And' – I said faintly – 'what *were* your charges?'

'I charged a flat rate of one hundred pounds for the morning session, but only because he was a regular.'

'One *hundred*–?'

I broke off and stared at Coco, mentally working out Derek's financial outgoings. So, including the afternoon session, that would have been an outlay of one hundred and fifty pounds. And to think, when our daughter had raised the subject of a junior bed for Mo, he'd told Ruby that he wasn't made of money, and to instead look on eBay. Bastard!

I swallowed down the last of my tea. Suddenly it was imperative to get out of this house.

'Thank you for your time,' I said.

I set the cup down on the tray and stood up. Kelly followed my lead, briefly fighting her way out of the sofa's confines.

'Anytime, love,' said Coco. She followed us out to the

hallway. We stood aside as she opened the front door. 'You take care now.'

'Thank you, and you,' I muttered.

As the door shut behind us, Kelly and I were brought up short by the sight of Mabel Plaistow once again hovering on her daughter's doorstep.

'Oh no,' Kelly groaned.

'Jus' want to give me condolences,' said Mabel. She tightened her cardigan over her vast bosom. 'Sorry about what 'appened with yer 'usband. Bad business that. Gawd, I 'ope I never pop me clogs in a sex dungeon.'

# Chapter Thirty-Six

By the end of the afternoon, I was feeling completely spaced out.

Kelly, bless her, had accompanied me to the hospital. Identification had blurred into talk about autopsy arrangements which had blurred again into a phone conversation with a funeral director.

By the time we were done, I felt as though Saturday had stretched into a hundred hours. As we finally headed out of the hospital, the pair of us felt exhausted.

'Come on,' said my bestie. She slung an arm around me as we tottered across the carpark. 'Let's get you home.'

'But Betty is still at Trosley Country Park,' I protested.

'Wends, with the greatest respect, sod Betty. You're emotionally drained and not driving anywhere. Also, you need to talk to Ruby, preferably before some well-meaning Little Waterlow resident delivers the bad news before you.'

'Omigod, yes,' I wailed.

'Betty will still be in the carpark tomorrow. Ruby can drive you there.'

'You're right.'

Minutes later, Kelly pulled up outside my house.

'Do you want me to stay the night?' she offered.

‘That’s really kind of you, but you’ve done enough for me today.’

Apart from anything else, I wanted to tell Ruby about her father’s demise in private.

I leant across the handbrake and gave Kelly a hug, then hopped out. As I stood on the pavement, she buzzed down the passenger window.

‘Go and have a stiff drink,’ she advised.

‘I will.’

‘And ring me if you suddenly have a bad dose of the collywobbles. You never know, it might unexpectedly creep up on you.’

She drove off with a cheery toot-toot that belied the gloominess of the day.

Slowly I turned and walked up the path to my front door.

# Chapter Thirty-Seven

Ruby was shocked to say the least, but more than anything she was furious.

She put Mo to bed so we could talk properly, without interruption. We were now sitting at the kitchen table, both armed with a brandy.

'My God, Mum,' she ranted, then swiped angrily at a tear rolling down one cheek. 'I feel so embarrassed for you.'

'Don't be, darling,' I said tiredly.

I'd brought Ruby up to date with everything apart from the bit about her father dressing up as a giant rabbit. Some things weren't appropriate to share with your child, however old she might be.

'Dad made an idiot of you,' she raged. 'And of all the people who happen to live next door to *that woman*' – she spat the last two words – 'it flipping well had to be Mabel Plaistow's daughter.' She took a slug of brandy, then banged down the glass. 'I can't imagine how you must have felt spotting Mighty Motormouth as the welcoming committee. This gossip will be all around the village by tomorrow.'

'It doesn't matter,' I shrugged.

Well, it did matter, but then again, a hundred years from now, it wouldn't. So why expend energy fretting about it?

'I should have said,' Ruby muttered under her breath.

'Should have said what?' I frowned.

For a moment she appeared to dither on whether to tell me.

'Because I knew,' she conceded.

*'Whaaat?'*

'I sooo wanted to tell you, and I nearly did after that set-to you had with Dad. Remember? It was just after you'd paid a visit to the dishy solicitor. You were telling me all about your future plans. We didn't realise Dad had quietly come in and was eavesdropping.'

'Yes, I do remember. He kicked off, and you stepped between us, and he told you to have some respect.'

'Which I threw back in his face. I said, "Respect? One word. Coco."'

'That's right,' I said, my mind flipping back to last Monday's kitchen drama. 'I watched your dad's face drain of colour and couldn't understand why you were both behaving so oddly about hot chocolate. Not cocoa, but *Coco*.'

'Mum, honestly, you must be the only person in this village who doesn't know about Coco Rowbotham. Sharon Plaistow was the first to notice the steady stream of men going in and out of her neighbour's house. It goes on all day, apparently. Sharon gossiped to her mother who made short work of putting the info about. Coco probably didn't even need to put an advert in the local paper thanks to Mabel Plaistow. That old boot could give social media a run for its money when it comes to spreading rumours. Apart from anything else' – Ruby's face momentarily crumpled – 'a little while ago, quite by chance, I saw Dad going into Coco's house.'

I reached for her hand and patted it reassuringly.

'How on earth did that happen?' I asked gently.

Ruby shrugged and slowly shook her head.

'I can't properly recall. I think it was due to roadworks and a traffic diversion. Whatever the reason, I found myself detouring home, and that was when I spotted Dad. He was standing outside Coco's house, presumably having rung her doorbell. I slowed down and craned my neck to see better. He was looking very furtive and holding a huge bunch of flowers. A woman answered the door and he immediately thrust the blooms at her. That was my first glimpse of Coco Rowbotham. She looked a lot older than you,' said Ruby loyally.

'She is,' I nodded. 'She's also far more glam than me.'

'Only because she trowels on the makeup. She's not a patch on you, Mum. It's simply that you don't bother with yourself. Sorry,' she sighed. 'I shouldn't have said that. You don't need lipstick or eyeshadow. It's just' – she sighed again – 'I do sometimes wonder why you don't make the most of yourself.'

'Because there's not much call for buying up half of Boots cosmetics' counter when you spend your day walking dogs.'

'You should still make some sort of effort, Mum,' Ruby urged. 'For your self-confidence if nothing else. I'd also like to mention – now that you're footloose and fancy-free – that going around looking like you've had an argument with one of the trees at Trosley Woods isn't conducive to attracting another man.'

'Sweetheart!' I gaped at my daughter. 'Your father isn't even buried yet. The last thing I want in my life is another man.'

'Well, not now, no, but at some point, surely?'

'No!'

'Why not?'

'Because… because' – I spluttered – 'for heaven's sake, Rubes. I'm forty-seven. Hardly love's young dream.'

'So? I have a classmate whose mum is fifty-two. She's dating again and having loads of flirty fun. She was out last weekend with a thirty-nine-year-old guy.'

'Bully for her, but the last thing I need – or want – is a man in my life, and definitely not a toyboy.'

'You shouldn't knock it until you try it,' Ruby grinned.

'You can talk,' I said, nudging her playfully. 'I'd like to see you letting your hair down and having some fun now and again with a nice young man. I know you had a bad experience with Simon, but there must be a few decent lads out there somewhere.'

For a moment Ruby looked secretive, as if wrestling to divulge something. The need to share got the better of her.

'Actually, I have been talking to someone.'

'Really?' I said, surprised but also delighted. 'Who?'

'I'd rather not say,' she demurred.

'Oh?' I raised my eyebrows. Since when had my daughter been bashful about a boy? And then a nasty thought popped into my head. 'Please tell me he's not married.'

'Crikey, Mum,' she tutted. 'What do you take me for? I'm not up for stealing another woman's husband. No, it's nothing like that. He's...' – she paused briefly before adding – 'it's simply very new. We're carefully feeling our way.'

Right. It must be someone at her college. I gave her an encouraging smile.

'I'm pleased for you. Presumably he knows about Mo?'

She gave a strange laugh.

'Yes, he knows.'

'Remember, if you want to go out together one night, I'm happy to babysit.'

'Yeah,' she said, momentarily looking wistful. 'We're only at the talking stage though.'

I squeezed her hand, then tried stifling a yawn, which set Ruby off too.

'Look at the pair of us,' I laughed. 'It's not even that late.'

'After the events of today, I feel emotionally empty. I'm sure you do, too.'

'Yes,' I agreed with a sigh.

For a moment, neither of us said anything. We remained sitting quietly side by side, lost in our own thoughts as the kitchen clock quietly ticked away on the wall. It seemed odd suddenly noticing its steady rhythm. It was almost like a heartbeat. And then I thought of Derek whose heart was no longer beating, and wondered where the essence of him had gone. A part of me believed in life after death, although I wasn't sure what form that took. Was Derek now a ball of light? Or was he still Derek but without the overcoat of skin, muscle, and bone? In other words, invisible and – effectively – a ghost? In which case, could he be sitting here in this kitchen, alongside Ruby and me, once again eavesdropping?

A chill ran down my spine. Abruptly, I stood up and went to the fridge, peering within.

'Have you eaten?' I asked.

'Not properly. I cheated earlier and fed Mo some jarred food. She very sweetly invited me to share with her. However, mushed up toddler food isn't really my thing.'

'Shall we get a takeaway?' I said impulsively.

Ruby's eyes lit up.

'Yes please,' she beamed. 'Curry?'

'Sounds good.'

'But can we afford it?' she frowned.

I thought about Coco taking Derek's money. A hundred and fifty smackers no less – and I didn't mean of the kissy kind. Things around here were about to change, and for the better.

'Yes,' I smiled. 'We can.'

# Chapter Thirty-Eight

Ruby and I enjoyed a companionable takeout together. We ate off our laps in front of the television.

It was strange not having Derek around, jeering as we mentally junked out on reruns of *Friends*. It was also blissful not having the remote control snatched away. My husband had always pointed out that, as he paid the bills, he and he alone would determine what programme to watch. As his choices were almost entirely sport – of which Ruby and I had little interest – the lounge had consequently been Derek's domain.

Later, when Ruby had gone up to bed, I picked up the phone and rang Mum and Dad. I knew they'd still be up because they were night owls. As I waited for the line to connect, I imagined the two of them sitting on their roof terrace having a final nightcap.

'Darling!' said Mum. 'Dad and I were just talking about you. Were your ears burning?' she chuckled.

It was so good to hear Mum's voice. Suddenly I felt overwhelmed with tears and couldn't speak.

'Wendy? Hello? Are you there? Must be an awful line. I can't hear a word you're saying.'

'Sorry,' I gasped, swallowing down the gobstopper of

emotion that had lodged in my throat. I took a deep breath. 'I was just collecting myself.'

Mum immediately picked up on my mood and went into panic mode.

'Omigod, what's happened?'

'I have some terrible news.'

'Gawd,' she squawked. 'Nigel. NIGE! Put that sambuca down and get yourself over here. It's our Wendy. She'd got bad news.'

'Are you sitting down?' I asked.

'Nigel, Wendy wants us to sit down. NIGE! I said SIT!' My mother turned her attention back to me. 'Now what's happened? Is Ruby all right?'

'Yes.'

'And Mo?'

'Yes, yes,' I assured. 'They're both fine, and I'm fine too, but Derek isn't.'

'Derek? Well, we're not bothered about him,' said my mother dismissively. 'Horrible little toad of a man. Anyway, I thought you said you were divorcing him.'

'Well, now I'm not.'

'Oh GAWD! Did you hear that, Nigel? NIGE! She's changed her mind about the divorce. Yes. Yes, I'll tell her. Dad says he isn't pleased to hear this and that if you're thinking about a reconciliation then it's a huge mistake.'

'Mum, the reason I'm not divorcing Derek is… he's died.'

'Derek has died? Did you hear that, Nigel? NIGE!' she whooped. 'Derek has popped his clogs. Yes, I'll pass that on to Wendy. Dad says he's delighted for you, darling. Obviously, we mean that in the nicest possible way. I mean, it's heartbreaking that Derek has left us' – my mother didn't sound remotely sad – 'but look on the bright side. It's very convenient.'

I stared at the wall ahead of me. It was quite something when you delivered shocking news to your parents, and they couldn't muster up a few tears between them.

'How did he die?' asked Mum.

'A heart attack,' I said, omitting the Coco details.

'Really?' said Mum. I sensed her blowing out her cheeks at the other end of the line. 'Mercifully quick, I guess. Let us know about the funeral arrangements, darling. Now get yourself to bed. Dad and I are finishing this last drinkypoo and then we'll turn in too. Sending lots of love, darling.'

'Lots of love back,' I said dazedly.

That night I slept fitfully in the marital bed. It wasn't because I missed Derek's presence – it was a joy not to be disturbed by his thunderous snoring. It was more because of the endless questioning narrative that kept playing on a loop in my head.

In the early hours, exhausted, I finally walked the corridor of sleep. At some point, the dreaming began. A huge oak door stood before me. I opened it cautiously and, just like Alice in Wonderland, encountered a large rabbit dressed in a waistcoat. The creature turned, revealing itself to be Derek in full costume. He stroked his whiskers as he stared at me.

'So, you discovered my little secret.'

'Yes, and I'd like to know–'

'What?' he demanded. 'What is it you want to know?'

I threw up my palms.

'Just…why?'

'Why not?' he retorted.

'Look, Derek. If you found comfort in dressing up, then fine. But why go to Coco Rowbotham and pay for it? That money could have been spent on Ruby and Mo and–'

'That's the trouble with you, Wendy.' Derek waggled a paw at me. 'You never understood my needs. You totally failed me.'

'You could have talked about it! I might have sympathised. Certainly, I would have tried my best to understand.'

'What, and joined in? Dressed likewise? Would you have twitched your cottontail and sat alongside me on the sofa?'

'Well, maybe not–'

'*Exactly*, Wendy. It was always about you. You, you, you, you, you. But let me tell you something that might now enlighten you. As a spouse, you were a complete let-down.'

I stared at my dead husband, aghast. Then suppressed rage came from nowhere and I flew at him. Two giant furry paws shoved me hard and I fell backwards, falling… falling. Terrified, I stuck out my hands, ready to break the impending fall, only to have my palms slam down on the mattress. Shocked, my eyes flew open, and I shot upright, breathing hard. Sweat beaded my forehead.

Staring around the grey gloom of the bedroom, my eyes landed on Derek's dressing gown hanging from the back of the door. One sleeve had caught on the door handle. It seemed to wave reproachfully at me.

As I waited for my pounding heart to steady, I glanced at the bedside clock. It wasn't quite yet six in the morning. Suddenly I didn't want to be in this room with hallucinogenic images still semi-dancing through my brain, or stare at a dressing gown that appeared to have taken on a life of its own.

Snapping on the bedside lamp, I squinted in the sudden glare. Relief flooded through me. I was grateful for the soft illumination lighting up four solid walls and the mundane objects within: the wardrobe with its squeaky door hinge, the dressing table with my hairbrush upon it, and Derek's loose change.

I flung back the quilt, pushing my feet into my slippers. The central heating's timer hadn't yet come on, and the house seemed exceptionally cold. Shivering, I reached for my own robe draped across the bottom of the bed.

Ten minutes later, washed and dressed in warm clothes, I quietly let myself out of the house, having left a note for Ruby.

Outside it was still dark, but that didn't bother me. Shutting the door behind me, I headed towards Trosley Country Park where Betty still idled in the carpark.

As I walked, I reflected on the events of yesterday. How could I have been married to someone for twenty-seven years and yet not truly have known them? And then, like one of November's recent fireworks, fury whooshed up from nowhere. It started in my feet, fizzing and popping. Then made its way up my calves. Thighs. Torso. Shoulders. Through my neck. Up into the skull. Then it exploded out of my crown in what felt like a million tiny pieces of angry oranges and reds.

Suddenly I found myself shifting from a brisk walk to a jog. Then a full-on run. In that moment I had unspent rage. It powered my body in a way that wasn't the everyday normal. I found myself belting along at a speed I hadn't achieved since a child in a school race.

My feet thumpity-thumped along the tarmac as I ran and ran and ran. And as I did so, I cursed my dead husband for his selfish ways, while equally thanking my creator – whoever that was – for releasing me from such an unhappy and loveless marriage.

When I arrived at Trosley, the security gate was still padlocked. Non-plussed, I slipped under the metal barrier and let myself inside Betty. I sat alone with my thoughts until the sun rose and bathed everything in rose-pink and gold light. Then something occurred to me.

This was the first day of the rest of my new life.

# Chapter Thirty-Nine

By the time Monday rolled around I was desperate for some sense of normality.

Visiting the village shop for provisions, I became aware of whispers behind hands. Picking up my wire basket was a defining moment. Some customers had been chatting animatedly, but they immediately went quiet as I moved through the aisles. Plucking a carton of milk from a refrigerated shelf, the postman's wife quietly approached me. She murmured words of condolence. Head bowed, I thanked her.

At the checkout, the lady on the cash till quietly told me I was very brave, while the packing assistant gave me a knowing look that morphed into pity.

Once home, I put the shopping away and then headed off to my first dog-walking client of the day. Daisy was a cute looking poodle but had major attitude. If she'd been in a Disney movie, she'd have been portrayed as the canine aristocrat who put the local bit of rough into a complete tailspin.

It was whilst walking around the local park that I remembered Mum's words. My new status of *widow* negated any divorce. Daisy paused to check out the leg of a park bench upon which many other dogs had left their calling card. While she sniffed and snorted, working out which way to shift her backside and then jettison the requisite amount of liquid on a pre-determined spot, I took advantage of her dilly-dallying and clamped my mobile to my head.

Rosie at Gardener and Stewart Solicitors answered almost immediately. She put me through to Gabe, but his phone went to voicemail.

'Hello, this is Gabe Stewart. I'm either away from my desk or on another call. Please leave a short message with your name and number and I will get back to you.'

There was a beep, but as I opened my mouth to speak, Daisy finished her wee and decided to squat.

'Damn,' I swore, instantly cringing at my opening comment as I set about scooping the poop. 'Sorry, I meant to say hello. So, er, hello. It's-'

But before I could say anything further, a huge German Shepherd, off-lead and looking for fun, trained its eyes upon Daisy. Uh-oh. I knotted the bag and tossed it into a nearby wastebin while quickly weighing up the situation. The dog's owner was male and distracted due to flirting with a woman holding a chihuahua.

Daisy, sensing eyes upon her, looked up. For a moment, the two dogs gazed intensely at each other. Something unspoken passed between them, then suddenly a vast black-and-tan blur was streaking towards my charge.

'Shit,' I squeaked, as Daisy catapulted towards her new love interest. The extendable lead unravelled like a fish fighting a rod's line. Seconds later I was pulled after her.

'Daisy!' I yelped, as the dogs initially collided, but then shot past each other.

The German Shepherd jammed on his brakes. Spinning round, he glued his nose to Daisy's bum. Deciding this wasn't gallant behaviour, she peeled back her lips and bared tiny sharp teeth. This didn't go down well with the German Shepherd. He narrowed his eyes and growled his displeasure at Madam's hoity-toity attitude.

'Good boy,' I quavered, just as Daisy nipped him on the nose.

The dog gave a squeal of pain, while Daisy prepared to launch a second attack.

'Oh no you don't,' I warned.

Dropping my mobile, I darted forward and scooped up the wriggling pompom of curls. Infuriated, the German Shepherd reared up and thumped two huge paws against my chest. Switching to weightlifter mode, I hoicked Daisy up in the air like a dumbbell. Suddenly I was up close and personal with an enormous whiskery muzzle, two furious black eyes and a pair of ears big enough to rival Little Red Riding Hood's wolfish grandma.

'Nice doggy,' I cooed.

The Alsatian decided I wasn't a nice human for snatching up its object of desire and began furiously barking. As halitosis and hot breath wafted over my face, I had a serious moment of wondering if this might end badly. Right now, the newspapers could have a field day with me, what with Derek demising in a sex worker's house and his wife possibly following in his heavenly footsteps while at the park. I could imagine Mabel and Fred Plaistow devouring the local paper's headlines.

*WOMAN MAULED AFTER POODLE'S CANOODLE*

*Things have gone from bad to worse for Little Waterlow resident Wendy Walker. Mrs Walker's late husband, Derek, died in compromising circumstances after visiting divorcee Coco Rowbotham's boudoir where anything goes in kinky clothes. Like her name, Mrs Walker likes walking and regularly exercises dogs for a living. However, she has a track record of un-fur-tunate episodes with her four-legged friends including a paw-sitively hairy encounter with a barking mad Alsatian. Mrs Walker, when asked to comment from her hospital bed, said that the episode had been both scary and ruff, and left her more than a little husky.*

As I stood there, eyeballing a row of sharp fangs that Dracula would have envied, it seemed that now might be a good moment to start praying.

'Dear Lord,' I intoned. 'Forgive me for I have sinned.' Well, in the moment, it seemed like a good opening line. 'Please deliver me from German Shepherds who look like they haven't eaten for a week and… ARGHHH!' I screamed.

The dog had dropped back on all fours and had grabbed the hem of my coat, tugging hard.

'RANDY!' shouted the owner, finally tearing his eyes away from the girl with the chihuahua. 'HEEL!' The dog instantly released my jacket and took off across the park. 'Sorry,' the man called. 'No harm done, eh?'

‘N-No harm done,’ I repeated shakily, setting Daisy down. I retrieved my discarded mobile and once again put it to my ear. ‘H-Hello,’ I stuttered into the mouthpiece. ‘Sorry about that. Anyway, please could you call me when it’s convenient.’

Trembling with the after-effects of a doggy drama, I left the park failing to realise that I hadn’t left my name or number on Gabe Stewart’s voicemail.

# Chapter Forty

At four o'clock my mobile rang with a withheld number.

'Hello?' I said cautiously.

'Wendy, it's Gabe. Sorry if you didn't know who was calling. The switchboard here automatically hides the number.

'That's okay. Thanks for returning my call.'

'You're lucky that I am because you didn't leave your name and number.'

'Oh, my goodness, I do apologise.' I slapped my forehead. 'So… how did you know it was me on the voicemail?'

'Because there was an awful lot of commotion at the other end of the line which involved expletives, some ferocious barking, a prayer asking for deliverance from mad dogs, followed by a scream so piercing I had to hold the phone away from my head. There's only one woman I know who walks dogs and creates mayhem, and that's you.'

'I see,' I said, trying not to bristle.

'So, what can I do for you?'

'Basically, I no longer need a divorce.'

There was a pause before Gabe spoke again.

'Okay,' he said briskly. 'I take it a reconciliation has

taken place.'

'Crikey, no,' I spluttered. 'Nothing like that. It's… it's…' Suddenly my eyes inexplicably filled with tears. 'It's D-Derek,' I quavered. Oh, my goodness. Why was I crying? 'S-Sorry, I think I'm having a delayed reaction.'

'A delayed reaction to what?' asked Gabe gently.

'My husband has died.'

Gabe didn't miss a beat.

'I wasn't expecting you to say *that*. Wendy, I'm very sorry. My sincere condolences.'

'Th-Thank you,' I stuttered. 'But I'd be a liar to say I'm devastated. I was divorcing the man. I don't even know why I'm crying.'

'That's simple. It's shock,' said Gabe. 'Look, I'm about to go into a meeting but if you come along to the office at, say, five-ish, we'll have a chat. You might need help with probate. Don't worry, the advice will be free. Or have you not even had a chance to think that far ahead?'

'No, I haven't,' I said, foraging up one sleeve for a tissue to wipe my nose.

I'd only just started liaising with the funeral director, never mind dealing with all the red tape that went with the death process. I had a fleeting moment of seeing myself disappearing under a mass of paperwork. Thank goodness Gabe could point me in the right direction.

'Then I'll see you later,' he said.

'Okay, bye.'

I disconnected the call and rubbed my temples, massaging away a headache that threatened. I wasn't even sure Derek had a Will. Certainly, I'd never made one. Who thinks about dying when you haven't even yet drawn your pension? Not many people, surely.

Returning home, I spent the next few hours divesting Derek's wardrobe of clothes. Folding everything neatly, the garments were then bagged up, ready for the local charity shop. Some would say, "So soon?" But I wanted his stuff out. Somehow it felt cathartic. My husband had led a double life – and a very strange one at that. I wanted his belongings gone, as if it would somehow exorcise the more recent unpalatable memories.

I carefully checked pockets to make sure nothing of value was inadvertently given away. The last thing I wanted was someone having a lucky find, like Derek's bank cards or house keys. I came across a half-opened packet of spearmint. It struck me as odd that my husband would never again peel back the foil wrapper and put one in his mouth. Likewise, he would never know what happened in the next chapter of the book still residing upon his bedside table.

I shook my head in bemusement as I carried on patting and feeling. I pulled a fiver from the back pocket of a pair of trousers. From another, the business card of a rival painter and decorator. And then I came across a scrap of paper. A phone number was written upon it. Under the digits, was one word. *Coco.*

I inhaled sharply. Well, my husband wouldn't be needing *that* anymore. But it was when I reached into the garment's front pocket that I found myself needing to sit down. I put my head between my legs.

*Breathe, Wendy. Breathe! Inhale. Exhale. And repeat.*

I felt the blood rush to my head as I sat there, viewing the base of the bed from an upside-down position, my face currently in line with my ankles. I squeezed my eyelids together to block out the image of the small snapshot that lay upon the carpet at my feet. After slowly counting to ten, I opened my eyes again.

It was a picture of Derek and Coco. Their heads were inclined together, and they were both dressed as rabbits.

# Chapter Forty-One

I left a note for Ruby advising her of my whereabouts, then lugged all the black sacks out of the house and into the back of Betty. There was still enough time to catch the charity shop before it closed for the day.

The boot was crammed with almost all of Derek's clothes and footwear. Only a suit, shirt, tie, and a smart pair of shoes remained in the marital bedroom's wardrobe. This was at the behest of the funeral director who would dress Derek before his final send off.

Grimacing, I shunted the gear into first, and set off.

After depositing the bags, I headed off to Gardener and Stewart Solicitors. As previously, Annabelle greeted me.

'Sorry to hear about your husband,' she said, as we walked along the now familiar corridor to Gabe's office. 'I'm also so sorry about that hideous typo on your divorce application.'

'It couldn't matter less,' I assured.

'I got a right bollocking from His Highness.'

'Between you and me' – I smiled – 'I thought it quite inspired.'

'Thank you for taking it in good humour.' She paused for a moment outside Gabe's office. 'By the way, I just want to say that – despite all your current stress – you look absolutely amazing.'

'Thanks,' I said in surprise. I was unused to compliments.

She opened the door and ushered me in.

Gabe looked up from his desk. His eyebrows went up, but he made no comment about my appearance. I realised this was probably the first time he'd seen me looking presentable. My hair had been brushed and was currently falling in soft waves past my shoulders. Thanks to a light makeup foundation, my skin was glowing. I'd added a bit of blusher, followed up with a slick of lipstick, then finished with a spritz of perfume. The latter had been swiped from Ruby's dressing table. My daughter's recent words about me looking a perpetual scruff had stung. Also, if I'm honest, seeing Coco's glamour had shamed me into making some effort with my appearance before leaving the house.

'Wendy,' said Gabe. He set down a Dictaphone machine, then briefly rubbed the bridge of his nose. He looked tired. 'So.' He steepled his elbows as he regarded me. 'I won't offer you my condolences because I've already done that. We've also established that you're shocked, but not devastated.'

'That's about the sum of it,' I said, collapsing into the chair on the other side of his desk.

'This is all very sudden. Did Derek meet with an accident?'

'No, he had a heart attack.'

'Stress?'

'Who knows?' I shrugged. 'I discovered that he was

keeping a whopping secret, which perhaps had a detrimental effect on his health.'

'And is his secret going to stay a secret, or are you prepared to share?'

'I might as well tell you,' I sighed. 'After all, ninety percent of Little Waterlow now know.'

'I don't listen to tittle-tattle. Rest assured that whatever you say within these walls will be in the strictest confidence.'

'Brace yourself. I discovered that my husband had a thing going with, um, a lady of ill repute.' If Gabe was shocked, he didn't show it. 'Also' – I took a deep breath – 'Derek had a dressing-up fetish.'

'Women's clothes?'

'Ha, I wish!' I hooted, but without humour. 'No, Derek's *thing* was quite different. He also paid the lady in question to dress up with him.' My brow furrowed as I thought back to that snapshot I'd discovered. 'I can only presume that he was Benjamin Bunny, and she was Lily Bobtail. No doubt their couplings were – to put it bluntly – like the rabbits they were pretending to be. Then, during one particularly energetic session, Derek keeled over.'

'He died on the job?' said Gabe, looking aghast.

'Yes.'

'Geez, Wendy.' He sucked on his teeth for a moment. 'And how the heck are you feeling? I mean, *really* feeling?'

'I'm not sure. Angry. Disbelieving. Shocked. Embarrassed.'

'But you're not in bits?'

'No,' I said carefully. 'Not in bits. Does that make me a

bad person?'

'Of course not,' Gabe assured. 'Listen, probate isn't my field, but I'm assuming you only have a small estate without overseas properties or Swiss bank accounts?'

'Definitely not,' I smiled wanly.

'Did Derek leave a Will?'

'I don't think so. I'm sure if he had, he'd have suggested I make one too.'

'And you haven't ever made a Will yourself?'

'No,' I said, suddenly feeling a bit foolish.

'Many people of your age don't, but I strongly urge you to do so. My partner, Roy Gardener, can assist. Meanwhile, let me help you sort things out. It's likely a straightforward legal matter and will relieve you of some of the stress at what is nonetheless a challenging time.'

I hesitated before answering.

'That's very kind, but I really don't want to run up a solicitor's bill. If sorting things out is an uncomplicated matter, then I can do it myself.'

'I won't be charging you.'

I blinked.

'Why would you do that for me?'

Gabe didn't answer. Instead, he leant forward and logged off the computer.

'I've had enough for one day. Also, I haven't eaten since this morning, and I'm famished. As you're no longer officially my client, would you like to join me?'

My stomach rumbled by way of response.

'That's settled then,' he said.

# Chapter Forty-Two

Gabe led the way from his office to reception, through the double doors and out into a cold and chilly late afternoon.

We set off on foot at quite a pace. Within a minute or so, I was puffing away.

'I'm pretty good at powerwalking, but you are borderline sprinting. Slow down!'

'Sorry,' he said, easing up a smidgen. 'Food is calling me. Anyway, judging from your stomach's earlier growls, fuel is urgently required for you too.'

'Lately I've been forgetting to eat,' I confessed, scampering after him. 'There's been so much going on, I haven't really felt like eating. When my emotions run high, it seems to interfere with the enjoyment of food.'

'Fair,' he said, striding on. 'It can go two ways with folks. Some use food as a comfort blanket, so a crisis will see the weight piling on. Others go right off it and, almost overnight, shed pounds. You need to watch yourself though, Wendy. I've noticed you shrinking. While you look great, take care not to go too far, eh.'

'Yes, okay,' I said, reeling slightly from the compliment within his words. He thought I looked great! Now, why was my heart singing?

*Careful, Wendy. He's just being kind. Remember Annabelle's tale of Ms Gucci Belt. Proceed with caution regarding all matters of the heart.*

He's my solicitor, I countered. Plus, I've just been widowed. What do you take me for?

*A vulnerable woman who has been starved of love and is ready to lap up every tiny crumb of kindness – potentially making a fool of herself in the process.*

Thanks for the warning, I acknowledged, as gloominess threatened to envelop me.

'Here we are,' said Gabe, interrupting my thoughts.

He'd stopped on the High Street outside a cosy looking bistro. Pausing, he opened the door for me.

'Thanks,' I said, liking the gentlemanly gesture.

Derek would have opened the door for himself and then let it swing back in my face.

'Ah, Mr Stewart,' said a pretty waitress, hastening over. She plucked two menus from the nearby bar's counter. 'Your usual table?'

'Yes, please, Amanda,' said Gabe.

We followed Amanda as she weaved between tables, heading for a corner at the rear of the restaurant. I couldn't help noticing her pert little bottom in those tight black trousers. The dangling ties from her white linen apron jiggled in time to her swaying hips. What a sexy walk. Perhaps I could try and emulate her. It might make me feel more… self-confident, or empowered, or… well, something like that.

I sucked in my stomach and minced along, sashaying my pelvis as I tried to copy Amanda's gait. Unfortunately, I was broader in the beam than her and my left hip caught a nearby chair, toppling it over.

'All right, Wendy?' said Gabe, turning to see what the noise was about.

'Yes, fine,' I gasped, nearly tripping over the upended legs.

A waiter zoomed over.

'Let me help, Madam,' he said, grabbing the chair and righting it. 'No harm done.'

I caught his expression. He was endeavouring not to snort with laughter. Okay, he'd seen my attempt at strutting my stuff and knew I'd failed miserably.

'Thanks,' I muttered.

I returned to my usual slouch and drooped after the other two.

'Here we are,' said Amanda, pulling out a chair for Gabe first.

She gave him a smile so dazzling that it surely could have lit up a football stadium without floodlights. I pulled out my own chair and sat down.

Amanda was now shaking out a white linen napkin and laying it over Gabe's lap. There was a lot of attention to detail as she straightened it out at the corners, smoothing away imaginary creases. Blimey, talk about touchy-feely. I wondered how close her fingers had come to touching Gabe's crown jewels, and instantly got hot under the collar at the very thought.

*Get a grip, Wendy.*

'Can I get you the wine list,' asked Amanda, dimpling

prettily.

'Sounds good,' said Gabe. 'Is that okay with you, Wendy?'

The thought of a long cool glass of wine was extremely tempting.

'I'd really like to, but Betty is waiting in your carpark,' I said.

'Betty?' said Gabe frowning. 'Does Betty want to join us or – no, don't tell me – you're one of those people who give their wheels a name, right?'

Amanda's gaze was now upon me. She was flashing me the sort of look that let me know I was dafter than Basil Brush.

'Betty is my Citroen Picasso,' I said defensively. 'And yes, I would love a drink, but I have to drive later.'

'So we'll share a bottle, and then have half a dozen coffees until it's okay for you to return to' – his lips twitched – 'dear Betty and see her safely home. This place doesn't shut until midnight.'

I instantly perked up at the thought of having Gabe all to myself for the next six-and-a-bit hours. Likewise, Amanda's eyes lit up like a pinball machine at the prospect of this good-looking guy being in her restaurant for a lengthy period. It dawned on me that she might wiggle over every few minutes to interrupt our conversation.

*It's called customer care, Wendy.*

Actually, it's called being a bloody nuisance.

*Don't you listen to anything I say? You'll be making Ms Gucci Belt look like Mother Teresa if you're not careful.*

I sighed. God, what was the matter with me?

'What do your tastebuds fancy?' said Gabe, looking up from the wine list.

They'd like to taste your kiss.

*I can't believe you just had that thought.*

Neither can I.

'I'm not a wine connoisseur,' I replied.

'Neither am I,' Gabe smiled.

'Prosecco, please.'

'I was hoping you'd say that,' Gabe twinkled, handing the wine list back to Amanda.

Was it my imagination or had our waitress's smile suddenly become a little brittle?

'One bottle of Prosecco coming up,' she said, eyes firmly on Gabe. 'I'll leave you both to look at the menus.'

'So,' said Gabe, as Amanda sashayed off. 'It's Friday evening. The end of the working week. Time to wind down.'

He loosened his tie and undid the top button of his shirt, immediately revealing biscuity-coloured skin. My fingers instantly itched to undo the rest of those buttons and peel away that shirt.

*Oh my flipping God! Do you really want to do that? If so, you're in deep trouble.*

I know. Help! H-E-L-PPP!!

*Don't drink too much. You don't want to say something you might later regret.*

Good advice.

I tore my eyes away from Gabe's shirt buttons and

instead concentrated hard on the tip of his nose. That was better. Noses weren't sexy. Noses were, well, breathing apparatus. They were quite weird looking things when you paused to properly study them. Gabe's nose was aquiline straight. No bumps. No flaws. No nasal hair – which was always a bonus.

'What are your plans for the weekend?' I asked breathily.

'I'm hoping to–'

He broke off to peer at me.

'Are you okay, Wendy?'

'Yes,' I said to his nose. 'Why do you ask?'

'Because you've gone a bit cross-eyed.'

'O-Oh,' I blushed, refocussing. 'Yes, it… it happens sometimes.'

'Really?'

'Only when my eye test is overdue.'

*What flipping nonsense are you spouting, woman?*

Suddenly I felt horribly tongue-tied. Oh no. How was I going to get through an evening with Gabe if I couldn't think of anything to say?

'Um… do you ever wear glasses?'

*Riveting conversation, Wendy.*

'No.' Gabe shook his head. 'The last time I saw my optician he asked what I could see, and I replied, "Empty airports, closed football grounds, shut theatres and locked up pubs." And the optician answered, "Absolutely perfect, Mr Stewart. You have 2020 vision."'

I stared at Gabe blankly, belatedly realising he'd cracked a joke.

'Sorry,' he apologised. 'That was terrible.'

'No, it wasn't,' I assured, as laughter bubbled up and burst out of me.

Thankfully it swept away that shy moment.

'I'm glad it made you chuckle,' he smiled.

His eyes crinkled attractively at the corners. I wondered what it would be like to trace those lines with my fingertips.

'You look lovely when you laugh,' he added.

Immediately my laughter petered out. Was he flirting?

'And I'm not flirting,' he said, as if reading my mind.

Oh. Shame.

'Just making an observation,' he explained.

Amanda chose that moment to deliver the Prosecco in an ice bucket. As she faffed about polishing glasses and popping the cork, I made a conscious decision to simply relax and enjoy the evening. If Gabe thought I looked lovely when I smiled, then maybe I'd make sure I spent tonight beaming like the sun on a clear day in Spain. I picked up my glass of pale gold bubbles and raised it in the air.

'Cheers,' I grinned.

## Chapter Forty-Three

The Prosecco was going down a treat, along with a complimentary ramakin filled with stuffed olives. Despite ordering fifteen minutes ago, our starters had yet to appear. The wine, on an empty stomach, was giving my brain quite a buzz.

Ruby had often joked about me being a lightweight, so I reminded myself to sip the wine slowly, and not knock it back out of nerves. Meanwhile, Amanda had returned to our table and was doing an unnecessary amount of hovering.

'Wine okay?' she asked Gabe.

'Perfect, thanks.'

'Celebrating?' she enquired, smile firmly in place.

'Yes,' said Gabe, not elaborating.

'What are you celebrating?' she persisted, refusing to budge.

'Lots of things.'

'Like?'

'The end of an exhausting week.'

'I *soooo* know that feeling,' she gushed, rolling her eyes. 'The best thing for unwinding is a massage. Full body,' she added. 'Every nook and cranny.' She gave Gabe a meaningful look. 'I know the perfect place, and if you want to give it a try, we could go together.'

As I was so obviously excluded from this conversation, I took a few more sips of wine.

*Hellooo, Wendy? Are you going to sit there like one of those stuffed olives and not see this bitch off?*

Blimey, language!

*You've had alcohol. Therefore, inhibition is being swiftly removed from my vocabulary.*

Okay, but I'd like to point something out. I'm not Gabe's girlfriend, so if Amazing Amanda wants to come on to him, there's damn all I can do about it.

*Don't be so bloody wet. Get rid of her. Now!*

'I'm *soooo* exhausted too,' I interrupted.

I took another slug of wine, then suggestively licked away some of the liquid from my lips. Amanda swivelled her head and regarded me with distaste.

'Oh?'

'Yes, totally knackered. Perhaps you can include me' – I waved a hand carelessly – 'in the massage thingy.' I regarded her innocently. 'I'm always up for new experiences.'

*Whaaaat? Talk about innuendo. You wally. You sound like you're inviting her to have a threesome.*

Well *you* were the one who told me to see her off. Two's company and three is a crowd, right?

*What if she swings both ways and takes you up on your offer?*

'E-Except' – I stammered – 'I only have massages with… men.'

Gabe's eyes were now rounder than the stuffed olives.

'I mean' – I blustered – 'it must be a man giving the massage. They have better… finger technique.'

*Oh geez…*

'Tell you what' – Amanda turned her back on me, addressing just Gabe – 'let's skip the massage parlour. Instead, come over to my place. I have a variety of essential oils, and there's absolutely nothing wrong with my' – she gave a dirty laugh – '*finger technique*.'

I stifled a groan and slung some more Prosecco down my throat.

'Oy, Amanda,' called a male voice. She turned to regard the maître'd who was ringing up another client's bill. 'Stop gassing and give Table Nineteen their starters.'

'I'll be right back,' she said to Gabe.

'Please don't hurry,' I muttered.

Gabe was looking at me with amusement.

'You're a dark horse, Wendy. When have you visited massage parlours?'

'Since never,' I admitted, draining my glass. 'Fill me up, Gabe.'

*Wendy, pleeeeez. Now you sound like you're wanting sex with the guy.*

'The glass,' I gasped.

Gabe looked at me curiously.

'Naturally.'

As he refreshed my drink, I leant across the table and hissed conspiratorially at him.

'Are you aware that Amanda likes you?'

'Really?' said Gabe. He took a sip from his own glass.

'How can you tell?'

I stared at him incredulously.

'Did you not twig that Amanda was inviting you back to her place for sex?'

Gabe looked bemused.

'The S word was never mentioned.'

'Then what do you think she was going to do with her essential oils? Give you a facial?' I asked, snorting at the very idea. I took another glug of wine. 'You need to watch yourself, Gabe. You're clearly an innocent.'

*He doesn't look like an innocent, Wendy.*

Don't you think?

*No. He looks like a lady killer.*

Looks can be deceptive.

'You need to learn to read the signs,' I cautioned.

'Tell me more,' said Gabe, leaning in.

'Like body language.'

I gazed squiffily at him. Dear God but he was attractive. Such amazing eyes. The blueness. The golden flecks. Those dark irises that – was it my imagination? – seemed to be dilating to the size of the nearby ice-bucket.

'What sort of body language?' he asked softly.

We seemed to be in the middle of an eye-lock.

'Like the way she was twiddling her hair around one finger while looking at you,' I said, twiddling my hair around one finger. 'And the way she leant towards you,' I added, leaning closer.

'Starters,' said Amanda, shoving between us two bowls of *soup of the day.*

Gabe and I sprang apart, and I let out a shaky sigh. Blimey, for a moment something had been going on there. Or had I been imagining things?

This time Amanda was unable to linger because, almost immediately, the maître'd called her away to seat new customers. Oh, goody. Now I could try and recapture that lost moment.

*I told you to go easy on the wine, Wendy.*

Yes, yes, YES.

*Don't go saying those three words out loud, otherwise you'll sound like you're having an orgasm.*

Let's not talk about orgasms, please.

I mentally waved away my inner voice. Gabe was tucking into his soup. I took a rather noisy slurp of mine.

'Wow, this is amazing,' he said.

'Mmm, orgasmic,' I agreed.

*WHAT did you just say?*

'I mean' – I cast about wildly – 'you know, cosmic. Orgasmically cosmic. It's one of Nigella Lawson's pet phrases.'

'Is it?' said Gabe, looking at me speculatively. 'Are you into Nigella Lawson.'

'God, no!' I gasped, slurring slightly. 'I'm totally heterosexual.' Gabe momentarily appeared to choke on his soup. 'But I love her cooking programmes,' I continued. 'She's so… suggestive.'

'Do enlighten me,' he said, giving me a wicked look.

'Oh you know… she's always fondling aubergines. Waggling cucumbers. Making saucy innuendo to camera about her sweet sorbet and stiff raspberry ripples.'

'My goodness, I had no idea these television channels showed such titillating programmes. What a sheltered life I've led,' he said, mouth twitching.

'You need to educate yourself, Gabe, in the ways of alluring women,' I said, licking my soup spoon suggestively.

'Perhaps you could teach me,' he murmured

Was it my imagination, or was there a dangerous gleam in those amazing eyes?

'Soup okay?' said Amanda, thrusting her face between us.

# Chapter Forty-Four

Gabe Stewart was the urban dictionary's definition of *sex on legs,* and I could see why our waitress was attracted to him. Nonetheless, Amanda's attempts to crowbar her way into my time with him, was seriously starting to annoy me.

Now, I don't mind sharing things in life. After all, I did it all the time with Mo, from dividing up a cream cake to letting her "borrow" one of Nanna's lipsticks. But I was suddenly feeling proprietorial about the man sitting opposite me, and I was *not* up for sharing his company.

Amanda was once again presenting me with her back while she asked Gabe if his starter was satisfactory. I prodded her shoulder blade. As she spun around to face me, her expression was one of immense irritation.

'What?' she scowled.

'Do you really want to how our shtarter was?' I slurred.

'Excuse me?'

'The. Shoup.' I enunciated.

'Why, is there a fly in it?' she sniggered.

'No.' I glared at her. 'There's a woman in it.'

'Eh?'

'You heard.'

Possibly my tone was a little raised, but alcohol blurs

inhibitions, and currently I didn't give a damn if the whole restaurant heard me. I was done with people looking down their noses at me, whether it was Derek, Mabel Plaistow, or this snotty waitress. If Gabe had been my husband, I'd have had every right to tell Amanda to sling her hook. Okay, Gabe wasn't my husband, but he was my solicitor – or at least he had been – and if this had been a working meeting it would have ratcheted up a bill that *I'd* have been paying. And anyway, why was I even trying to justify myself? I'd been invited out to dinner. The reason why I was here didn't matter. The fact remained that the evening was being spoilt by a waitress with attitude. I took a deep breath and gave it to her with both barrels.

'I'm trying to have a private conversation which you keep constantly interrupting.'

'What's going on?' said the maître'd', whizzing over.

The last thing he wanted was a fracas at Table Nineteen. I smiled at him sweetly.

'Your employee wants to rub her lavender and geraniums all over my dinner companion.'

'Madam,' said the maître'd, looking most perplexed. 'I'm not sure I understand.'

'Could you please ask someone else to serve us. Preferably a man.' Yes, that would be better. 'One who isn't gay,' I added, just to be on the safe side.

'I will make sure Henri serves you both,' said the maître'd. 'My sincere apologies for the handsome man and his beautiful wife being disturbed,' he said, bowing and scraping, before half-dragging the outraged Amanda away.

‘Oh, but Gabe’s not my hus–’ I protested, but I was talking to the air.

‘Well done, Wendy,’ said Gabe, trying not to snort with laughter. ‘I was just about to diplomatically ask Amanda if she could perhaps be not *quite* so attentive, but you saved me the bother.’

I immediately turned the colour of the sundried tomatoes in the soup.

‘Sorry, but I’m not psychic,’ I mumbled.

‘It’s fine,’ he assured. ‘It’s been a long time since a woman rushed to defend me, especially one as attractive as you.’

I opened my mouth to say something and then shut it again.

*Ooooh… did you hear that? ONE AS ATTRACTIVE AS YOU!*

Yes, of course I heard it. I’m sitting opposite the guy.

‘It was rather nice,’ Gabe added.

‘Was it?’ I asked tentatively.

‘Yes,’ he nodded. ‘I haven’t been part of a couple for a long time. For a moment it made me feel’ – he suddenly looked coy – ‘cherished, I guess.’

‘Oh,’ I said, momentarily flummoxed. ‘That’s good. I think.’ I didn’t know what to say. I’d drunk half a bottle of wine on a virtually empty stomach and my soup was now almost cold. ‘Sometimes we all need to feel as if someone has our back,’ I said, picking my words carefully. ‘Sorry for behaving like a Rottweiler seeing off a dodgy door-to-door salesman.’

'It couldn't matter less,' Gabe assured.

'But hang on,' I frowned. 'Annabelle said-'

'Oh no, Annabelle again? Go on. What did my secretary say? Spit it out.'

'Well, referring to the word *cherished*' – I could feel myself reddening again – 'Annabelle said you had someone special in your life. Lisa. Doesn't she make you feel cherished?'

'She's an *ex*-girlfriend,' Gabe reminded.

'Okay, so she's an ex. But didn't she make you feel loved?'

'She did her best but...' he trailed off.

'Was it because of' – my brain was rapidly sobering up, but I wanted to be sure my mouth was keeping up and didn't make a hash of words – 'those *romantic scars?*'

'You've lost me.'

'It was Annabelle who mentioned them. You see, I asked her – when I was initially looking for a divorce – whether you had empathy with your clients. She assured me you did because of your romantic scars. So, I deduced you'd been divorced yourself. But maybe Lisa added a few more wounds along the way. Am I right?'

'Wrong on both counts.'

'Now *you've* lost me,' I said, confused.

'I haven't ended a marriage through the divorce courts. And as for Lisa…' – Gabe blew out his cheeks – 'she was never in the running for being the second Mrs Stewart.'

'The second–?'

I broke off. I was *so* not following this conversation. And then Gabe said something that completely knocked me for six.

'Wendy, I *do* have empathy with my clients. I know exactly what it feels like for a relationship to end. I know the hurt. The pain. I've been besties with mental turmoil. I've walked the path of grief. But I'm not a divorced man.' His ice-blue eyes bored into mine. 'I'm a widower.'

# Chapter Forty-Five

'You're a widower?' I gasped. 'You mean...' – my brain struggled to process this new information – 'you had a spouse but now she's dead?'

*Brilliant, Wendy. Nothing like stating the obvious.*

'Yes. My wife died five years ago from sudden adult death syndrome.' He shook his head as if still not quite believing it. 'She was here one minute, then gone the next. I kissed her goodnight, put the light out, and in the morning discovered-'

His voice caught, and he didn't finish the sentence, but no further words were required. It was obvious that he'd awoken to find his wife had passed away.

'Gabe, I don't know what to say.'

'There's nothing *to* say. We go through life and stuff happens. That was my "stuff". I sold the house. Couldn't bear to be there for a moment longer than necessary. I moved out and tried to move on.'

'I'm so sorry.'

'If I had a pound for every time someone said those words, I'd be very wealthy.'

I looked at him helplessly. He pushed his empty soup bowl away, then folded his hands, one over the other. They were within touching distance. Without even thinking about it, I reached out. Slowly, his fingers unfurled. Gently, they folded into mine. Sparks of electricity zigzagged through my wrist, up my armpit, through the back of my neck and out into the space around us. I'm amazed the energy didn't cause a power surge along the high street.

'I truly am sorry,' I repeated. 'There are no adequate words.'

'They say time heals,' he said. 'That's true. As the months – and then years – went by, it became less raw. There is an acceptance.' He shrugged. 'Maybe "acceptance" is the wrong word. More… a coming to terms with the situation. Getting on with life. Trying to do the routine things to stay sane. Cleaning your teeth. Remembering to put the lid down – even though she's no longer there to remind me. Putting the kettle on and making a cuppa for one, and not a pot for two. Going to work. Thank *God* for work,' he added.

'How on earth did you manage to concentrate?' I asked.

'I'm one of those people who, once behind their desk, manage to switch off the outside world. Immersing myself with clients and their problems pushes personal issues away. Well, for a while. Certainly, long enough to press the pause button on heartache. I'm aware that I'm now a workaholic and not the sunniest of people to work for, hence my poor track record of keeping a secretary. If you hadn't dropped by the office with your outrageously rumbling stomach demanding food, I'd probably have stayed at my desk until nine o'clock this evening.'

'You should work to live, Gabe,' I said gently. 'Not live to work.'

'Yeah, I know,' he sighed, squeezing my hand by way of acknowledgement. 'My brother-in-law has said the same thing. He suggested cycling as a release. I find it very therapeutic.'

'That's good. Do you cycle together?'

'Not so much these days. If I'm honest, he struggles to keep up with me. I'm not one for moseying along. I'd much rather be frantically peddling, using all the adrenalin that can rush up from nowhere, making me want to shake my fists at the sky and curse a so-called God for taking my wife.'

I thought back to when I'd been walking William Beagle at Manor Park. How Gabe had been hurtling along before flying over the handlebars. So that was why he rode at such speed. To run from the torment chasing at his heels.

'What was your wife's name?' I asked.

I had a sudden burning desire to know more about the woman that he'd loved and lost too early in life.

'Heather,' he said. 'We were married for ten years. Don't think it was the perfect love story because it wasn't all a bed of roses. Sometimes we fought like cat and dog. But there was passion too. A lot of laughter as well as huge rows.'

'Are you a bit of a hothead?' I asked gently.

'Not at all,' Gabe laughed. 'However, Heather was. I don't really go in for all that astrology lark, but she was a Leo. If you believe the character traits, then it's true to say she fitted the feisty description. She could roar when she put her mind to it. She was never afraid to speak her truth – which often upset people. She was always falling out with her brother and sister-in-law, but not intentionally. Heather wasn't deliberately unkind, she just said things how they were. The single biggest argument we ever had was about having children. Heather didn't want them, and I did.'

'That's a shame,' I said. 'But equally, if someone doesn't feel maternal, then I guess there's not much you can do about it. At least she was honest with you.'

'Yes, she was honest, but I'd secretly hoped that she might one day change her mind. That her nesting instincts would kick in and her hormones metaphorically yell in her ear, "It's time to make a baby – NOW!"' He sighed. 'At least, when she died, there was no child to comfort or raise single-handedly. I was spared that distress.' He smiled bleakly. 'Are you glad you had children, Wendy?'

'Well, I only have the one. A big family didn't happen for us, but I think that might have been a blessing. I wouldn't be without Ruby for the world. She was the sweetest child. She turned into a bit of a Tasmanian Devil as a teenager. We were unexpectedly landed with a granddaughter, but Mo is a delight and the apple of my eye.'

'Is Mo short for Maureen?'

'Er, no,' I said, looking a bit embarrassed. 'My daughter went through a stage of zealously following celebrities. She was heavily influenced by the names that some reality stars give their children. She named her newborn Moonbeam-Fairy.'

'It's not so bad,' Gabe smiled.

'Ruby now rather regrets it, but that's the name on Mo's

birth certificate.'

'And do you love being a grandma, Wendy?'

'Totally,' I smiled. 'But less of the *grandma* word, please. Mo calls me Nanna.'

'Was Derek delighted to be a granddad?'

My smile faded.

'No. Derek wasn't a great dad, and he certainly wasn't a doting grandpa. Mo called him Grumpa, and the name was spot on. Derek would have made Grumpy – Snow White's dwarf – seem like a stand-up comedian. My husband was a miserable man who squashed all the joy out of life. I wish I could find some warm memories to look back upon, but currently all I can recall is the endless unpleasantness.'

'What about when you were first married? There must have been some love and laughter in the beginning.'

'Maybe some happy memories will eventually filter back to me.'

'So you're not missing him?'

I opened my mouth to speak, but nothing came out. I had an overwhelming urge to be brutally honest and to hell with what Gabe – or anyone else for that matter – thought.

'No, I'm not missing him. Not one little bit. That must sound callous and cold. I truly wish I felt differently, but I don't. The only thing I *do* feel is embarrassment at sitting here splurging it all out to you like a sinner confessing to a priest.'

'You don't need to feel ashamed, Wendy.' Gabe squeezed my hand again. 'Not all marriages are made in heaven. Mine wasn't, but nonetheless I loved Heather. I put her on a pedestal in the beginning, but I'm more realistic about her memory now. I simply miss having that special someone in my life.'

'Look, Gabe' – I hesitated, unsure how to phrase what I wanted to say – 'please don't think I'm coming on to you or something, because I'm not–'

'I wouldn't presume,' he assured, giving me a smile that threatened to singe my eyelashes.

'You are an incredibly fit guy.'

'I'm flattered.'

'Seriously, I mean it. What I'm trying to say in a cackhanded way… is that I'm flabbergasted you haven't been snapped up by someone and marched into the nearest registry office.'

'There have been one or two invitations,' he grinned.

I raised my eyebrows enquiringly.

'Ms Gucci Belt?'

He chuckled.

'No. Females like her only want the honeymoon stage of a relationship, then they're happy to spit you out and move on. I have had, very recently, someone prepared to do the whole washing-your-smelly-socks thing, along with ironing shirts, and cooking lavish meals before turning into a tart in the bedroom.'

'Blimey,' I murmured, feeling a ridiculous stab of jealousy. 'Are you talking about Lisa?'

'Yes.'

'So… why didn't you go down on one knee?'

'Because, despite her being a sweetheart, she didn't make

my heart sing.'

Wow, his standards must be high. From what Annabelle had said, Lisa was also an absolute knockout in the looks department.

'I'm sure there's someone out there for you, Gabe, and when she comes along it won't just be your heart singing. An entire orchestra will be playing in the background.'

'I know.'

'Do you?'

'Yes, and actually' – he hesitated a moment before continuing – 'I've already met her.'

'Really?' Suddenly all those earlier Prosecco bubbles were popping, leaving me feeling inexplicably flat. 'Then why aren't you pursuing her?'

'Because the timing isn't right.'

'When is timing ever right?' I countered. 'People spend their lives saying those words. Like delaying buying a house because they want to accrue a bigger deposit. Then what happens? The price of property rises faster than they can save. Or' – I cast about for another example – 'they hold off starting a family because they want to wait for a promotion. Meanwhile, the house they had their eye on is snapped up by someone else, and then they discover they didn't make the grade on that promotion. Also, they missed out on their wife's ovaries producing two eggs in one month which would have netted twins.'

'Do all women think like you, Wendy?' Gabe smiled.

'I don't know,' I sighed. 'All I'm saying is, there comes a point in life where you have to stop thinking about timing and trust your intuition.'

I rattled to a standstill and stared bleakly at our hands across the table. Our fingers were still entwined. It felt so right to me, but I knew he wasn't feeling it. Not the way I was. Not when he was mooning over someone else. I'd taken his hand to offer comfort, and he'd accepted it, but not because of any romantic notion. That was now being underlined to me, for he'd confided about his feelings for another woman. My heart sank as I realised he was well and truly out of my reach.

*Were you seriously entertaining the idea of hooking Gabe Stewart?*

No. Yes. Oh, I don't flipping know.

*And do you still think it feels right holding his hand?*

It does to me.

*Then tell him how you feel. Be brave. Take your own advice. Bugger timing.*

I can't do that! I'm a woman. It's for the man to say such things.

*I don't think Germaine Greer would agree.*

Too bad. I'm all for women being independent and whatnot, but I'm not up for rejection. The guy has just confessed to having huge feelings for someone else, so what chance have I got?

*None, if you don't seize the moment.*

Oh, get stuffed. I'm a forty-eight-year-old grandmother. Gabe Stewart is out of my league. Also, he said he wanted kids. He could easily find a gorgeous twenty-something like the pneumatic Amanda. She could pop out babies like peas from a shell.

*Having children is very overrated. And anyway, you could still be in with a small chance. After all, he did say you were attractive.*

Kate Middleton is attractive. It doesn't mean Gabe wants a fling with her.

Henri arrived at our table holding two platters of steak. Reluctantly I let go of Gabe's hand and picked up my knife and fork.

# Chapter Forty-Six

The evening continued. Our mains were divine, and the dessert delicious.

As we ate, we talked about anything and everything. By the time we'd reached the coffee stage, I knew a hell of a lot more about Gabe Stewart than when I'd first walked into the restaurant. It was fair to say he also knew quite a bit about me.

We had discussed our respective families. Childhood holidays (his spent on windswept Cornish beaches, mine on the Brighton coast thanks to Mum and Dad having a static caravan at Newhaven). Our ambitions (he'd already fulfilled his by becoming a partner at Gardener and Stewart). Our respective bucket lists. Australia was next on his, while I had yet to move on from visiting Mum and Dad in Spain.

'So, tell me, Wendy,' said Gabe, stirring sugar into his cappuccino. 'Despite the mini earthquakes that seem to go on in your life – from discovering your recently deceased husband wanted to be a rabbit to your scrape with a dog intent on pursuing Daisy-Doodle the Poodle – what's next for you?'

'Some peace and quiet, I hope,' I said with a small smile. 'Oh, and a trip to the hairdresser. I counted two more grey hairs this morning. I'm surprised I've not gone white overnight.'

'You have beautiful hair. In fact, given all the stress you've had in your life, you look amazing.'

'Thanks,' I said, noticing the compliment and feeling delighted.

*Amazing* was a nice word, but I knew it didn't mean anything, as such. *Amazing* simply suggested that I didn't look haggard after everything that had happened over the last few days. Still, at least Gabe thought my hair was beautiful. I made a mental note to stop the hairdresser cutting off anything other than a few split ends.

'I know it's early days for you' – he continued – 'and that you're sailing through unchartered waters, but do you see yourself possibly settling down again one day?'

'You must be flipping joking.' The words were out of my mouth before I could stop them. 'I mean–'

'That was a stupid question,' he quickly interrupted. 'Forgive me for being so tactless. You're still coming to terms with being a widow.'

'It's not that,' I protested. 'It's… well, lots of things. My daughter is still at home and needs supporting – emotionally and financially. And then there's my granddaughter. I spend a lot of time with her. Between the two of them, my free time is limited.'

'But you managed to get out this evening,' he pointed out.

'Tonight is a one-off,' I countered. 'If I made a habit of it, Ruby would probably get peeved. Plus, I can't see many men being up for taking on the emotional baggage I'm carrying.'

'Lots of people start again with kids from other relationships. They're called "blended families".'

'Yeah, I know. But… I'd be concerned that if I couldn't give my all to a new partner, he might eventually look for company elsewhere.'

'Like Derek, you mean.'

'Well, yes. Although Derek and I were floundering long before Ruby joined the Pudding Club while still a kid herself. However, throwing myself into my new role of Nanna probably didn't do my marriage any favours. I loved sharing the nightshift with Ruby. And I was in heaven assisting her when Mo was screaming the house down with colic. My attention to Ruby and Mo drove Derek barmy. He was moody and bad-tempered all the time. This was a man who seemed unable to bond with his own flesh and blood. Based on that, how would a new guy – one who wasn't even biologically related – find affection for Ruby and Mo?'

'If that man was kind, caring and in love with you, then he would.'

'Hm,' I frowned. 'Unfortunately, there isn't anyone like that on the horizon.'

'Keep scanning it,' said Gabe. 'You might be surprised.'

'I don't think so,' I sighed, my mouth quirking downwards.

I didn't want to find another man. And even if I did, I wouldn't know where to look. At the local pub? Or the supermarket? Trawl the aisles hunting for a man holding a wire basket that contained a microwave meal for one? Or go on some online app, like Sadie Farrell had done. She'd been lucky finding her perfect match in Jack. But some dating websites gave women nightmare experiences. And anyway, I'd already found a man who – as Gabe put it – made my heart sing. He was sitting right opposite me.

*Oh my God, you're finally admitting it.*

Bloody hell, I thought you'd disappeared for the night.

*I'm back!*

And now I'm mentally pressing the delete button on your voice. Bye-eeeeee!

'Why are you suddenly looking sad?' asked Gabe.

'Was I? Sorry.' I consciously lifted the corners of my mouth and flashed him a grin. 'Anyway, never mind trying to pair me off with someone. Tell me all about this lady you've met.'

'What do you want to know?' he said, looking amused.

'The romantic bit,' I said dreamily. 'Women love a bit of romance.'

'There hasn't been any.'

'Well you can't have a relationship without romance,' I pointed out.

'But there is no relationship,' he protested. 'I told you I'd met someone. However, the person in question has no idea how I feel.'

'What… not even the slightest scooby-do?'

'Is that Mo talk for *clue*?'

I smiled at the mention of my granddaughter.

'I guess so. At least tell me the basics about this lady.'

Gabe took a sip of his coffee and, for a moment, considered.

'Well, I think she has a very generous heart. She strikes me as someone who will do anything for anyone while expecting nothing back in return. I suspect she's the sort of person who, once in a relationship, will give her partner a stable, loving, and peaceful environment.'

'Like Heather did?' I asked. 'Sorry, that was a bit thoughtless mentioning your wife.'

'It's fine,' Gabe assured. 'And no. Not like Heather. I loved Heather, but her energy was chaotic. Whereas this lady…' He looked pensive for a moment. 'I've seen a feisty side to her, but mostly she's a serene soul.'

'That's good,' I said.

Who couldn't use a bit of serenity? Indeed, where was my Angel of Tranquillity when I needed her – or him? Lately my sole visitor had been The Angel of Havoc.

'She's also' – Gabe continued – 'determined, sensitive and very beautiful.'

'I was wondering when you'd stop gushing about her characteristic traits and tell me what she looked like. How old is she?'

'About your age.'

'You surprise me. Why not go for someone younger? Especially when you want children.'

'*Did* want children,' Gabe corrected. 'That ship has sailed.'

'Really? You could do a U-turn. I'm sure you could have your pick of younger women with excellent childbearing hips. Girls who would be totally up for having your babies.'

'But that's no longer what I want. Anyway, I'd rather take my chances with this lady.'

'How on earth are you going to do that if you don't make your feelings known to her?'

'Maybe one day I will.'

I drained my coffee.

'Well, if you want my advice, you'll get a move on. After all, if this female is as incredible as you make her out to be' – *ouch, that sounded so bitchy, Wendy* – 'then you should pull your finger out before she gets snapped up by someone else.'

'I'll bear that in mind,' said Gabe, eyeing me over the rim of his cup.

'Good.'

Yes, jolly good. Jolly, jolly, jolly bloody good.

# Chapter Forty-Seven

The restaurant presented their bill just after midnight. Gabe snatched it up, refusing to let me pay my share.

'You're making me feel awkward,' I complained.

That said, I'd fleetingly caught a glimpse of the total, and the figure had given me heart palpitations.

'Absolutely not,' he said, waving away my protestations. 'I invited you out. Therefore, it's my tab.'

'Oh dear,' I fretted. 'How can I repay you?'

*Careful with the wording, Wendy! And whatever you do, NO asking him back to yours for a coffee. It could be misconstrued as a "take me I'm yours" scenario. Apart from anything else, you don't want to end up sexually frustrated if he declined.*

Cheers for that. Anyway, Ruby and Mo are at home. I'd hardly risk the pair of them wandering into the lounge while Gabe and I have a nightcap in our birthday suits – *your* insinuation, not mine!

At the thought of Gabe, perched on my sofa, stark bollock-naked, I had a violent hot flush. Were his pecs really as defined as my imagination seemed to think? And were those thigh muscles truly as toned as my mind's eye wanted to believe?

'I'll tell you how you can repay me,' said Gabe, interrupting my thoughts, which had been on the cusp of turning pornographic. 'Buy me a coffee sometime.'

'Sure,' I said eagerly. 'How about Saturday?'

'*This* Saturday?' said Gabe, looking startled.

*Try not to sound so desperately keen, Wendy. The guy was simply giving you some dignity over a stonking bill that you hadn't a hope in paying.*

'Only if you're not doing anything,' I said, hastily back-peddling. I belatedly attempted nonchalance. 'I mean, if you have plans for – you know – trying to see this lady you like, then I'll totally understand and–'

'Noooo,' said Gabe quickly. 'Not at all. Not yet anyway. She's… on ice. For now. Saturday would be great. I'm doing damn all else anyway. Usually, I go to the office and crack on with dictation. Annabelle's Monday morning expression is akin to a slapped arse. Mind you, I can't really blame the girl. Her desk is loaded up with files before she's even taken her coat off.' He smiled ruefully. 'Anyway, It's either work or a thirty-mile bike ride. I can do that on Sunday instead. I'd much prefer to let you buy me that coffee. Honest.'

I inwardly sighed with happiness.

'That's a date then.'

*No, it's not a date, Wendy.*

Oh God.

'I mean–'

'Yes, it's a date,' said Gabe. 'Where shall I meet you?'

'Well, I usually walk William on Saturday mornings, but afterwards I always go to the Bluebell Café and treat my–'

'Would this be William Beagle?' Gabe interrupted.

'Er…' Oh heck. Gabe didn't have the happiest memories of this particular canine client. ''Fraid so,' I confessed.

'Just to show I have no hard feelings about Mr Beagle, what about I keep you company and walk with you too?'

'Oh,' I said, taken aback. 'Well, that would be lovely.'

*Lovely?*

Oh for…

'I mean, yes, if you want to,' I said, feigning casualness. 'Be warned though. I take him to Trosley Country Park. At this time of year, it can be very muddy.'

'I know the place, and a bit of mud doesn't bother me. I have hiking boots.'

'Okay. Well, if you're up for it, then it would be nice to have some company.'

*That's better. Be reserved. Play it cool. He's not interested in you, remember? He's interested in Mysterious Lady. But as she's not on the scene – for now – there's nothing to stop you enjoying his companionship. And for goodness' sake, Wendy, don't let him know you're so excited that you're counting the days off on your fingers.*

'Good,' he smiled. 'I'm already looking forward to it.'

'R-Right,' I quavered, trying not to vibrate with joy.

'Shall we?' he said.

Gabe pushed back his chair, indicating we leave the restaurant.

Outside, it was bitterly cold. We stood on the pavement for a moment, pulling up collars against a stiff wind. The breeze lifted my hair, instantly turning my earlobes to ice-cubes.

Hands in respective pockets, we walked side by side back to Gabe's office carpark. He waited alongside me while I held out the zapper and popped Betty's central locking. Suddenly I felt hideously awkward.

'It's been a lovely evening,' I said politely. 'Thank you.'

'The pleasure was all mine, Wendy,' said Gabe, rather formally.

He made no attempt to remove his hands from his pockets to draw me into his arms, and I felt faintly disappointed.

'Well, goodnight then,' I chirped, opening the driver's door.

'Drive carefully,' he said, before moving forward and briefly brushing his lips against my cheek.

It was the most platonic of kisses. Nonetheless it set off a series of explosions in both my brain and heart.

When I finally arrived home and let myself into a dark and silent house, I could still feel the heat on my cheek where his mouth had touched.

## Chapter Forty-Eight

I crept along the darkened hallway and made my way into the kitchen, intent on grabbing a glass of water to take upstairs to bed. As my hand felt along the wall for the light switch, the lamp on the nearby dresser came on, startling me.

'Aye, aye,' said Ruby. 'And what time do you call this, Mother?'

I clutched my heart with one hand and clung onto the door frame with the other.

'For heaven's sake, Rubes. I thought you were in bed. You've just aged me by about ten years.'

My daughter grinned and sat back down at the kitchen table. A mug of something frothy was steaming away in front of her.

'Sorry,' she apologised. 'I've not long since managed to get Mo off to sleep. She's been an absolute nightmare this evening. The neighbours must love us. Not. She's been screaming the house down, thanks to another tooth coming through. A big one, by the looks of things. Her little gums look so pink and sore. I came downstairs to make myself a hot chocolate and wind down.'

She tossed her phone to one side. It occurred to me that she'd been talking to someone. I wondered who.

'I was on FaceTime,' she said, as if reading my thoughts.

'Anyone interesting?'

'Maybe,' she said carelessly.

'Tell me more,' I said, flopping down at the table opposite her.

'No.' She shook her head. 'I don't want to jinx it. Anyway, I'd rather hear about *your* new love interest.'

'Don't be daft,' I spluttered.

'Hm. Is it normal to have a meeting with your *solicitor*' – she emphasised – 'at gone midnight? Anyway, would you like one of these?' My daughter nodded at her hot chocolate.

'That would be lovely,' I said, glad to get off the subject of what I'd been doing and who with.

Ruby stood up and reached for the washed-up saucepan she'd left on the drainer.

'I got your note,' she said, filling the pan with milk and popping it on the stove to heat. 'I'm all ears by the way, and not dropping the topic. Tell me about your evening with the handsome lawyer.'

'How do you know I spent it with him and not Kelly?' I deflected.

'Because I rang Kelly earlier to see if you were with her.'

'Ah. Miss Smarty Pants, eh!'

'Just call me Miss Marple. Obviously, I put two and two together and deduced that your "meeting" for legal advice had run into considerable overtime.' She added chocolate powder to a mug and eyed me speculatively. 'Am I right or am I right?'

'You are an excellent detective,' I smiled. 'Gabe took me

out to dinner.'

'I see,' she said, her voice taking on a teasing tone. 'And did he kiss you goodnight, too?'

'Rubes, what is this? A police interrogation?'

'Ho-hum. I observe that my mother wants to discontinue this line of questioning.'

She placed the cup of hot chocolate in front of me and sat back down.

'C'*mon*,' she wheedled. 'Tell me all about it.'

'There's nothing to tell,' I protested. 'Gabe gave me some probate advice. Then my stomach rumbled loudly, and he said he was going to have some dinner and asked if I'd like to join him. Words to that effect, anyway. I simply kept him company.'

'It is now quarter to one in the morning,' she pointed out. 'He must have been bloomin' good company for you to be out until this hour.'

'Yes, he was,' I agreed. 'But before you jump to any further conclusions, Detective Pepper Anderson–'

'Who?'

'Sorry – that one is before your time. As I was saying, before you jump to conclusions, we discussed probate matters, and then simply spent the rest of the evening chatting.'

'As all good solicitors do with their clients,' she said wryly.

'He's not interested in me.'

'How do you know?'

'Because he told me so.'

'Charming,' Ruby tutted. 'How the heck did that little gem of info creep into the convo?'

'Somewhere around the topic of our respective demised exes,' I shrugged. 'He let it be known that he has met someone, but that it is very early days. Apart from anything else, Rubes' – I softened my voice – 'your dad isn't yet six feet under. It would hardly be fitting for me to step out with someone new, would it?'

She gave a snort of laughter.

'Step out. Is that what your generation say?'

'You know what I mean.' I rolled my eyes. 'Apart from anything else, I wouldn't want the population of Little Waterlow gossiping behind their hands about me.'

'Why not?' She gave me an old-fashioned look. 'They're already talking about you because of Dad's antics, so where is the harm in giving them something else to chunter about?'

I took a sip of my hot chocolate and considered.

'Maybe they'll talk about me anyway because, when I walk William Beagle this Saturday, Gabe will be keeping me company.'

'Is that so?' Ruby raised her eyebrows speculatively.

'There's absolutely no romance to it,' I quickly added. 'It's only because he insisted on paying the bill at the restaurant – which was humungous, by the way – so I said I'd buy him a coffee to say thank you.'

'And throw in a free walk with William Beagle,' she winked. 'Go for it, Mum.'

'Honestly, Rubes, there's noth–'

'Shhh,' she said, putting her finger to her lips and

standing up. 'Not another word. I'm going to bed. Sweet dreams.' She stooped to kiss my cheek. 'Although I have a feeling yours will be,' she chuckled, before sweeping out of the kitchen.

It was only after Ruby had gone that I noticed she'd left her phone behind. It suddenly lit up in the gloom with a text. There was no name against the upside-down number display, but the message was clear to read.

*Night, babe. Love you xxxxx*

# Chapter Forty-Nine

I stared at the message until the phone switched to dark mode and the words disappeared.

Who was this mystery man? Whatever romance my daughter was enjoying, it was clearly hotting up if the chap in question was declaring his love.

I was tempted to go through Ruby's phone, but two things stopped me.

First, it would have been morally wrong.

Second – and more honestly – I didn't know her passcode.

*You mean you WOULD have been nosy if you'd had that passcode?*

I'm just curious. That's all.

*Shame on you.*

Look, would you stop berating me? I'm not touching the flipping thing, okay! I totally get where you're coming from. After all, I wouldn't appreciate Ruby going through my phone. Not that there's anything titivating to read.

*Not true. You have messages from Kelly logging all her knee-trembling supermarket encounters with Steve.*

Hardly X-rated stuff. Now if you don't mind, I'm going to bed.

I drained my cup, then washed it up and left it to airdry upside down on the drainer. Leaving Ruby's phone exactly where she'd left it, I switched off the lamp and tiptoed upstairs.

When I finally lay back against the pillows, there were an awful lot of thoughts going round in my head. Someone had declared their love for my daughter, yet I didn't even know the person's name. And Gabe was smitten with some woman but hadn't wanted to reveal *her* name. Secrets. Why did people always have secrets?

Despite knowing that Gabe was out of bounds, I nonetheless found my thoughts returning to him. I lay there, my eyes closed, mentally back in the restaurant and dissecting every word of our earlier conversation. And despite knowing that he was hoping to start a romance with a mystery lady, I had no control over my subconscious. When sleep eventually claimed me, I found myself dreaming vividly.

I floated in the ether. It was a black void but filled with glittering stars and a glowing white moon. Naturally, Gabe was there too.

'Hello, Wendy,' he said. 'I've been waiting for you.'

I took his hand and gave him a dazzling smile. He led me out to a space where the stars seemed to shine extra brightly. And then, holding me tightly, he waltzed me through the universe.

# Chapter Fifty

The week progressed.

I finally caught up with notifying friends and relatives of Derek's demise. There was much sympathy for Ruby and me but, astonishingly, not one person said they were able to attend my husband's funeral which was due to take place at Eltham Crematorium on the last Monday in November.

'Such a long way for one to come,' apologised Susie, an old schoolfriend who – admittedly – I only kept in touch with these days via social media.

'Shame it's a weekday,' said another. 'I can't possibly get the time off work as my few remaining days of annual leave have been set aside for Christmas.'

Derek's parents were long gone, and his brother was in Australia.

'You're thousands of miles away, love,' said my brother-in-law. 'We'll raise a glass to him here in Melbourne.'

'Oh, darling, we can't,' said Mum when I FaceTimed her and Dad.

'Why ever not?' I said, aghast.

'We've both tested positive.'

'But you'll surely be okay by then,' I protested.

'Best not take any chances,' she said, giving an

unconvincing little cough. 'Come out to Spain after the funeral, sweetheart. Recuperate. It will do you good. Bring Ruby and Mo too. We'd love to see the three of you. Anyway, must go, darling. I'm absolutely whacked.'

As I ended the call, I realised there weren't going to be many attendees at Derek's send off. I'd been all set to book The Angel, Little Waterlow's largest pub. The place regularly hosted hen nights, birthday bashes and, on occasions, wakes. However, it seemed a bit pointless if I could count on two hands the number of people attending.

Oh well. Whoever turned up at the crematorium would instead be invited back to the house. Yes, there was nothing wrong with having a wake at home. I'd be sure to serve food that Derek had loved.

There was no shame in buying pre-made foods either. I would take a trip to Costco. Purchase some trays of party sandwiches with lots of different fillings. Derek had loved roast beef. Turkey and gammon were also popular choices. I'd throw in a nice quiche and lots of salady bits too. Maybe I should place some photographs of Derek near the buffet. It would give a point of conversation. Perhaps it would lead to us all trading stories about him – but preferably not of the bunny variety.

I had a sudden queasy moment imagining a couple of guests pausing by the tray of crudités.

'Oh, I say. Look, chopped carrots.'

'You'd have thought Wendy would have omitted those.'

'Whatever for? They were one of Derek's favourite foods.'

'I suppose. After all, he was part-rabbit.'

I made a mental note to stick to Pringles and a dip.

# Chapter Fifty-One

By the time Saturday rolled around I was almost beside myself with excitement at seeing Gabe again.

Ruby passed me in the hallway, Mo on her hip. She watched me carefully as I sat on the second stair, lacing up my hiking boots.

'You seem very buoyant this morning, Mother.'

'And why shouldn't I be? After all, it's a beautiful day outside.'

I nodded at the view beyond the hall's window. Harsh cold light showcased some ominous looking grey clouds. My daughter gave me an incredulous look.

'Are you mad? I don't know what the temperature is out there, but I'd hazard it's somewhere between bloomin' chilly and bloody freezing.'

'Bluddy freezin',' Mo repeated.

Ruby and I froze and stared at each other.

'That's right, darling,' Ruby cooed. '*Freezing*. Clever girl.'

I carried on lacing up.

'It's not cold if you wrap up sensibly.' I pointed to my rollneck sweater. Underneath was a thermal t-shirt for extra warmth. 'Right.' I stood up. 'I'm off to walk William Beagle.'

'Ah, yes.' Ruby put Mo down and folded her arms across her chest. 'I remember now. You're also meeting a certain sexy solicitor for "coffee".'

'Cawfee,' Mo repeated, also folding her arms across her chest.

'Honestly, just look at the two of you,' I said, laughing. 'My daughter with her Mini Me soaking up every word and mimicking Mummy's body language. Watch out, Rubes. In a few years' time you might be getting the third degree from young Mo here about who *you're* having coffee with. Or' – I added slyly – 'do you want to enlarge upon the young man you're *already* having coffee with?'

Ruby quickly unfolded her arms and scooped up Mo again.

'There's nothing to tell,' she said, her tone deliberately vague.

'Really?' I said, volleying back an enquiring look of my own.

'As I said the other day, I'd rather not jinx it by talking about it.'

I pulled my Barbour off the banister rail and gave her a frank look.

'Sharing info about your new romance won't jinx anything, Rubes,' I said, posting my arms into my coat.

'There's a lot at stake,' she said, suddenly very serious.

'Such as?' I asked, zipping up the jacket.

'His family for starters,' she said cautiously. 'I'm not sure they want someone like me being around their son.'

'It's nothing to do with them,' I bristled. I didn't like the idea of this boy's parents judging my precious daughter. Thinking her not good enough. 'What *is* important is how your young man feels about *you*. And hopefully he won't be spineless, like Simon was.'

'Mum, that's not fair. Simon was just a boy at the time.'

'That as may be, but he was still old enough to father a child.' I was aware that my tone was taking on some heat. 'And where is he now?'

'Leave it, Mum,' Ruby muttered. 'I don't want an argument.'

'Sorry, darling.' I gave her shoulder a quick squeeze. 'I just feel outraged that you were the one left to singlehandedly deal with the consequences.'

'But I wasn't on my own,' she protested. 'I had you.'

'I know, but that's not quite the same, is it? Since then, time has passed. It would have been nice if Simon had found the wherewithal to get in touch. But then again, maybe he will one day.'

'Maybe,' said Ruby quietly. 'Anyway, you enjoy your walk with William and Gabe.'

'Thanks,' I said, suddenly feeling bad at mentioning Simon. 'Tell you what. When I'm home again, do you fancy going out somewhere? I'll treat you and Mo to something nice.'

After all, there was no longer a husband keeping a stranglehold on our finances. Also, I'd since received a letter from the insurance company. They'd advised that Derek's life cover was currently being processed. Two hundred thousand pounds would be in my bank account within the next seven working days.

'What would you like to do?' I continued. 'Go girly shopping?'

'Shopping,' squeaked Mo, clapping her little hands together. 'Toys!'

'It's fine, Mum. You don't need to do that.'

'I want to,' I protested.

'That would be lovely, but some other time.'

'You're still offended,' I said, my mouth drooping.

'I'm not.' Now it was Ruby's turn to insist otherwise. '*Really* I'm not. I promise. It's just that' – she was looking cagey – 'I'm meeting… someone. A little later. With Mo.'

'*Ohhh*,' I breathed, as the dawn came up. My daughter was seeing the fella who had declared his love in the text message I'd seen. 'I'm so pleased for you.'

'Are you?'

'Of course,' I assured. 'I want my girl to be happy.'

'I am happy,' she said, rewarding me with a smile. 'He's… very special.'

I looked at my daughter's face. Anxious, yet hopeful. What could it be like being her? She'd missed out on so much fun. She'd made a monumental decision that had catapulted her into adulthood, and she had a beautiful baby girl to show for it. However, Mo had come at a huge emotional cost.

I leant forward and kissed her on the cheek.

'Have a lovely day, darling.'

‘Thanks, Mum.’ She gave me a watery smile. ‘And you.’

Turning, I let myself out of the house.

# Chapter Fifty-Two

When Betty chugged into Trosley's carpark, I saw that Gabe was already there. He was sitting in his BMW reading a newspaper.

As I parked alongside him, he folded up the paper and flashed me a grin. I returned it, hoping that my face wasn't lit up like Mo's when entering a sweetshop.

'Hi,' he said, as we clambered out of our vehicles at the same time.

'Hello,' I beamed. 'Let me get Sylvie and William out of the boot, then we'll be off.'

'I remember Sylvie,' said Gabe. He peered through Betty's rear window. 'She's the obedient one.'

'That's right.' I released the boot lid. 'Generally she's a good influence on William. Unless, of course, he's distracted by squirrels.'

'Then he will be in his element here. While I was waiting for you, I spotted several swinging through the trees like miniature Tarzans.'

The dogs leapt down from the boot. William immediately bounced over to Gabe, stretching up his jeaned legs for a muzzle rub. As Gabe obliged, I momentarily envied William. What was it like to touch those thighs while having your cheek caressed? My loins unexpectedly twanged, and I hastily batted the thought away.

'I'd better make a fuss of you too,' said Gabe.

For one ridiculous moment I thought he was talking to me, and felt slightly foolish when he instead stroked Sylvie's silky head.

*Put your tongue away, Wendy. You're emulating one of the dogs.*

I closed my mouth and gathered up trailing leads, before locking up Betty.

'Which way shall we go?' asked Gabe.

'Let's do the circular route. It's nice and straightforward, also relatively flat. We'll skip the goats' fields because the return path climbs a hill that's steeper than a skier's black run. When it's muddy – like now – it's hellishly slippery. I've always been wary about losing my footing and accidentally ending up cartwheeling down it.'

'We're on the North Downs and parts are incredibly steep,' Gabe acknowledged. We moved through the carpark and joined the main path and its starting point. 'Have you ever been skiing?'

He might as well have asked if I'd ever bungee-jumped from a bridge.

'No.' As we were now well away from the carpark, I let the dogs off their leads. 'That type of holiday was never taken in the Walker household. To be honest, it's not something I'd even have thought of trying.'

'Why not?'

I shrugged.

'We didn't always go on holiday and, if we did, Derek was the one who chose where we went.'

'So where did you end up?'

I felt a bit uncomfortable telling Gabe about Derek's stinginess.

'Well, before my parents moved to Spain, it was either a staycation at home or a week at Camber Sands. However, whenever we went away in the UK, the weather always seemed to conspire against us. It was usually cold, wet, and miserable. In the end, Derek said he wasn't wasting his hard-earned money staying at a seaside town where you couldn't eat fish and chips on the beach without getting soaked.'

'That's England for you,' Gabe laughed. 'It's always the Law of Sod that a heatwave comes along when you're back at work.'

'Exactly.'

'But you mentioned your parents living in Spain. Don't you sometimes go there?'

'Yes. When my folks left Blighty, Derek would jump at visiting them. That was because he didn't have to put his hand in his pocket and could take advantage of freeloading. All rather embarrassing. Especially on our last trip. Derek expansively suggested we all eat out. My parents accepted his invitation, believing he was showing some generosity after two weeks of free board and lodging. But when the bill came, Derek disappeared to the toilet. He was gone for a good twenty minutes. Unbeknownst to him, Dad told the waiter to come back when Derek had returned to the table. I can still remember Dad's expression. He looked livid at

Derek's tactic. His lips had turned into a tight, thin line. Mum was looking awkward and studying her fingernails, while I chatted inanely to Ruby. When Derek returned, he said, "Sorry to take so long, folks. Thanks for settling up, Nigel." Whereupon my father said, "Oh, but I haven't, dear boy. After all, you invited us out. Therefore, the cost on *this* occasion is yours." Derek went redder than the lobster he'd eaten and there was a bit of a row. On the flight home, Derek said he never wanted to see my parents again.'

'Oh dear,' said Gabe. His foot connected with a large stone, and he kicked it out the way. 'I know from personal experience that it's tricky when a spouse doesn't see eye to eye with one's parents.'

I glanced sideways at him.

'Was that the case with Heather and your folks?'

Gabe made a seesaw motion with one hand.

'My parents found Heather's assertiveness a little overbearing at times. They were also secretly disappointed that she wouldn't give them a grandchild. Not that they held that against her. But' – he paused for a moment to reflect – 'she didn't put herself out to get along with them. She was one of those people. Take me as I am.'

'In other words, like it or lump it,' I grinned.

'That too,' Gabe agreed. 'I loved my wife but was aware she wasn't everyone's cup of tea.'

'At least you loved each other,' I said wistfully.

We were silent for a moment.

'Do you regret not leaving Derek years ago?' said Gabe eventually.

'In hindsight, yes. But at the time it all boiled down to that old chestnut. The one about a child having two parents. I wanted Ruby to have her father around. Perhaps, deep down, I knew that if I'd divorced Derek years ago, he would have drifted away and failed to keep in touch with his daughter. I told myself that some contact was better than none.'

'It's amazing how many absent fathers do eventually disappear,' Gabe acknowledged. 'I've seen both sides thrash out access details. Then, when the parties have signed on the dotted line and a Court Order has been drawn up, suddenly the father meets a new ladylove and buggers off without a backward glance.'

'I can't imagine doing that,' I said, aghast at the very thought. Never see Ruby again? I'd rather die.

'There are plenty who do,' said Gabe. 'Are your parents coming to Derek's funeral?'

'No. Mum said she and Dad have tested positive and neither of them want to take any chances.'

'Fair enough.'

'I wasn't sure if it was an excuse, to be honest. There was no love lost between them.'

'I'm sure they would fly over to support their daughter if they could.'

My shoulders slumped. Of *course* they would. Why had I even doubted their loyalty? My eyes momentarily brimmed. Was I turning into some sort of mean-minded dowager destined to be miserable and drive people away with her wretched attitude? I hastily blinked, forcing away the unshed tears.

William had disappeared amongst the trees. Every now and again I could hear his joyful bark as he spotted a squirrel. I could see him in my mind's eye chasing a fluffy-tailed creature before it shot up a gnarled trunk, then disappeared into the safety of overhead branches. Sylvie remained at our heels, steadily keeping pace with us.

'So do you ski?' I asked, abruptly returning to the question Gabe had asked earlier.

'I do now. It was something I always wanted to try when Heather was alive, but she didn't like the idea. After she passed away, I decided to give it a go. I loved it. You should try it too.'

'Really? I'm not sure I fancy standing on the side of a mountain with a blizzard blowing in my face.'

Gabe laughed.

'I go in March. It's rare to get caught in a snowstorm. Italy is spectacular with its combination of sunshine and snow. Even if you're a rubbish skier, there's always the scenery to admire. Seeing a snowscape smothered in thousands of Christmas trees is staggeringly beautiful, especially when viewed aerially from a gondola. It's also incredibly invigorating spending the morning on the slopes, then the afternoon in a deckchair enjoying a beer at a mountain restaurant.'

'You make it sound magical,' I said wistfully. 'But I wouldn't know who to go with.'

Not Ruby. Her idea of a decent holiday was sun cream in one hand and ice cream in the other, while dangling her legs over the edge of her grandparents' swimming pool. Nor could I see Kelly being a companion. I could imagine her now shrieking, "You want me to freeze my tits off while sliding down a mountain with no brakes? Sorry, Wends. Count me out."

'If you're interested' – Gabe continued – 'I could let you know when I'm going, and you could join the crowd I go with.'

'That's very kind but…'

I could imagine the group. Likely all husbands and wives, or partners at the very least. I was aware that Gabe was single, but he'd mentioned a lady he had his eye on. Would she still be on ice by next March? Somehow, I doubted it.

'But what?' Gabe prompted.

'I couldn't impose. By March you might be with your new lady. I don't think she'd want me tagging along. Especially if everyone else is all partnered up. I'd be the spare person. There's nothing worse.'

'Aren't you rather jumping to conclusions?' Gabe laughed. 'I haven't even asked the lady out yet.'

'Well, when you do, she'll say yes.'

'What makes you say that?' he said carefully.

'Oh, come off it, Gabe,' I tutted. 'Why would she *not* say yes?'

He was suddenly looking at me intently.

'You tell me.'

'Because you're extremely good looking and excellent company.'

'Is that so?' he said quietly.

*Steady, Wendy. You're giving yourself away here. Don't make a fool of yourself.*

'Well honestly' – I spluttered as my body heated up with embarrassment – 'you must realise that you're something of a catch.'

I fiddled with the zipper of my coat, momentarily wishing I'd not worn a rollneck sweater *and* a thermal vest. I felt like I was about to melt all over the woodland floor.

'I mean, you're only in your forties,' I continued. 'No emotional baggage. A partner in your own law firm. If you popped up on a dating app, you'd have every heterosexual female ticking your box.'

'Thank you for the glowing reference,' he grinned. 'I might have to ask you to assist with my profile details should I ever join such a site.'

'You're welcome,' I said, unzipping my jacket in an attempt to cool down.

Gabe was grinning away. I noticed that he now had a spring in his step which hadn't been there before.

*Not surprising really. You've basically just told him he's God's gift to women.*

Oh shut up.

We walked on for a bit in companionable silence, then Gabe insisted on seeing the goats.

'We've passed that trail,' I said.

'Won't we come across the trail's end point further on?'

'Yes, but I wouldn't advocate taking the path in reverse.'

'Why not?'

'Because of that steep hill I mentioned earlier. Instead of

ascending the gradient, we'd be sliding down it.'

'Come on, Wendy,' he teased. 'Are you scared?'

'Er, yes,' I admitted. 'You've not seen this hill.'

'If it makes you feel safer, you can hold my hand.'

I pretended to think about it for, oooh, at least an entire second.

'Okay.'

*Are you mad? You'll both go arse over tit!*

Language, please!

Never mind the possibility of falling over and the pair of us breaking our necks. All I could think of was the offer of some handholding. Suddenly, I had a spring in my step too.

As we arrived at a turnstile that revealed the immediate sharp descent, I felt a frisson of excitement. The dogs were at our heels and furiously wagging their tails. For a moment we both stood there and simply observed. From this angle, the slope had an illusion of looking like a vertical wall. William gave a yap of excitement and took off, his back legs practically going over his ears as he hurtled downwards. Sylvie barked a "wait for me", then chased after William.

'Come on,' said Gabe, grabbing my hand.

The shockwaves from his touch nearly sent me into the stratosphere, but the tether of his handhold propelled me forward.

We instantly began slipping and sliding, moving into a half run, half crouch, as we extended our free hands to balance us. Putting the weight in our heels, we tightly clung onto each other as we sped after Sylvie and William. Every now and again, I thought we'd topple like skittles. Then, somehow, we'd right ourselves and charge on, all the while laughing aloud or – occasionally – shrieking at the top of our lungs.

The strong North Downs' wind acted as a buffer, pushing into our torsos, almost bending our spines into the hill as we continued our fast-paced descent, which was both terrifying and exhilarating.

Never had I felt so alive.

# Chapter Fifty-Three

When we eventually reached the bottom of the hill, the pair of us were out of breath and giggling like schoolkids who'd just played a game of *Dare*.

'I can tell you now, Wendy' – said Gabe, panting hard – 'that skiing is far less scary than what we just did.' He jerked his head at the mound behind us.

'I believe you,' I wheezed, desperately trying to catch my breath.

My heart was still racing from the adrenalin rush. It was also emulating the big bass drum in a brass band because Gabe was still holding my hand – which was just as well because suddenly my legs were turning to jelly. I had an overwhelming urge to sink down and park my backside on the cold wet earth.

'Are you okay?' puffed Gabe.

'Not sure,' I confessed, eyeballing the ground. There was a particularly tufty bit of grass at my feet which looked invitingly cushion-like. 'Can we sit for a moment?'

'Where?' said Gabe, looking about wildly. 'I don't see a handy bench anywhere.'

'The ground will do,' I muttered, as my knees started to buckle.

'Come on,' he said, releasing my hand and instead wrapping strong arms around me. 'Lean on me for a couple of minutes until your pins have stabilised.'

*MAYDAY, WENDY! MAYDAY! DO YOU READ ME?*

What?

*AN INVITATION TO SWOON HAS BEEN ISSUED. COMPLY IMMEDIATELY!*

Omigod, you're right.

'Thanks,' I muttered, collapsing against his chest. Oh, but that felt good. Mmm. I took advantage and snuggled into him, but my legs were still weak.

*STAY UPRIGHT!*

I'm trying!

*This is the perfect moment for him to hold you tight.*

He is! Omigod, it feels so wonderful. But my legs won't stop misbehaving.

'I've got you,' Gabe assured.

'Thank you,' I mumbled, aware that I was leaning on him heavily and must have felt like a dead weight.

'Put your arms around my neck and hold on tight,' he instructed.

I did as he said, still panting hard, but the breathlessness was nothing to do with racing down that hill.

'I shouldn't have made you do it,' said Gabe, sounding cross with himself.

'Nonsense,' I gasped. 'It was fun.'

'That as may be, but you've expended a bucketload of adrenalin in the process which has now left you debilitated.

It's the fight or flight thing. It sees you through the moment, but afterwards catches up. Now you're paying for it.'

'It's fine,' I assured, privately thinking that being draped over him was a price I didn't mind paying.

'How are you feeling now?' asked Gabe, as I continued to vibrate away.

'Still wobbly,' I replied truthfully. That said, I wasn't sure if the shakes were now due to my body trying to recalibrate after that adrenalin surge, or whether it was because I was up close and personal with Paul Newman's doppelgänger.

'No rush,' he assured. 'Hold on for another minute or two, and then we'll test out those legs.

'Okay,' I said, happily nuzzling into his neck and fighting the urge to kiss it. If I died right now, I'd die happy. I wondered if Ruby would think to have my tombstone etched accordingly:

*Wendy Walker*

*1974-2022*

*Vibrated her way into the Great Beyond*

Immediately, I thought of Derek's upcoming funeral. Shame he was being cremated because in that moment I had an epiphany about what would be appropriate on *his* tombstone.

*Here lies Derek Walker*

*Golfing enthusiast*

*At last a hole in one*

I shook my head. I didn't want to think about Derek. I only wanted to concentrate on Gabe and the "now" of this moment. It was blissful. I sighed with happiness. And was it my imagination, or were those arms hugging me tighter? I could feel Gabe's warm breath against my ear. A delicious shiver travelled down my spine. It would be the work of a moment to lean back slightly, look up at him enquiringly and whisper, "Do you want to kiss me?". But… wait. Something was happening. Gabe was… yes! He was pushing me back a little. And now… oh!… *he* was the one looking at *me*. His eyes were searching my face. Something was definitely going on here. As I met his gaze, it seemed as if the real world rapidly receded. The nearby barks of William and Sylvie simply faded away.

Suddenly the two of us were no longer standing in a bracing wind at the foot of a hill on the North Downs. Instead, we were in our own encapsulated bubble with red hearts pulsing outwards, filling the space around us.

'Wendy,' Gabe murmured.

'Yes?' I whispered.

'Can I–?'

*SECOND MAYDAY, WENDY. HE'S GOING TO ASK IF HE CAN KISS YOU.*

I know, so butt out.

'Yes,' I said, before Gabe could even finish his sentence.

I gave him a sultry look, then closed my eyes, anticipating a passionate lip lock.

*Any moment now!*

For God's sake, go away. Let me enjoy this in peace.

I kept my eyes tightly shut, trying not to tremble with anticipation, desperately willing my hands not shoot up to his head and pull it down to mine. He seemed to be taking an awfully long time to get on with it. What was the problem?

I opened my eyes again and was slightly perplexed to see him frowning at me.

'Is something wrong?' I whispered.

Oh no. Did I, perchance, have halitosis? I tried to remember what I'd eaten in the last twenty-four hours. Nothing with onion. Or garlic. Oh, wait. Those falafels last night had been rather spicy. Oh Lord, poor Gabe. While I'd been hoping to pucker up, he'd been subjected to me billowing all manner of herby seasoning over him.

'Can I–?' he repeated.

I stared at him. What? WHAT! Just spit it out, man.

'Let you go?' he concluded.

Let me go? Surely that was an entirely retrograde action. If he let me go, how would he be able to kiss me?

'It's just that' – his tone was apologetic – 'when William Beagle recently knocked me off my bike, I injured my shoulder. Your weight is reminding me that the rotator cuff isn't yet fully healed.'

# Chapter Fifty-Four

Forty-five minutes later Gabe and I were seated opposite each other outside The Bluebell Café.

I'd recovered from the mortification of my weight nearly pulling Gabe's arms out of their sockets, and the two of us were now sipping hot cappuccinos.

Sylvie was sitting with her head in Gabe's lap, silently willing his sausage sandwich to levitate off his plate and into her mouth. William Beagle was parked alongside me on the wooden bench, staring intently at my food. A six-inch saliva strand was dangling from one side of his muzzle.

'Thanks for this,' said Gabe, tucking in.

'You're very welcome.'

'I must confess that the walk – especially in this cold weather – has given me quite an appetite. That said, I can't cope with Sylvie making goo-goo eyes at me. I'm going to have to share with her.'

But as Gabe pulled a piece of crust from his sandwich, William completely lost the plot. He sprang to his feet, launched himself across the trestle table – dangly saliva and coffee cups flying – and snatched the morsel, swallowing it down before Sylvie could claim it.

'WILLIAM!' I roared, as milky liquid puddled across the

table's surface.

The little beagle immediately began slurping up the spilt coffee, tail wagging furiously.

'My fault,' said Gabe, attempting to mop up with some flimsy paper serviettes.

But William was having none of it and lapped even faster. He looked like a video on fast-forward. Gabe jumped to his feet.

'I completely forgot about this breed being obsessed with food. Let me replace our cappuccinos. Back in a jiffy.'

'No, I'll do it,' I protested, getting to my feet.

William instantly took advantage of my momentary distraction and hurled himself at my plate. In a trice he'd gobbled up the rest of my food, then lunged forward again, this time snatching up the remainder of Gabe's uneaten sandwich. William gave me a naughty look as he endeavoured to cram everything down his oesophagus as fast as possible, just in case his dog walking companion dared to open his jaw to reclaim some bread. Sylvie, meanwhile, was looking outraged at not getting anything at all.

'Oh dear,' I said in dismay. William had scoffed our brunch in a matter of seconds. 'I'll get us two more sausage sandwiches as well.'

'Absolutely not,' said Gabe. He leant across the table and pushed me back down. 'You've already forked out once. You're not doing it a second time. And you, young man' – he pointed a finger at William – 'will sit over there, tied up to the fence, and keep your thieving chops to yourself.'

Gabe lifted William off the table and walked him over to

a low post-and-rail affair, looping his lead around the top of the fence.

'Right, Mister. Your punishment is to sit and watch us eat our food. You can dribble away to kingdom come because you're not having another scrap. Do you hear?'

I snorted behind my hand. Gabe seemed unaware that he was talking to William as if he were a wayward child. I liked him even more for it. It was exactly the sort of thing I did – but usually when nobody was listening.

'Won't be a mo,' said Gabe. He flashed a smile that instantly caused my heart to somersault. 'And as Sylvie missed out, I'm going to buy a sausage sandwich for her too.'

'She'll love that,' I grinned.

As Gabe strode off like a man on a mission, I watched him go, lust no doubt shining in my eyes. Not that it mattered because he couldn't see me studying his beautifully shaped bum. It was definitely a very well-defined derriere. Very… grabbable.

I steepled my elbows on the tabletop, resting my chin in my hands as I continued to watch him, unobserved. He was now smiling at the lady behind the counter and – I didn't think I was imagining it – she appeared to be giving him an appreciative once over before scribbling down the order on her notepad.

I sighed wistfully. What must it be like to turn heads wherever you went? For that was what Gabe was. A head turner. And he appealed to all ages. His secretary was only in her twenties and had cosily informed me she "wouldn't say no" if Gabe crooked a finger her way. Then there were his army of female clients only too happy to treat him like Tom Jones, and metaphorically throw their knickers at him.

Annabelle had also recently confided that one of Gabe's clients, in her early sixties no less, had made it abundantly clear she was up for bedroom games. "She barged into his office while I was returning files to the cabinet. She didn't see me lurking in the corner, and I heard everything. She was sporting a newly lifted face and was dosed up to the eyeballs on HRT. She didn't bandy her words and came straight to the point, offering him two grand in cash if he spent the afternoon in bed with her."

'A penny for them?' said a familiar voice.

I looked up and saw Kelly standing there with Alfie at her heels.

'Hello,' I said in surprise. 'Have you finished your walk or are you about to start?'

'About to start, but Alfie can wait a few minutes. I tried to get hold of you earlier. I thought you might be walking today, but you didn't pick up.'

I frowned.

'Really?' I reached for my phone and peered at it. 'Oh, silly me. I had it on silent.' I flicked the ringer's side switch.

'I've copped a load of your companion,' Kelly said. She gave me a smutty look. 'Now I know why you didn't invite me to join you this morning.'

I rolled my eyes.

'Don't be daft. You weren't deliberately excluded. I simply owed my solicitor a coffee. Do you want to join us?'

'I wouldn't dream of intruding.' Kelly gave me a sly

smile. 'And since when did solicitors have coffee with clients unless it was in a boardroom? I take my hat off to you, Wends. Quick work.'

'It's not what you think,' I tutted. 'Truly it isn't.'

'Don't give me that.' Now she was the one rolling her eyes. 'I was quietly observing you before coming over, and your eyes were glued to that guy's backside.'

'Well it's a lovely bottom,' I protested. 'There's no harm in looking.'

'It's not just his botty that's lovely either,' she grinned. 'The whole package is extremely easy on the eye.'

'Yes,' I agreed. 'Gabe is a very attractive man. So now that we've established that, shall we move on to a different topic of conversation?'

'I'm happy to stick with him being the main subject matter,' she winked. 'At least, until he comes out of the café.'

'Which will be at any moment,' I pointed out. 'So, do you want a coffee with us, or not? Make up your mind quickly, while he's still got the server's attention.'

'Nooooo.' She shook her head. 'I'll crack on walking Alfie. Meanwhile, I've left Henry pushing the vacuum around, and then he's taking me out to lunch in West Malling.'

'Blimey,' I said, blowing out my cheeks. Henry doing housework? And then wining and dining Kelly? 'I detect things are going well in the reconciliation department.'

She gave a happy sigh.

'You betcha. Right now, Henry can't do enough for me. We've fallen madly in love with each other, all over again.

Isn't that slightly bizarre, after so many years of marriage?'

'Not at all. Sometimes it takes a blip to make one realise what we are in danger of losing.'

'True words,' she agreed. 'Oh look. Your handsome solicitor is returning. I'll make myself scarce.'

'Stay,' I urged. 'Say hello.'

'Another time,' she said, quickly gathering up Alfie's lead. 'But ring me if you have any juicy details to share.'

'He's my *solicitor*,' I stressed.

'Yes, and I suppose my uncle has tits, right?'

'Erm, I think you meant to say that if my aunt had balls, she'd be my uncle.'

'That too,' she twinkled, before smartly walking off.

# Chapter Fifty-Five

William was very vocal while Gabe and I settled down to Take Two of dining al fresco, especially when he saw Sylvie tucking into her sausage sandwich.

The sun broke through and, for a while, sitting outside became a pleasant experience. After an hour or so, a bank of dark clouds crept across the sky, blocking out the light. Within minutes my fingers and toes began to get cold. Gabe's nose took on a pink tinge, indicating that he too was feeling the drop in temperature.

'Come on,' he said, stacking our empty plates and cups back on the tray. 'You look frozen. I'll take this lot back inside the café, then we'd better get ourselves home to warm up.'

The way he'd phrased that, for just one moment, had made it sound like we lived together. That we would shortly be heading back to *our* home. Sit in front of *our* cosy fire. And maybe watch an old film together on *our* telly.

I momentarily allowed myself a little daydream. There was Gabe. Shoes off. Feet up on a pouffe. And there was me, snuggling into his side. His arm was around my shoulders. His fingers were playing with a tendril of my hair. Now he was turning his head just enough to drop a kiss on my forehead before saying–

'Excuse me.'

I looked up to see Mabel Plaistow bearing down on me. Oh, for heaven's sake. Why was I always bumping into her these days? She looked miffed.

'Good morning, Mabel,' I said politely.

'It's the afternoon now,' she said tartly.

'Is everything okay?' I asked, psyching myself up to hear what she so clearly wanted to get off her chest.

'That dog,' she said, pointing a quivering finger at William. 'I don't know 'ow yer can sit there oblivious to the racket he's makin'.'

'I think it's called *zoning out*, Mabel,' I said, smiling sweetly. 'After a while, one simply doesn't hear it.'

'Well bully for you,' she huffed. 'Me an' Fred can hear 'im from inside the café an' 'e's playin' 'avoc with Fred's new 'earin' aids.'

'Sorry,' I apologised, getting to my feet. I picked up Sylvie's lead. 'We're going now. William won't be bothering you any further.'

'Thank gawd for that,' she snapped.

'Hello,' said Gabe, reappearing. 'Are you one of Wendy's friends?'

'Potentially 'er new neighbour,' said Mabel, looking slightly taken aback at the vision standing before her. 'An' who are you?'

'Gabe.' He held out a hand to Mabel. 'I'm a friend of Wendy's too. Pleased to meet you.'

*Did you hear that, Wendy? You're a friend. Not a client.*

*Progress!*

'And you,' said Mabel, instantly charmed as Gabe took her gnarled hand in his.

'I caught what you were saying to Wendy about William. Sorry he's given your husband a headache.'

'Oooh, that's orright, luv,' she said, beaming away. 'William is no bovver really. It's jus' Fred who was moanin'. Silly old fart. Last year 'e was depressed an' miserable. This year 'e's turned 'imself around. Now 'e's miserable an' depressed,' she guffawed. 'Anyways, luv' – she gave me a sly look – 'I 'eard yer was seein' a new man. Now I've met 'im, I want to be the first to wish yer all the best.'

'Oh, Mabel, that's simply not true. Gabe is–'

'Look after 'im now and 'ave many 'appy years togevver like me an' my Fred. An' don't listen to the rumour mongers,' she said firmly. 'You tell 'em what to do with their gossip an' judgements.'

'We will,' said Gabe smoothly, keeping a straight face. 'Come on, darling.' He offered me his elbow, rendering me speechless in the process. 'Let's get you back to the warmth of the car.'

Dumbstruck, I linked my arm through Gabe's.

'That's it,' Mabel cackled. 'You look after each other. You've a good'un there, Wendy, so 'ang on ter 'im.'

She waddled off looking mighty pleased with herself.

'What on earth–?' I spluttered, puce in the face.

'Just playing along with her,' said Gabe, his eyes twinkling with mischief.

'But she's going to tell Fred that we're an item. It will be the talk of Little Waterlow by this evening.'

'Does it matter?' Gabe shrugged. 'People around here are always gossiping. If it isn't the truth, then they simply make stuff up. So why worry about it? Meanwhile, you take Sylvie and I'll take William. No, don't let go of my arm, Wendy. Mabel is still watching.'

As he led me over to the post-and-rail where William was impatiently waiting, I glanced at Gabe in bemusement.

'Are you enjoying this?'

'I haven't had so much fun in years,' he chuckled.

As we strolled arm in arm back to the carpark, any onlooker would have thought we were just another couple out walking their dogs. The effect upon me was cataclysmic. Every cell in my body was glowing, just like Oxford Street's Christmas lights, and my feet no longer seemed to be touching the ground. As I floated to a standstill by Betty, Gabe finally released me.

I unlocked the boot and let the dogs jump inside.

'Thanks for keeping me company today,' I said. I suddenly felt a bit awkward after both the darling endearment and the public display of affection. I reminded myself it hadn't been real and had simply been Gabe hamming it up for Mabel's benefit. 'And sorry about William's earlier behaviour.'

'I've enjoyed every moment,' Gabe assured. He was standing very close to me. 'I can honestly say I've never had a day like it.'

'Hopefully in a good way?' I gave him a rueful grin.

'Absolutely,' Gabe assured. 'When Annabelle asks on

Monday morning how my weekend was, I can put my hand on my heart and truthfully tell her that I raced down a sheer drop, tightly held a hyperventilating female, had my brunch stolen by a pillaging beagle, and was congratulated by a stranger on my upcoming nuptials.'

'Sorry about that bit,' I said, blushing furiously.

'Couldn't matter less,' Gabe laughed. 'The way news travels around these parts, it might even reach Ms Gucci Belt. That will save me a lot of hassle.'

'Bonus,' I agreed.

'And I meant every word. I really have enjoyed today.' He gave me one of his blowtorch smiles and I tried not to visibly palpitate. 'You've been lovely company.'

'You too,' I said shyly.

And then he leant forward and kissed my cheek. Was it my imagination or did his lips linger for a moment longer than was necessary?

'Take care of yourself, Wendy.'

'I will,' I nodded, playing for time, hoping he might suggest we repeat today again, and very soon.

'If you need any further help with legal matters, you know where I am.'

Oh. That didn't sound indicative of another get-together. My euphoria began to slowly sink down to my hiking boots. Okay. There wasn't going to be any further invitation to spend time together.

*He already has a romantic interest elsewhere, Wendy. Had you forgotten?*

Yes, I had. Thanks for reminding me.

Gabe turned and pointed the zapper at his car. Seconds later he was tucking himself behind the steering wheel and pulling the driver's door shut. I did likewise, sliding into Betty's driving seat.

As our respective engines roared into life, I slowly followed his BMW out of the carpark, over the sleeping policemen, and back to the main road. At the junction, Gabe signalled left, and I indicated right.

And then we went our separate ways.

# Chapter Fifty-Six

Sadie was already home when I dropped William and Sylvie back.

'I'm so sorry to hear about Derek,' she said, giving me a big hug. 'How are you coping?' she asked, her voice concerned as she released me.

'I'm doing fine. Honest,' I assured. 'Remember, we were getting divorced anyway, so the love had gone. However, I won't deny that his sudden departure from this planet was one heck of a shock.'

*Especially given the circumstances.*

Wow, you just keep on giving with those reminders today!

'I'll bet,' said Sadie with feeling.

Her tone left me in no doubt that she'd heard the rumours, and knew that Derek had travelled through the tunnel of light via Coco's cottage.

'But life goes on' – I said brightly – 'and all those other hackneyed clichés.'

'It does,' she nodded. 'So now that you're officially a singleton again, I guess you won't be wanting to buy Clover Cottage.'

'On the contrary,' I said quickly.

'Really?' she said, looking puzzled.

'I want a fresh start. A new home where I can make new memories.'

'Okay,' she said, looking pleased.

'Let me get the funeral out of the way, and then I'll put my house on the market. Hopefully it will sell quickly, and the conveyancing can begin soon afterwards. I already have a solicitor in mind,' I assured.

Well, Gabe wasn't a conveyancer, but I knew he could point me in the right direction. Gardener and Stewart Solicitors had a property department. My heart did a few skippy beats at the prospect of knowing there was a valid reason to get in touch with him again.

'There's no rush at all,' Sadie assured.

'Thank you. Anyway, never mind me,' I said, changing the subject. 'How's you and Little Bump?'

It had only been a couple of weeks since I'd last seen Sadie, but there was now a hint of swelling around her midriff.

'Little Bump is doing just fine. I had a scan earlier this week, and look!' She walked across the kitchen and picked up a snapshot that had been tucked behind the condiment jars. 'I put it here for safekeeping. Here is Baby Farrell.'

'Oh my goodness.' I took the pic from her and peered at the alienlike image. 'This is incredible. When I was pregnant with Ruby, the scan result was so grainy. Yours is as clear as a photograph. Technology is a marvellous thing.'

'It certainly is,' she agreed, retrieving the image, and smiling fondly at it.

‘Right,’ I said, jingling the car keys in my coat pocket. ‘I’d best be off and leave you in peace.’

‘It’s always lovely to see you, Wendy.’ She gave me another quick hug. ‘I hope all goes well at the funeral. Do you want to skip helping me with the dogs for now? You must have a lot on your plate.’

‘Good heavens no!’ I protested. ‘William, Sylvie, et al are currently keeping me sane.’

‘As long as you’re sure.’

‘I am.’

We said our goodbyes and I headed back to Betty. Starting up the engine, I pointed the bonnet towards home… blissfully unaware that a shock was waiting.

# Chapter Fifty-Seven

I unlaced my hiking boots, pulling them off my feet outside the house. The shoes were caked in mud, and I didn't want mess trekking inside.

Hopping about in my stockinged feet, I picked up the boots with one hand and, with the other, stuck the key in the lock.

Stepping into the hallway, the first thing that caught my eye was a pair of size ten trainers parked on the doormat. I stared at them in surprise. Ruby was always complaining about her big feet, but it was unlikely her toes had suddenly sprouted an extra inch.

Quietly shutting the door behind me, I became aware of the noise coming from the kitchen. Seemingly, a lot of merriment was going on. Mo was making delicious chuckling sounds and Ruby was snorting with laughter.

'I think I've found yoooo!' sang a male voice. 'BOO!'

Cue peals of laughter from Mo.

'More, more,' said my granddaughter, squealing with joy.

'Okay, if you insist. Are you ready? Steady? GO! Oh nooo. Where's Mo gone?' said the stranger. 'I can't find her anywhere. Is she in the larder? No. Is she hiding under the table? No. Where can she be?'

'Can't find meee!' shrieked Mo joyfully.

'I'm going to have to look much harder. Let me see. Is she under the sink?' I could hear cupboard doors opening and closing. 'Is she *in* the sink?' I could now hear the washing up bowl being lifted and then set down again. 'Nope. I think I'm going to have to give up. Mo's hiding place is too hard to find.'

More squeals of excitement from Mo.

'But… wait,' said the stranger. 'What's this? I can see a tea towel. And why is the tea towel moving all by itself?'

Mo sounded thoroughly overexcited at the possibility of her hiding place being discovered.

I crept along the hall, pausing in the kitchen doorway just in time to see Mo, a dishcloth over her face, crouching down in one corner. She was clearly under the impression that if she couldn't see anyone, then they couldn't see her.

Ruby was sitting at the kitchen table fondly looking on, clearly delighted at the happy scene taking place before her. A man was playing peekaboo with Mo, but as he wasn't facing me, I couldn't see what he looked like.

'What's this in the corner?' said the guy.

Mo snorted and clapped two little hands over her mouth.

'Is it a wobbly jelly? Is it a fluffy cat? Is it a teddy bear?' He leant in and whipped the cloth off her face. 'It's my little Mo,' he crowed, scooping her into his arms.

*My* little Mo?

The tea towel fell to the floor as the stranger whirled my granddaughter round and round, Mo all the while shrieking her delight. My presence went unobserved, until the stranger set her down again on the floor. Mo suddenly caught sight of me.

'Nanna,' she beamed, toddling towards me. 'Nanna home.'

'Hello, sweetheart,' I said, picking her up for a cuddle.

Startled, the guy turned, and Ruby sprang to her feet.

'Mum,' said Ruby, struggling to recover her composure. She came over and pecked me on the cheek. 'I didn't hear you come in.'

'Probably because Mo was hooting with laughter.'

I dredged up a smile, even though I wanted to grimace. What was this lad doing here? You see, I knew him, although it had been a long time since our paths had crossed.

He'd grown several inches. That explained the size ten shoes on the doormat. His hair was shorter now, and trendily styled. His shoulders had broadened too. There was no sign of the spotty boy who'd once stood alongside my daughter in this same room. He, looking grey and terrified, while Ruby – in her school uniform – had brandished a pregnancy test, defiantly announcing she would soon become a mother.

'Hello, Wendy,' said Simon.

# Chapter Fifty-Eight

'Hello,' I said to Simon. My smile remained in place, but I was on my guard.

'How are you?' he asked.

'Surprised,' I said honestly. 'It's not every day your granddaughter's absent father turns up in your kitchen.'

'Mum,' Ruby muttered.

I caught the warning in her tone. She didn't want me making a stink about Simon's reappearance. Equally, she was letting me know that if I shot from the hip with some acid comments, then she would defend Simon all the way.

I sighed. The last thing I wanted was a row, and certainly not in front of Mo.

My mind suddenly flipped back to last Monday night. More specifically, returning home after being out with Gabe. It had been late. Ruby had been in the kitchen, hot chocolate in one hand, phone in the other. Eventually she'd gone upstairs to bed, accidentally leaving her mobile behind. Seconds later, the screen had lit up with a message.

*Night, babe. Love you xxxxx*

She'd mentioned previously that "someone" had made an entrance in her life but had refused to elaborate on the grounds of possibly jinxing things. I'd assumed this “someone” to be a fellow student at her college. But I’d been wrong. It had been Simon. It was Simon who she’d been talking to on Monday night, and it was Simon who’d signed off his goodnight message with a declaration of love. So, what the heck was going on here?

‘I can tell from the look on your face that there’s a million questions going around in your head,’ said Simon.

‘You can say that again,’ I agreed. I moved over to the kitchen table and pulled out a chair. Sitting down, I suddenly felt incredibly weary. ‘How about the pair of you give me an update?’

Simon pulled out a chair and seated himself alongside me.

‘Where do you want me to start?’

Ruby scooped up Mo and strapped her into the highchair. Mo looked momentarily mutinous until Ruby waved a packet of chocolate biscuits at her. No doubt an apple would have been better for her tiny teeth, but Ruby and I both knew that if we wanted to talk without interruption, then we’d have to employ the help of Mr McVitie.

‘The beginning is always a good starting point,’ I said. ‘Or maybe, to be brutally frank, the end. After all, that’s the last time we saw you.’

Simon blew out his cheeks.

‘I understand you’re angry, Wendy.’

‘I’m not,’ I protested. ‘I’m simply sad. You left Ruby pregnant and in an emotional mess.’

‘Wendy, I think what you need to remember is that I

was still a minor myself. I was living with my parents, very much under their thumb, and having to comply with their rules. They insisted I had no responsibility for Mo because, legally, I was still a child myself. Apparently, a father under the age of eighteen cannot be declared an adult. At the time, Ruby was still a minor too. A guardian should have been given temporary responsibility.'

I paled at his words. We hadn't taken any sort of legal route through all the emotional mess at the time. Partly out of ignorance. Partly out of fear. And partly because I'd automatically stepped in to support my daughter – as any mother surely would for their rebellious but terrified child.

'But now' – Simon continued – 'I'm older. Wiser. Also, I've left home. There is no parental control holding me back, and I'm finally able to acknowledge Mo. That's something I always wanted to do, but my parents wouldn't allow it. And now, because I *can* acknowledge my daughter, that officially makes me Mo's father. I'm now legally an adult. I no longer need to make an application to the court asking for official responsibility. Incidentally, that was something else I wanted to do, except my parents thwarted me.'

'Oh,' was all I managed to say.

'They feared legal consequences at the time. When they announced that the family home had been sold and we were off to Scotland, I didn't want to go. But they told me I didn't have a choice. It was either go with them or have the police after me. Wendy, I was a frightened school kid. So, I did their bidding. But I never forgot about Ruby or our unborn child. I got my head down at the new school. Studied hard.

Then, rather than go to university, I secured an apprenticeship in the Greater London area. Once I was back in the South of England and off the parental leash, I found digs and then re-established contact with Ruby. I was so relieved you hadn't all moved away. Meanwhile, I have thrown myself into work. It will take me three to four years to get qualified. Financially, I'm only just about making ends meet, but I don't care. The end result will be worth it. When I'm finally an accountant, I'll be able to properly support Mo – and Ruby too, for that matter. You see, more than anything, Wendy, I want to be with Ruby and our daughter. I always knew Ruby was the girl for me, even when we were schoolkids.'

I looked at his face. It was earnest. Kind too. Simon had always been a nice boy, but *boy* had been the word. He hadn't been one of the kids who'd had endless detentions at school. Nor had he roamed the streets in a gang. He'd never vandalised bus stop shelters or the last of the public phone boxes leaving broken glass, cider cans and an absent dial tone. Instead, he'd unwittingly found himself in a different kind of trouble. But now the boy had become a man. Even though he was still only eighteen, he had a maturity about him beyond his years.

Simon leant across the table and took my daughter's hand.

'I want to be with Ruby and Mo. I know I'm going to have to play a lengthy waiting game for that to happen, but I don't care.'

'Nor me,' Ruby murmured, her fingers curling around

Simon's hand.

For a moment the three of us were silent and the only sound was that of Mo sucking soggy crumbs from her chocolatey fingers.

'I'm pleased for you both,' I said eventually. 'I mean it. I think you've been very brave breaking away from your parents, Simon, and no doubt risking their disapproval. Do they know you're in touch with Ruby?'

'They do now.'

'And how do they feel about it?'

'They're coming to terms with it.'

'And what do they think about you living down south again? After all, you're a long way from Scotland.'

'Ah, I didn't finish that bit of my story. My folks never really settled there. They're currently in the process of moving back down here again. Mum and Dad recently exchanged contracts on a house in Brighton. They'll be relocating just in time for Christmas. Also' – he looked bashful for a moment – 'they are now desperate to meet their granddaughter.'

'Right,' I said, trying not to feel a little sour about that. A small part of me – the resentful bit – thought it was all very well belatedly waving olive branches. It would have been nice if they'd financially contributed in some small way upon the birth of their own flesh and blood. Baby equipment wasn't cheap – even when second-hand.

*Don't dwell upon it, Wendy.*

No?

*You can't change the past. The future, however, is a*

*blank page waiting to be written upon.*

Right. I guess Simon's parents were running scared too.

*Obviously.*

'My goodness,' I said, blowing out my cheeks. 'This is such a lot to get my head around. It's all been happening, hasn't it? For everyone.'

'So it would seem,' Simon agreed. 'Um… I'm not asking to move in, Wendy, but I'd like your permission for me to visit Ruby and Mo every weekend and, if possible, stay overnight? It would be so great to have some family time together.'

I looked at him for a moment. A germ of a thought was brewing in my head.

'Actually,' I said. 'I have a better idea.'

# Chapter Fifty-Nine

As the last Monday in November rolled around, Ruby, Simon and I waited for the funeral car to arrive at the family home.

Much had happened since I'd first walked in on Mo's daddy playing peekaboo with her in the kitchen. The biggest change was that, in the last few days, the house I'd raised my child in had become an empty nest.

When Derek's life cover funds had finally cleared, I'd wasted no time in returning to Gabe's firm, asking for the conveyancing to begin on Clover Cottage. Gabe had also organised an interim rental agreement between Sadie and me, bridging the gap between now and completion.

Gabe had seemed delighted to see me. He'd introduced me to a colleague in the Property Department then, as his lunch hour approached, insisted on taking me out for a coffee and a sandwich just off the high street.

I'd enjoyed his company, and he'd twinkled at me in a most charming way with gentle teasing and lots of banter. I'd even kidded myself that things had gotten slightly flirty. But later, I'd accepted that it had been an overactive imagination on my part, because he hadn't been in touch since.

*That's because he was acting for you professionally, not*

*romantically.*

Quite.

As soon as Sadie had handed over the keys to Clover Cottage, in turn I'd passed them on to Ruby.

'Here you are,' I'd said. 'The key to your new home. We'll review things after Simon has qualified. For now, live there together as a family and concentrate on getting your hairdressing business up and running.'

Workmen had already been in to convert the little outbuilding Sadie had originally used for her pottery business. It was now a small salon for Ruby to work out of.

'Thank you so much, Mum,' Ruby had said, fighting back tears and flinging her arms around me.

'I don't know what to say' – Simon had looked suitably gobsmacked – 'other than a massive thank you.'

'And that's all that needs to be said,' I'd assured.

Meanwhile, I was still in the marital home. By myself. Hating every moment. Dithering about what to do next. Sell it and downsize? Somehow, I couldn't see myself being in a one-bedroomed flat. I'd spent so much time in my head living at Clover Cottage that I could no longer envisage being anywhere else other than a charming stone building with oak beams and whitewashed walls.

*Wait and see. Sometimes the universe has a surprise in store.*

I think I've had enough surprises lately, thanks very much.

'All right, Mum?' said Ruby.

She touched my arm, bringing me back to the present. It

was time to say goodbye to Derek.

'Yes, darling. I'm fine. And you?'

'I'm okay,' Ruby said, although she looked very pale dressed in black. It wasn't her colour.

I was wearing a simple navy skirt and matching jacket. Simon was kitted out in the suit he wore to work. He'd borrowed a black tie from a colleague. The house seemed even quieter without Mo. Earlier, Simon had taken her to crèche. No doubt my darling granddaughter was currently elbow deep in a rainbow of finger paint, thankfully oblivious to the sombre mood at home.

Ruby and I had been up bright and early overseeing the buffet for the wake. I had no idea who would be coming back to the house, but it was better to be prepared for a small army, just in case.

'Derek's here,' said Simon.

A shiny black car pulled up outside. The coffin, with its single wreath of flowers, lay within. A matching vehicle parked closely behind.

Quietly, we made our way outside. The driver held open the door to the limo that would follow behind the hearse.

The funeral director, for a short distance, led the cortege on foot. Then we properly set off, but at a respectfully sedate pace. Upon arrival at the crematorium, the funeral director once again briefly led the cortege on foot.

As the limousines came to a stop, I was surprised to see a sizeable crowd. Puzzled, I peered at the unfamiliar faces. Had Derek really known all these people? I mentally reviewed the buffet waiting at home and told myself not to panic. There should just about be enough food. Then realisation dawned. There were two chapels. It was the second chapel that had attracted this substantial gathering. These people were nothing to do with Derek.

We were directed into the first chapel where one mourner was already in situ. I blanched.

'Oh God.'

Coco Rowbotham was sitting in the front row.

'How very *dare* she,' hissed Ruby, outraged. 'Simon, see that tarty looking woman in the leopard print dress with a matching bow in her hair? Tell her to move. She's nothing to do with us.'

'Who is she?' asked Simon, confused.

'The local bike,' snarled Ruby, anger colouring her pale cheeks.

'Um, right,' said Simon, looking bewildered. 'I think I understand.'

He moved off to whisper in Coco's shell-like. I pretended not to noticc her as Simon subsequently guided Coco to a seat further back. Silently, Ruby and I moved into the front row. We kept our eyes trained ahead as Derek's coffin was carried in and placed on the catafalque.

I had rather ambitiously printed twenty copies of the Order of Service. Most lay upon empty chairs. I did a quick recce of the chapel and my spirits lifted as I spotted Kelly and Henry coming in. They were closely followed by Derek's pal Bill, and his wife Jackie.

Kelly discreetly waved, instantly making a beeline for the row behind me.

'All right, sweetie?' she stage-whispered. She stooped to drop a kiss on my cheek, leaving half her lipstick behind in the process.

'All the better for seeing you,' I murmured.

Henry gave me a comforting squeeze on the shoulder.

'We're here for you, love,' he said.

'Yes,' Kelly agreed. '*You.*'

I noted her emphasis on that last word. They'd come to support me. Not wave bye-bye to Derek.

'I just want to say, Wendy' – Henry's face was earnest – 'if you ever need a man to change a lightbulb or provide a screw, just say the word.'

'Careful how you phrase things, darling,' Kelly snorted, nudging Henry in the ribs with her elbow.

Ruby turned to see what all the suppressed giggling was about.

'Hey, guys,' she said to Kelly and Henry.

'Hello, sweetheart,' Kelly whispered back, just as Simon returned to his seat and sat down next to Ruby. 'Oooh, is this your young man?'

My bestie had never been backward in coming forward.

'Yes,' Ruby beamed. 'Simon, meet Kelly and Henry.'

'Pleased to meet you,' said Simon, getting to his feet. Turning to face them, he shook their hands. 'We have met, but it was a long time ago.'

'I thought you looked familiar,' said Kelly, her brow furrowing. 'Where have I seen you before?'

'He's Mo's daddy,' said Ruby helpfully, visibly swelling with pride. 'And yes, we're together.'

'That's the best news I've heard in a long time.' Kelly clapped her hands together in delight. 'I'm chuffed to bits for the pair of you.'

I was distracted from listening to any more of their conversation by a hovering Bill and Jackie, who both wanted to say hello before the service began.

'Lovely to see you, Wendy, although I wish the circumstances were different,' said Bill.

'Likewise,' said Jackie.

'I know, and thank you for coming,' I murmured back.

Bill looked genuinely upset. My heart went out to him as he and Jackie made their way to a row on the other side of the aisle.

I glanced quickly around the chapel to see who else was here.

Coco was sitting on her own a few rows back but... wait. I groaned. Oh no. Mabel and Bill Plaistow were creaking their way down the aisle.

Mabel's eyes swivelled over to Coco. Her wrinkled old face twisted into an expression that indicated a bad smell had passed under her nose. Coco, sensing someone glaring at her, volleyed back a supercilious look of her own. Mabel promptly stuck her nose in the air and slid into the same row as Bill and Jackie. Her gaze fell upon me.

'Cooee, Wendy, luv. Hope yer don't mind us bein' 'ere. Fred an' me never like to miss a funeral when someone local kicks the bucket. We're 'ere ter pay our respects, even though your Derek was a bit of a prat.'

'Er, thanks, Mabel,' I said, as Kelly snorted again.

'Blimey,' she whispered. 'Trust that old biddy to say it how it is. She'll be gate-crashing the wake next and–'

Anything else Kelly had been about to say was drowned out by the music starting up. As the chapel filled with the notes of AC/DC's *Highway to Hell,* Ruby and I looked at each other in horror.

The music abruptly stopped. There was a shocked silence.

'So sorry,' said the funeral celebrant. 'That track is for the next service. The deceased had a sense of humour.'

As the notes of *Here I Am, Lord* then proceeded to fill the chapel, I was suddenly consumed with a dangerous need to giggle over the earlier musical mistake. It was likely due to nerves. Nonetheless it wasn't appropriate for a bereaved wife to be seen splitting her sides at her husband's funeral.

Quickly, I pulled a pack of tissues from my handbag. Burying my face in the Kleenex, I hoped that anyone seeing my shaking shoulders would construe it as an outpouring of grief.

# Chapter Sixty

As Kelly had predicted, Fred and Mabel Plaistow came to the wake.

They hoovered up platefuls of sandwiches, scoffed several slices of cake and left late afternoon with various serviette-wrapped goodies stashed in Mabel's oversized handbag.

'What a dreadful woman,' said Kelly, as the Plaistows finally tottered off, sated and stocked up for the next day or two.

'She's not that bad,' I protested.

'She's not that good either,' said Kelly. 'Thank heavens you escaped having her as your neighbour at Clover Cottage.'

'Instead Simon and I have the Plaistows as our neighbours,' Ruby grinned. She now had Mo on her hip, after Simon had nipped out and collected their daughter from crèche. 'And I can confirm' – Ruby continued – 'that Mabel is the biggest Nosy Parker in Little Waterlow. Simon keeps teasing Mabel with fake gossip.'

'I hope you're not winding Mabel up,' I said.

'Noooo,' Simon assured. He held up his hands, revealing crossed fingers.

'Ha!' Ruby harrumphed. 'Simon told Mabel he'd seen an

alligator in our garden.'

'No, I didn't,' he protested. 'I told her I'd seen an alligator *in a vest* in the garden.'

'And she believed you?' I asked.

'Totally,' said Simon, straight-faced. 'Mabel rushed off, all in a flap. I could hear her yelling to Fred to ring the police. I called after her, "Don't panic. It turned out to be an *in-vest*-igator."'

'Simon!' I said, trying not to laugh. 'Please remember that Mabel is an old lady. Nobody wants her keeling over from fright.'

'That's not all he's done,' said Ruby, trying and failing to look reproving. 'Tell Mum about the deodorant stick.'

Simon flashed me a naughty look.

'I was in the bathroom and the window was open. I could hear Mabel outside in the garden berating Fred. She was standing over him as he swept up leaves, and giving him hell for missing a few. When she went back inside the house, Fred let rip with a noisy fart. He growled under his breath, "That's for you, you nagging witch." Whereupon Mabel stuck her head out the back door and shouted, "I heard that. Are you trying to stink out the entire neighbourhood?" So, quick as a flash, I grabbed an unused deodorant stick from the bathroom cupboard, nipped out, and rattled their door knocker. When Mabel answered, I presented it to her and said, "Here, give this to Fred as a present. The instructions say *remove cap and push up bottom.* He'll have trouble walking, but when he next farts it'll smell lovely."'

'And she believed him,' said Ruby incredulously.

'Just think' – said Simon innocently – 'it might even catch on. Can you imagine our Mabel at The Angel's next quiz night telling everyone about Fred's new-fangled fart fragrance?'

Kelly and Henry roared, and I joined in. It felt good to laugh, especially when things had ended so tensely at Derek's funeral.

As the service had reached its crux and the curtains in front of the coffin had slowly closed, there had been a shift in mood. Whatever I'd thought of Derek by the end of our marriage, the fact remained that he had been my husband. This was potentially the lowest and saddest part of the ceremony. Those present had to face the inevitable. Having celebrated the deceased's life, it was time to say that final farewell. Bill had been quietly weeping, but Coco had sobbed the loudest and longest.

After the committal, she'd sought me out. She'd asked if she could come back to the house and "raise a glass to my lover". Perhaps if she hadn't phrased it quite that way, I wouldn't have minded. After all, money doesn't change hands with true lovers, whether dressing as rabbits or not. But I'd been instantly reminded that my husband had been this woman's client – and so had Ruby, who'd overheard the whole conversation. My daughter had been livid. Coldly, Ruby had told Coco exactly where to go – along the lines of disappearing down a bunny warren.

But that was then, and this was now. I watched on fondly as Simon continued to keep the mood light, telling more and more outrageous stories about the Plaistows and how Mabel had asked what Mo's name was short for. Simon had solemnly told her that Ruby had been heavily influenced by celebrities and named their daughter Mo-the-lawn.

Eventually everyone peeled away. Ruby wanted to stay and help me wash up, but I was adamant she didn't need to.

Later, feeling very alone, I climbed the stairs to have a late-night bubble bath. Right now, all I wanted to do was soak away the tensions of the day.

It was strange not having Ruby here. Not hearing her singing to Mo. I was missing my daughter for sure, but oh how I also missed the daily cuddles with my little Moonbeam Fairy.

Just as I was climbing into bed, my phoned dinged with a text. Expecting it to be Ruby – who, since moving into Clover Cottage, had taken to texting me goodnight – I was instead surprised to see the message from someone entirely unexpected.

*Hope today went well. Was thinking of you. Gabe xx*

I immediately replied.

*Thank you. It went better than expected xx*

I didn't know what else to say. It wasn't a riveting reply but, then again, his text had simply been one of support.

There was no further message by way of response. Sighing, I switched off the light.

## Chapter Sixty-One

As December got underway, Ruby had telephoned insisting I drive over to Clover Cottage and help her and Simon put up a Christmas tree.

'You need to keep busy, Mum,' she'd insisted.

'I *am* keeping busy,' I'd assured.

Nonetheless, I'd jumped into Betty with alacrity, secretly delighted to be included in a family gathering.

A jolly-holly-time was had by all as we'd banded together dressing a real tree. Predictably, Mo had eaten some of the chocolate decorations along the way. The heady scent of pine needles had mingled with the delicious smells of home baking. Afterwards, we'd settled down by the woodburning stove and supped Simon's mulled wine and Ruby's homemade mince pies.

Meanwhile, Simon's parents had moved into their new home and had invited Simon, Ruby, and Mo to spend part of the festive period in Brighton. This included Christmas Day. Ruby was adamant they'd be back home again on Boxing Day morning.

'It will be lovely to spend time with Simon's folks, but we want you to be with us on the twenty-sixth, Mum. I'll be doing a high tea spread for the four of us.'

'No, don't do that,' I'd protested. 'Come to me instead. You'll be tired and wanting to get sorted out after being away. It's no bother to do a nice meal for us all over at mine.'

'The thing is' – Ruby had chosen her words carefully – 'don't take this the wrong way, Mum, but we'd prefer to have you at Clover Cottage. You see, I know you're not bothering with a tree or decorations this year. And that's fine. Totally your choice. But I want Mo to have the magic of Christmas all around her.' She'd waved a hand at the sumptuously decorated tree in the corner, and fairy lights twinkling prettily in the alcove. 'So please, tell me you'll join us on Boxing Day?'

In a flash, I'd understood where my daughter was coming from. Who wanted a turkey dinner in a house where not even a piece of tinsel was on display?

'Of course I will,' I'd assured. 'And thank you for asking me.'

Ruby had smiled her gratitude.

'That's settled then. Meanwhile, I'm sure you'll have a lovely time at Kelly's on Christmas Day.'

I'd not been able to look Ruby in the eye as I'd replied.

'Yes, absolutely.'

Ruby had frowned.

'You *are* going, aren't you?'

I'd sighed.

'Look, Rubes. Kelly invited me over, but I really don't want to intrude on her time with Henry and their boys.'

'But you can't spend Christmas Day all alone,' she'd cried.

'Of course I can! Honestly, it couldn't matter less, darling. I would much prefer that. I have an overwhelming need to… recalibrate. If you know what I mean. And then I'll have the joy of celebrating with the three of you on the twenty-sixth.'

'In that case we won't open our presents until we're all together,' Ruby had declared. 'After all, in the old days, that was when gifts were traditionally exchanged.'

'Lovely,' I'd said, glad that we'd come to an agreement.

Back home again, I'd then sat down with my address book and finally written out the annual Christmas cards and Round Robin letter.

Initially wondering what to pen had been quite challenging. A mischievous part of me had wanted to be truthful.

*Dear Kate and Paul*

*This year's card is just from me. Sadly, Derek recently passed away. He always used to say that he'd like to depart this world while having sex, and his wish was granted. At least you know it was quick.*

Instead I'd sighed and settled down to write something more traditional.

Meanwhile, the family home had been valued, photographed, and was now on the market. The estate agent, a plump balding man in his fifties, had been pleased to see a complete lack of decorations within.

'There's nothing worse than a brochure featuring a house with Christmas trees and tinsel when the month of December has given way to March,' he'd said. 'Prospective clients want to believe that everybody is after the house they're viewing – and we want them to believe that too,' he'd added.

'Oh, right. Well, your prospective viewers won't catch a whiff of pine needles in this house because I'm not bothering with decs this year,' I'd explained.

'Why is that?' he'd asked, intrigued. 'Are you a Jehovah Witness?' He'd paused to straighten a towel on the heated rail before pointing and clicking his camera. 'I heard that JWs don't celebrate the occasion.'

'No, it's nothing like that.'

'Oh? Don't tell me, you're an atheist,' he'd persisted, as we'd moved into Ruby's old room.

'Not at all,' I'd smiled. 'I don't particularly have any religious leanings, although I do believe in God.'

'Hmph,' he'd grunted. Pausing briefly to pull down the blind against white December light interfering with the camera, he'd adopted a pained expression. 'I have no time for bible bashers. Not after my wife turned into a religious nutter.' His lip had curled. 'Born Again Barbara. She ran off with a member of the congregation. They're out in Africa somewhere. Doing charity work apparently. She didn't even have the decency to tell me. Just upped and left without a word.'

'That's awful,' I'd said sympathetically. 'So how did you eventually track her down?'

'The vicar knew how distressed I was. He gave me her new mobile number. When I rang it, Barbara said she couldn't speak because she was in a missionary position.'

'Oh.'

'I wasn't sure if she meant overseeing a clean water project or lying back and-'

'Yes, yes I see,' I'd quickly interrupted.

'What about you?' he'd asked, as we'd eventually moved downstairs. 'Isn't Mr Walker partial to a Christmas tree?'

'My husband recently passed away.'

'Is that so?' He'd paused in the hallway, eyeing me speculatively. 'So, are you spending Christmas Day with family?'

'No,' I'd said, failing to read the signals. 'It will just be me, a sandwich and a Netflix binge.'

He'd handed me his business card.

'I'm finished here. The agency will be in touch. Meanwhile, my personal mobile number is under the agency's landline. Bottom left-hand corner. Ring me if you fancy sharing that sandwich. Although' – he'd waggled his eyebrows suggestively – 'there are better things to do than watch Netflix.'

He'd taken himself off to his car, leaving me so winded that I'd not had the breath to even wheeze goodbye.

When I'd told Kelly, she'd hooted with laughter.

'Welcome to the world of *Being Out There Again*. You'll soon be pursued all over the place. Good for you, Wends. It must have given your ego a lift, if nothing else.'

'Hardly. If he'd been a fit forty-something' – Gabe instantly sprang to mind – 'then maybe so. But not somebody who looked like Captain Mainwaring from *Dad's Army*.'

And then, two days before Christmas, I'd received a text from Gabe.

*Are you planning on walking a certain delinquent beagle any time soon? If so, I'd be happy to keep you company xx*

My heart had skipped several beats upon reading his message. The truth was, now that Ruby and Mo were in Brighton with Simon's folks, and Kelly was up to her armpits juggling visiting relatives, I was missing company. I didn't even have my four-legged clients to keep me busy. Their owners were either home for the holiday period, or had put their pooches in the back of the car and headed off to visit their own far flung kith and kin.

I'd tapped out a reply.

*I don't have any clients until the New Year. But if you're happy to go for that walk without any four-legged mayhem, then I'm free xx*

Gabe had texted back immediately.

*Tomorrow afternoon? Xx*

I'd frowned. That would be Christmas Eve.

*Aren't you busy? Seeing family, or something? Xx*

His reply had sent my skippy heartbeat into an erratic overdrive.

*I'm not seeing anyone – other than you (hopefully!) xx*

And so, joyfully, I'd agreed.

# Chapter Sixty-Two

It was with a sense of nervous anticipation that I drove to Trosley Country Park to meet Gabe.

Why, exactly, had he asked me to go for a walk with him?

*Why don't you ask him that question?*

Oh, hello. I wondered when you'd pipe up.

*I'm never far away.*

Evidently.

*So, as I was saying, ask him why he has sought you out for a walk.*

Okay. Oh heck. He's already here. Look. Over there. I'm feeling flustered.

*You look it. Try and be less William and more Sylvie.*

They're dogs. I'd rather be more, I dunno… Cameron Diaz.

*I know miracles happen at Christmas, but that's not going to be one of them.*

I unbuckled and got out of the car.

'Hi,' said Gabe, coming over. He made no attempt to hug me. Not that I was really expecting him to. Nor did he peck my cheek.

'How are you?' he asked.

'I'm good,' I replied.

Without my usual excess paraphernalia of dog leads, poo bags and canine water bottles, I suddenly didn't know what to do with my hands. My arms felt awkward and surplus to requirement, dangling inelegantly by my sides. I followed Gabe's body language and quickly stuffed them inside my pockets, even though they were already encased in woolly gloves against the cold.

'And you?' I added.

*I don't think Cameron Diaz would make such scintillating conversation, Wendy.*

Take your sarcasm and sod off.

Gabe paused before replying.

'I'm…' – he blew out his cheeks as if thinking whether to confide something – 'fine,' he eventually said. 'Shall we?' He jerked his head in the direction of the woods.

'Lead the way,' I smiled.

We walked across the almost empty carpark, then took the path that dipped down to the main tree-lined walkway.

'I can't believe how quiet this place is today,' I said, looking around.

'It's nice,' Gabe commented. 'Also, it suits my mood.'

'Oh?' I gave him a sideways look. 'What's up?'

'Nothing,' he assured. 'I simply meant that a large empty space can be very relaxing to wander through. It helps clear the mind – and mine has been overloaded these last few weeks.'

'Work?' I sympathised.

'My job is always fast paced, but I don't mind that. No,

my thoughts have been elsewhere. Wrestling with an entirely different matter.'

'Anything I can help with?'

'Maybe,' said Gabe, but he didn't enlarge. 'Fancy taking the path through the goats' field this time?'

'It will mean later scrabbling up that steep hill,' I reminded.

'Surely it will be less hair raising going up than the trip we took down,' he laughed.

'But I forgot to pack my crampons.'

'Me too. I guess we can always cling on to each other.'

'It's good to have a backup plan,' I grinned.

He flashed a smile back and I felt my spirits lifting. Oh goody. A spot of potential handholding might be coming up in the next thirty minutes or so. It didn't matter that it would be entirely innocent. I would take whatever was on offer.

*That's a bit desperate.*

Yes, okay, I'm desperate. Happy?

I cleared my throat, determined to get Gabe back on topic.

'So... er, what is it that I might be able to help you with?'

'It will keep,' said Gabe mysteriously.

Oh. How annoying. Especially as he'd piqued my curiosity.

'It was nice of you to suggest the walk,' I said.

'It was nice of you to accept,' he said casually.

*Yawn. Stop being wishy-washy and get to the frigging point!*

Give me a frigging chance!

I studied the ground for a moment, watching our feet moving forward in perfect synchronisation. Left. Right. Left. Right. Okay. Deep breath. Time to take the plunge.

'I must confess, Gabe, I was quite surprised to hear from you.'

'Really?'

'Well, yes. I mean, your colleague is handling the conveyancing on Clover Cottage. And you helped me with the probate matters, which is now all done and dusted.'

How did one say, "There was no need for us to ever see each other again – unless William Beagle and your bicycle happened to be on a second collision course."

'I hope you didn't mind me getting in touch,' he said matter-of-factly.

'Not at all.'

*Give him some encouragement, Wendy.*

What would Cameron Diaz say?

*I don't blooming know. Use your imagination!*

'Actually, I was delighted to hear from you,' I said boldly. I kept my gaze fixed ahead and willed my cheeks not to redden.

'Really?' he said, looking surprised. 'Why was that?'

*Yes, why was that?*

You're the mind reader. Why don't *you* tell me.

*Because this man is red hot in the looks department, and you have a crush on him bigger than Santa's Grotto. You've also had several erotic dreams starring Gabe Stewart in various stages of undress. Remember the last one? You bounced together on a waterbed the size of Wembley Stadium. And you know perfectly well that, right now, you'd like him to stop, pull you into his arms, lower his mouth to yours, and give your tongue a gymnastic workout.*

Would Cameron point all that out?

*I don't think so.*

'Because' – I squeaked as my voice involuntarily shot up an octave – 'our last walk together was such fun.'

*That is so LAME, Wendy.*

I know, I know. Can't you help me out?

Fortunately Gabe came to the rescue.

'Yes, it was fun,' he agreed. 'And the reason I texted you was–'

'Yes?' I asked breathlessly. Because you couldn't bear another day to go by without seeing me? Because you're mesmerised by my looks and fine line in witty repartee? Okay, not the witty repartee. I'm aware that's sorely lacking but–

'You were on my mind.'

'Really?' I gasped.

*Oh. My. God. You've been on his mind!*

I know!

'I left it for a few weeks because I wanted to give you some space after Derek's funeral.'

'No space was required. Honest. I've been fine.'

'Good. I simply wanted to check in and make sure there weren't any further matters the firm could assist with.'

'Oh,' I said, instantly deflating. This walk was nothing more than an out-of-office client meeting.

'After all, you've been our best customer this year. A divorce. Then probate matters. A rental agreement. Now the conveyancing. What can I help with next?' he bantered.

'Possibly a neighbour dispute with the Plaistows,' I said dryly. 'My future son-in-law delights in winding up Mabel and giving out false gossip. I'm not sure how chuffed she'll be when she discovers she's been spreading nonsense.'

Gabe laughed.

'It's good to know that you and your family will keep me in work.'

Having circumnavigated the goats' fields, we were now walking along a flat and winding footpath. We made small talk for a while. I mentioned that my house was devoid of a Christmas tree and updated Gabe about Ruby and Simon's reconciliation and how happy they were. As we approached the foot of the hill, I mentioned the estate agent's clumsy pass which made him chuckle.

'Are you really spending tomorrow alone?' he asked, suddenly looking concerned.

'Yes, and I'm fine with it. What about you?'

'I'm putting on my chef's hat and cooking at home.'

'Oh,' I said in surprise. Somehow, I couldn't see Gabe in the kitchen. 'How many do you have coming to Christmas dinner?'

'Two.'

'Only two?' I queried.

He gave me an old-fashioned look.

Ah. The mystery lady. The woman he'd been keeping on ice. Clearly there had been a development.

*Fuck.*

Do you have to say that word?

*Hey, it was YOU that was thinking it. I just repeated it.*

Do me a favour and go away.

'O-Oh, wow,' I stuttered, trying to dredge up some enthusiasm for him. 'You've made some progress with your lady.'

Gabe removed one hand from his pocket and made a see-saw motion.

'I'm so pleased for you,' I said, attempting sincerity.

'Thanks,' he smiled. 'Come on. It's time to see what we're made of and climb the hill. Ready?' He held out his hand.

I didn't hesitate and curled my fingers around his.

# Chapter Sixty-Three

By the time Gabe and I had completed our walk, the café had closed early due to a lack of customers.

He didn't suggest we find an alternative coffee shop. Or a cosy pub elsewhere. And despite it being on the tip of my tongue to suggest we do just that, unfortunately I lost my nerve.

'Well' – I chirped as we stood by our respective cars – 'Happy Christmas for tomorrow.'

'And you, Wendy,' he said quietly.

There was something about his tone that brought me up short. My breath inexplicably caught in my throat. I looked at him curiously and suddenly found myself in an intense eye-meet. The look went on and on, but he didn't say anything, and neither did I. Suddenly there seemed to be so many unsaid things going on between us. However, if you'd asked me to put in words what our respective thoughts were, I'd have been unable to do so.

He was the first to break the spell, leaning forward and giving me a perfunctory kiss on the cheek.

'See you later,' he said.

'Yes,' I murmured, before turning and pointing the zapper at Betty.

As I slid behind the steering wheel, I wondered why people said *see you later* when, most times, the phrase was entirely inappropriate. I mean, it was comparable to asking how long a piece of string was. Six inches or six feet? When people said *see you later* it sometimes meant next week, next month, or even next year.

With a sense of déjà vu, I followed behind Gabe's car. Slowly, our vehicles bounced over the sleeping policemen as we travelled towards the main road. Gabe signalled left, and I indicated right.

And once again we went our separate ways.

# Chapter Sixty-Four

Once home, I felt inexplicably at a loose end.

There was nothing to do. No hungry husband, daughter or granddaughter awaited. There wasn't even a cat to have a conversation with.

Sighing, I went upstairs. I'd have an early bath, change into my PJs, and then start my television binge a little earlier than previously planned.

By half past five, I'd drawn the curtains against the outside world. Armed with a cheese toastie and the remote control, I was just about to settle down when the doorbell rang. Pressing the remote's pause button, I cocked one ear, listening for carol singers.

An uncharitable part of me didn't want to be disturbed from my cosy snack-for-one in front of *The Holiday.* Well, if I couldn't *be* more Cameron, I could certainly *watch* her, along with the equally down-on-her-luck Kate Winslet. Even though I'd seen the film before, it was comforting to identify with two females swapping homes and subsequently falling in love with a couple of local guys.

I listened for a moment longer, but the air throbbed with silence. No sounds of *Good King Wenceslas* rang out nor any warbles of *Away in a Manger.* Choosing to ignore whoever it was, I pressed the play button again, taking care to turn down the volume so my guilty pleasure couldn't be overheard. Hopefully, whoever it was would get bored and go away.

I took an enormous bite of my toastie. Sighing contentedly, I ran my tongue over my lips, licking up a trail of warm butter running down my chin.

*Brrrr-inggggggg.*

Oh, for heaven's sake!

The bell then gave another long ring followed by three shorter intermittent ones.

Hastily swallowing, I rubbed the back of my hand across my greasy mouth and hastened out to the hall.

'Who is it?' I asked tentatively, unwilling to open the door.

No answer.

Terrific. No doubt some local kids were having a hoot, playing prank games before scarpering.

I peered through the spy hole, then blinked in confusion. There appeared to be a large Christmas tree on the doorstep.

'Who is it?' I repeated.

'Ho, ho, ho,' came the reply.

*It will be some local charity.*

Cosmic. Just when I thought I was going to have some peace and quiet.

*Grab your purse, then you can get rid of them.*

Good idea.

'Just a moment,' I called. 'I'll fetch some change.'

'No need,' said a muffled voice. 'Special delivery for Wendy Walker. All the way from the North Pole.'

'Very funny,' I said, putting the chain on the door before cautiously cracking it open. 'I don't want a Christmas tree, thanks very much. So, if you're trying to do a last-minute flog of supermarket stock that didn't sell then-'

'It's completely free,' the voice assured.

'Nothing in life is free,' I said waspishly.

I was now getting well and truly irritated. My cheese toastie was awaiting.

'Can I come in?' said the voice.

I gasped at the visitor's audacity.

'No, you flipping well c–'

The diatribe died on my lips as the tree swayed violently, before revealing the courier. Father Christmas, no less.

'Right,' I snapped. 'I'll have you know' – I ranted at the vast white beard and moustache – 'that you're spoiling my evening. If you're after festive good cheer, you've picked the wrong house.'

'Oh-dear-oh-dear-oh-dear,' said Father Christmas. 'I did try to pop by earlier, but one of the reindeer wouldn't co-operate.'

As if. I rolled my eyes.

'I'll also have you know that my cheese toastie is likely now stone cold.'

'Dasher, Dancer and Prancer are particularly partial to cold cheese toasties.'

'Very funny. You've also interrupted my movie night.'

'Oooh, I do love a movie night. What are you watching?'

'*The Holiday*, not that it's any of your business.'

'My favourite Christmas film,' Santa beamed.

His bright red, fur-lined hat accentuated a pair of ice-blue eyes. They were mischievously twinkling away.

I froze. Stared at them. Surely not.

'I have it on good authority' – Santa continued – 'that everyone in Little Waterlow has a Christmas tree, except for you.'

'That's right,' I whispered, suddenly unable to tear my gaze away from those eyes.

'So why don't you open the door and let Father Christmas fix that?'

'Er,' I hesitated. 'What about your reindeer?'

'Oh, don't worry about them. They're very patient creatures and don't mind waiting.'

'Um, right,' I mumbled. 'Just a moment.'

I shut the door. With trembling fingers, I removed the chain, before opening it again.

Moments later the pine tree was in the hallway shedding needles everywhere. Santa leant it against the wall, then turned to face me.

'Merry Christmas, Wendy.'

He pulled down his beard, revealing his identity.

'Merry Christmas,' I said faintly. 'Gabe, what on earth–?' I stared at him in bewilderment.

'I said I'd see you later and I always keep my promises.'

My eyes widened in surprise.

'I thought you meant *later.* You know, as in *later* later.'

'Or even *later today,*' he grinned.

'So what's with the outfit?' I said, recovering slightly.

'Wendy,' he said, suddenly serious. 'At the risk of making a bigger fool of myself than I already have, I wondered if we could spend the evening decorating this tree together. Then, tomorrow, would you do me the honour of sharing Christmas dinner with me?'

'W-What?' I stammered.

'You heard,' he said softly.

'B-But… whatever happened to your mystery lady? The one who, you know, you were keeping on ice.'

'That lady is you.'

'Me?' I gaped at him.

'Yes, you,' he said, putting his arms around me and pulling me into him.

'But it can't be,' I protested, as familiar electric shocks danced up and down my spine.

'It is,' he murmured. 'It was always you, but the timing wasn't right. And it *still* might not be right,' he added. 'But I'm prepared to take that chance.'

I stared at him in astonishment.

'Why me?' I whispered.

'Why not?'

'But you can have anyone. I mean *anyone*.'

'I could say the same of you,' he said tenderly. 'Darling Wendy. You have no idea how endearing or lovely you are. You captured my heart almost from the get-go.'

'Really?' I said, as a goofy grin spread across my face.

'Cross my heart. So, is that a yes to Christmas dinner with me tomorrow?'

I couldn't stop smiling.

'It is, but… can you cook?'

'Confession time. It's my secret passion. It's how I de-stress, along with the cycling. I'm also a big fan of Nigella Lawson. I also know for a fact that she has never ever said the words *orgasmically cosmic.*

'Ah,' I said, having the grace to blush. 'I guess the truth will always out.'

'You're right,' said Gabe, suddenly looking serious. 'And the truth of the matter is, Wendy, I'm head over heels in love with you.'

'Oh my goodness,' I whispered, gazing into those incredible ice-blue eyes. 'I love you too.'

As his mouth finally came down on mine, and wave after wave of joy crashed over me, I knew… just *knew*… that we were both speaking the truth.

Whatever would Ms Gucci Belt say?

THE END

# A Letter from Debbie

I'm not sure how this book got written. I wrote the words *Chapter One* on April Fool's Day and, boy, did life play a couple of hellish jokes.

The first was intensely private.

The second was when my ninety-one-year-old father took a tumble and broke his hip. My mother, afflicted with severe dementia, was unable to use the telephone to ring for an ambulance. Somehow, Mum found the wherewithal to open her front door and scream for help before her brain forgot why she was standing at the front door.

A big thank you to the unknown driver of an Abel & Cole vehicle who lifted my father into a chair while waiting for the ambulance.

The ripple effect of both events was traumatic and chaotic.

Consequently, disruption reigned throughout the entirety of writing this tale. There were many dark days when I felt too shocked by events to even write. Equally, there were other days when all I wanted to do was be with my fictional characters and "drop out" of the real world. All I can say is thank God for Wendy and her woes!

This is my seventeenth novel and sees a return to the

fictional village of Little Waterlow, which was the setting for my last three romcoms, *Daisy's Dilemma, Annie's Autumn Escape,* and *Sadie's Spring Surprise.* Little Waterlow is a small Kent village not dissimilar to my own stomping ground.

In *Sadie's Spring Surprise,* a small dog by the name of William Beagle is responsible for some serious matchmaking. As he was so well received by readers, I thought I'd bring him back in *Wendy's Winter Gift* and let him some work more of his mischievous magic. William Beagle is based upon my long departed old girl, Trudy Beagle, who was a crazy rescue dog with high energy and an obsession for food. It was a joy to remember her escapades once again as I wove William's antics between the pages.

I would like to say a huge thank you to fellow author and dog lover Rona Halsall for letting me use the story of her gorgeous girl, Maid, who disrupted a real-life marriage proposal. Maid is a crazy, beautiful rascal who also loves to wreck shoes and vacuum nozzles, and occasionally performs brain surgery on soft toys.

I love to write books that provide escapism and make a reader occasionally giggle. I hope this story will give readers a few smiles.

There are several people involved in getting a book "out there" and I want to thank them from the bottom of my heart.

Firstly, the brilliant Rebecca Emin of *Gingersnap Books*, who knows exactly what to do with machine code and is a formatting genius.

Secondly, the fabulous Cathy Helms of *Avalon Graphics*

for working her magic in transforming a rough sketch to a gorgeous book cover. Cathy always delivers exactly what I want and is a joy to work with.

Thirdly, the amazing Rachel Gilbey of *Rachel's Random Resources*, blog tour organiser extraordinaire. Immense gratitude also goes to each of the fantastic bloggers who took the time to read and review *Wendy's Winter Gift*. They are: *Tizi's Book Review; Comfychairandabook; Read & Tell Reviews; Books, Life and Everything; Ceri's Little Blog; Ginger Book Geek; Peacockbookreview; Books & Bubbles; Pickled Thoughts and Pinot; Bookshortie; Just Katherine; Little Miss Book Lover 87; Captured on Film; Staceywh_17; @webreakforbooks; onecreativeartist; School_librarian_loves_books; b for bookreview; Splashes Into Books; Tealeavesandbookleaves;* and finally, *Green Reads Books*.

Fourthly, the lovely Cindy Brouckaert for her sharp eyes when it comes to typos, missing words, and the like.

Finally, I want to thank you, my reader. Without you, there is no book. If you enjoyed reading *Wendy's Winter Gift*, I'd be over the moon if you wrote a review – just a quick one liner – on Amazon. It makes such a difference helping new readers discover one of my books for the first time.

Love Debbie xx

Enjoyed *Wendy's Winter Gift*?

Then you might also like *Stockings and Cellulite.*

Check out the first three chapters on the next page!

# Chapter One

'Happy New Year Simon.' I pecked my host's proffered cheek as a party popper whizzed over our heads. 'Absolutely fantastic party,' I lied.

'Thank you, Sandra.' He squinted at me.

'Cassandra,' I corrected.

Pillock.

Extricating myself from his drunken grasp, I scanned the whooping crowd for my husband. Perhaps Stevie was in the kitchen with a bunch of beered-up work colleagues? Either that or flirting outrageously with anything in a skirt.

I slipped out of the room and went upstairs to collect my coat. Party music pounded against my temples. A headache threatened. Elbowing open the door to the master bedroom, I froze. My brain struggled to make sense of the scenario.

I'd caught Stevie at it. On the job. Trousers down. Well, off actually. They were lying in a discarded heap on the floor along with his Designer shirt – a Christmas gift from me – and a tangle of female garments. Shockwaves hit my body. I felt peculiarly detached, as if looking down on the situation before me.

Stevie was on his back, spreadeagled across the bed. A plump woman was bouncing around on top of him. He was naked, apart from his socks. A part of me pondered whether he was wearing a condom, or if it was just socks he bothered about these days?

The woman had large porridge-like thighs, a stretch-marked tummy and banana-shaped breasts. Her nipples were both firmly in the grasp of gravity and my husband's hands.

The earlier glow of celebrating both my thirty-ninth birthday and embracing the New Year disappeared faster than water down a plughole. It seemed like an eternity but was probably only a matter of seconds before my presence registered.

Stevie's head snapped sideways, our eyes locked, and his hands froze mid-fondle. Suddenly he was shoving the woman off him. She let out a loud squawk and tumbled down to the bedroom carpet, pulling the duvet from under Stevie's buttocks in an effort to frantically cover herself.

'Cass!' Stevie spluttered. 'This honestly isn't what it seems. Believe it or not, there is a perfectly innocent explanation for what you think you've just seen.'

Did he say *think* I'd just seen?

Stevie began to dress, grabbing his shirt, hopping from foot to foot as he pulled on back-to-front underwear.

I didn't know what to say, or how to respond. The cat had been set amongst the pigeons and seemingly taken my tongue with it. Not one word of rebuke did I utter. Presumably it was shock.

So this was why my husband hadn't been by my side when Big Ben had bonged the midnight hour. Clearly, he'd been too busy doing his own bonging.

I extricated my coat from an untidy pile on the floor – at least they hadn't bonged all over my fake fur – before calmly walking out of our host's bedroom, down the staircase, and out of the house.

For a moment I stood on the pavement simply gulping in the freezing night air, then strode off towards the car. The engine turned over. I hit the accelerator, just as Stevie erupted through the front door doing up his flies.

Twenty minutes later, I pulled up on our driveway. As the engine died, I slumped over the car's steering wheel. Infidelity. That horrible deed that made the heart pump unpleasantly, turned legs to rubber, knees to jelly and was the surest way to losing a stone in weight without even trying. If infidelity could be manufactured as a diet, the financial ramifications would be endless.

Stevie didn't come home. I lay in our double bed, alone, dully contemplating the dark shapes of bedroom furniture in the gloom, listening to familiar background noises. The hum of the emersion heater as it warmed the water tank. The creaking of pipes. The drip-drip of a tap in the bathroom. All were sounds of an otherwise slumbering house.

As I lay there, utter devastation washed over me. I began to shake. Had my husband done this before? If so, how many times? I couldn't think straight. We'd more or less trundled through married life happily enough. Or so I'd thought. Oh, I'd always been aware that my husband was a flirt, and sometimes a downright outrageous one. But whenever I'd voiced aloud objections or suspicions, Stevie had thrown his hands in the air with a look of wide-eyed innocence. He'd protested such playful teasing was only a bit of fun for heaven's sake. How many times had I retreated, like a dog being scolded by its master, believing I was nothing more than a possessive wife who really should muster a grip on her overactive imagination?

So was my husband a serial adulterer? No doubt I'd been manipulated and lied to on more than one occasion. Dazzled by Stevie's good looks and fobbed off by his charm, I'd clearly become blind to any extra-marital sneakiness.

What the hell was I going to do? Leave my husband? Break up the family? Consign our twin children, Livvy and Toby, to a part-time father? It was either a case of put up and shut up or do something about it.

I stretched my legs, wincing as they encountered a chilly expanse of sheet from the unoccupied part of the bed. Turning over, I huddled into the foetal position and pulled the covers over my head. In a few more hours I'd collect the twins from Nell, my good friend and neighbour, and have a serious think about what – if anything – should be done.

With these thoughts tumbling over and over in my mind, sleep mercifully descended.

# Chapter Two

'Happy New Year Cass!' Nell enveloped me in a bear hug. 'You look a sight for sore eyes. Good party, eh?'

'Oh it was an absolute blinder,' I confirmed.

'Attagirl!' She laughed and nudged me heavily in the ribs. 'Must be great having a hubby who isn't a party pooper like my Ben. The minute anybody mentions a chance to partake in champagne celebrations, he goes straight into reverse. The mad bugger.'

'Who's taking my name in vain?' The man himself wandered into the hallway, distractedly scratching his balls before adjusting his trousers. 'Don't believe one word of my wicked wife's spin. It's all lies. I'm simply a homebird, and there's nothing wrong with that. If you want to go out whooping it up, Nell, then tag along with Cass next time.'

'I might just do that,' Nell threatened, nonetheless snuggling into Ben as he wrapped an arm companionably around her shoulders.

The pair of them seemed the epitome of wedded bliss. They were a couple who accepted each other's faults, but happily rubbed along together – sharing, dedicated, supportive and loyal.

I swallowed the sudden lump in my throat as my twins

appeared at the top of the stairs. Nell's young lad, Dylan, was two steps behind Livvy and Toby. An only child, Dylan always relished the company of my two.

'Aw, Mum. Do we have to go now?' Toby wheedled.

'Yep, come on. Let these good people have some peace and quiet.'

I gave my neighbours another hug, thanking them profusely for the extended babysitting service. With promises of doing the same for them and cries of any time, no problem, I gently extricated myself. Livvy and Toby followed me back across the grass strip that separated the two houses.

'Where's Dad?' asked Toby.

'He's, um, had to pop into work.'

'Oh. Fancy having a game on the PlayStation, Livvy? Come on, I'll race you to my room!'

As my offspring thundered up the stairs, I wondered whether the lack of their father's presence mattered more to me than to them.

Later that afternoon, the twins went out to play on their bicycles in the cul-de-sac. Dylan was with them again. They raced around, shrieking with laughter in the cold winter air, while I sat alone in the kitchen nursing a tepid cup of coffee.

The emotional numbness had lifted enough to permit an endless stream of tears to silently course down my cheeks. I wasn't actually crying. There was no heaving chest, or breathless gulping, or anguished howls. It was simply as if my eyes were leaking. Rather badly.

The sound of a key cautiously turning in the front door's barrel lock had my heartbeat quickening, but I remained motionless at the kitchen table.

'Cass?' Stevie called, before tentatively entering the kitchen.

I kept my eyes down, staring at the skin floating on my cold coffee. When Stevie spoke, it was clear any finger of blame was pointing firmly in my direction.

'You do realise you're blowing things out of all proportion, don't you?'

I continued to look at the disgusting coffee, aware that my mouth looked like an upside-down crescent moon.

'Don't you think you should at least give me the chance to tell you what *really* happened?'

I dragged my eyelids away from the brown liquid.

'Go on then.'

Stevie's explanation was so pathetically lame, it was almost laughable. Apparently Mrs Banana Breasts had been feeling faint. Stevie had taken her to the bathroom so she could splash her hot face with some cold water. However, the bathroom had been engaged. Undeterred, and ever the concerned party guest, Stevie had led Mrs Fat Arse into the master bedroom, whereupon she'd fainted enroute to the ensuite. Conveniently there had been a double bed for her to swoon upon.

'She was a big girl, Cass. You saw that with your own eyes. Her arm was around my neck, weighing me down. And when she keeled over – well, it couldn't be helped, could it? –I went down with her. Next thing I know, she's made this amazing recovery, flipped me over, pinned me down, stripped me off, and jumped on me.'

'How terrible,' I gasped. 'It's tantamount to rape.'

Stevie's eyes flickered.

'I'm telling you, she tricked me! I was set up good and proper. It might have looked like we were going at it. Certainly, she was trying. But good old Dick was having none of it. He was as limp as lettuce. And then you walked in! But I'm being absolutely honest, the intent was totally one sided. Hers, not mine.'

For one crazy moment, I nearly fell for it. Almost believed him. Which just left one outstanding question.

'Where were you last night?'

'Ah. Now you might not believe what I'm about to tell you, but I swear it's God's honest truth.'

Wearily I rubbed my red-rimmed eyes.

'Get out, Stevie.'

He went.

As the front door slammed behind him, I wondered if he'd go to *her*.

That evening, as I spooned baked beans over triangles of buttered toast, Toby regarded the empty space at the head of the table.

'When's Dad coming home?'

'Ah, yes,' I quavered brightly. 'I forgot to tell you both. Something cropped up at the office. Daddy's had to go away on urgent business.'

'But he didn't say good-bye,' frowned Livvy. 'He *always* says good-bye before he goes away. Where's he gone?'

'Well, here and there,' I replied vaguely. 'It's something frightfully important and all a bit hush-hush.'

Precisely what could be so top secret as to have a bog-standard surveyor taking off without any farewells fortunately bypassed the twins.

'When will he be back?' asked Toby, cramming an entire toasted triangle into his mouth.

'Not sure,' I mumbled miserably.

## Chapter Three

The following morning, as I stared at a soggy mass of cereal and willed my oesophagus to swallow a spoonful, the doorbell exploded with frantic ringing. It was Nell.

'Cass, you silly cow! Why the hell didn't you confide in me?'

'Probably because I was trying to come to terms with the situation before anybody else got wind of it,' I said, giving her a meaningful look.

There was almost nothing Nell didn't know about the residents of our cul-de-sac. I'd been deluding myself thinking that the infidelity fiasco would go unnoticed.

I chucked the congealed cornflakes in the bin and made some fresh coffee for us both as Nell settled down to spill the gossip beans.

It transpired that my love rival was a neighbour. She'd moved into the ivy-clad detached at the far end about a month ago. As I scalded my mouth on boiling coffee, I tried to silently count small blessings – well, just the one blessing. My house was the first in the road, and *hers* was the last. At least we wouldn't bump into each other on a Monday morning when the bins were put out. Nell also told me that my adversary was a divorcee, had four children, and Dylan was in the same class as *her* eldest boy. That was only one class down from Livvy and Toby. Oh God. I'd have to move.

'What's her name?' I hissed.

'Cynthia.'

'*Cynthia*?' I shrieked, making Nell jump. 'Who the hell is called Cynthia in this day and age?'

'Fat old bags?' asked Nell hesitantly.

'What am I going to do?' I wailed, massaging my temples.

Nell considered.

'Well, the way I see it, there are three options.' She held up her fingers and began to tick them off. 'Move. Stay put. Or-'

'Murder Cellulite Cynthia,' I growled.

Nell left about an hour later, eyes bright after such a gossip feast. This was the best scandal since Mr Witherspoon, a few doors down, had been rescued by Emergency Services. Although nobody had ever fully understood quite why he'd felt the need to shove his penis up the spout of the bath's tap. Especially the hot one.

Stevie sent a text proclaiming he loved me and had made a huge mistake. I let out a snarl and hurled the mobile across the floor. Fortunately we were the only house in the cul-de-sac never to have got around to laminate flooring. The mobile remained intact, unlike my heart.

Settling down with a notepad and pen, I made some financial calculations – essential if one was seriously considering going it alone – and happily discovered I was not necessarily financially dependent upon Stevie. Two years ago, my darling octogenarian parents had left me reeling when they'd died within weeks of each other. As their only daughter, they had bequeathed me the entirety of their worldly goods which, although modest, was not to be sniffed at. The money had been sitting quietly in an account earning a tidy bit of interest. If I was thrifty, it could easily support the twins and me for a while, at least until things were properly sorted out with Stevie.

On the pretext of wanting an early night, I was in bed soon after Livvy and Toby. In truth, I needed to privately release a torrent of weeping. Burying my face in the pillow to mute my howls of anguish, I wondered what Stevie and Cynthia were doing right now. Were they curled up together on the sofa watching telly? Cuddling? Kissing? Even worse, at it? The pain was so acute I thought it might dislodge my heart.

I eventually sank into a tortured mixed-up dream where, like Cynthia, I was sitting astride Stevie. Instead of groaning orgasmically, I was yelling, "Liar, liar, liar." As I pneumatically bounced around, Stevie morphed into my love rival. "Bitch! Tart! Home wrecker!" I shrieked, lashing out with my fists. She grabbed me by the shoulders and shook me furiously. "Cow! Pig!" I screeched, thrashing about, wishing she'd stop rattling me so violently because my brain was starting to hurt. If I could just bunch my fist up one more time and biff her really hard on the nose, it would be – *ouch* – it would be – *argh* – what was my rival doing to me?

'Mum! Can you hear me? Wake up!'

Toby was gripping my shoulders, shaking me like a terrier with a rag doll. Behind him stood Livvy. My daughter was managing to look both disdainful and pained.

'Do you know what time it is?' she admonished. 'It's nearly eight o'clock. We go back to school today, and there's no bread to make our packed lunches.'

Oh my goodness. What sort of parent was I? Aside from a heartbroken single one of course?

I leapt out of bed, experienced a bit of a head rush, then belted down to the kitchen to ransack cupboards for crackers, crisps, biscuits, and anything that bore the label Monosodium Glutamate.

Why couldn't I be like some of the other mothers at the school gates? Many of them were raising a vegetarian family, buying organic ingredients and knocking up nutritious home cooking? Perhaps, if I'd been more like that, I'd still have a faithful husband by my side. Meanwhile, bags of crisps, sugary drinks and stale crackers would have to do.

Shame washed over me as I realised that wallowing in self-pity had resulted in neglecting my precious offspring. Bugger Stevie for doing this to me. For the first time since the catastrophic events of *that* party, anger reared its head.

I slapped plastic lids on lunchboxes and frisbeed them to my patiently waiting children. Belting back upstairs, I ignored my burgeoning bladder and pulled a long coat from the wardrobe. Grabbing my handbag and car keys, the three of us legged it out to the car.

Eventually, after blowing noisy kisses to the twins' rigid backs (public displays of affection were apparently uncool) on impulse I headed off to Fairview Shopping Centre.

There was nothing quite like a spot of retail therapy to lift the spirits, and right now I needed to do everything possible to keep the pecker up. Just *visualising* handing over a little rectangular piece of plastic was putting some roses back in my pasty cheeks. This was definitely going to be good. I could feel it in my water. And talking of water, I really should find a loo very soon.

Inside the shopping mall, distraction was immediate in the form of glittery denim jeans in the window of River Island. Low rise, belted and boot-legged, they'd look absolutely terrific on an eighteen-year-old. I was a battle worn thirty-nine feeling furiously rebellious.

I strode into the disco-lit interior where blaring music instantly assaulted my eardrums. Businesslike, I began moving around the shop floor loading up. It was hot work. Ten minutes later I flung the garments over my shoulder and shrugged off my heavy winter coat. Instantly refreshed, I headed off to the fitting room vaguely aware that two teenagers were regarding me with ill-concealed amusement. When I swished the fitting room curtain aside with a flourish, the reason for the girls' mirth was apparent.

My reflection, caught in a full-length mirror and lit in a blaze of down-lighting, revealed a white faced black-eyed woman clad in nothing but a nightdress. I groaned and sank to the floor in mortification. At that moment I hated Stevie. How could I have let him reduce me to this?

Want to know what happens next?
You can order a copy from Amazon.

## Also by Debbie Viggiano

*Sadie's Spring Surprise*

*Annie's Autumn Escape*

*Daisy's Dilemma*

*The Watchful Neighbour (debut psychological thriller)*

*Cappuccino and Chick-Chat (memoir)*

*Willow's Wedding Vows*

*Lucy's Last Straw*

*What Holly's Husband Did*

*Stockings and Cellulite*

*Lipstick and Lies*

*Flings and Arrows*

*The Perfect Marriage*

*Secrets*

*The Corner Shop of Whispers*

*The Woman Who Knew Everything*

*Mixed Emotions (short stories)*

*The Ex Factor (a family drama)*

*Lily's Pink Cloud ~ a child's fairytale*

*100 ~ the Author's experience of Chronic Myeloid Leukaemia*

Printed in Great Britain
by Amazon

17040382R00214